HIS CURVY TREAT

A SMALL TOWN CURVY GIRL ROMANCE

BOOK BOYFRIENDS WANTED
BOOK THREE

MARY E THOMPSON

BOOK BOYFRIENDS WANTED

Welcome back to MacKellar Cove! It's so good to see you again. Never miss out on anything happening in town and sign up for Mary's newsletter.

Romancing the Curves comes with subscriber exclusive freebies, sneak peeks, and a first look at everything Mary has to offer. Be the first to know about new releases and sales and all the curves ahead!

SUBSCRIBE NOW AT MARYETHOMPSON.COM

Happy reading!

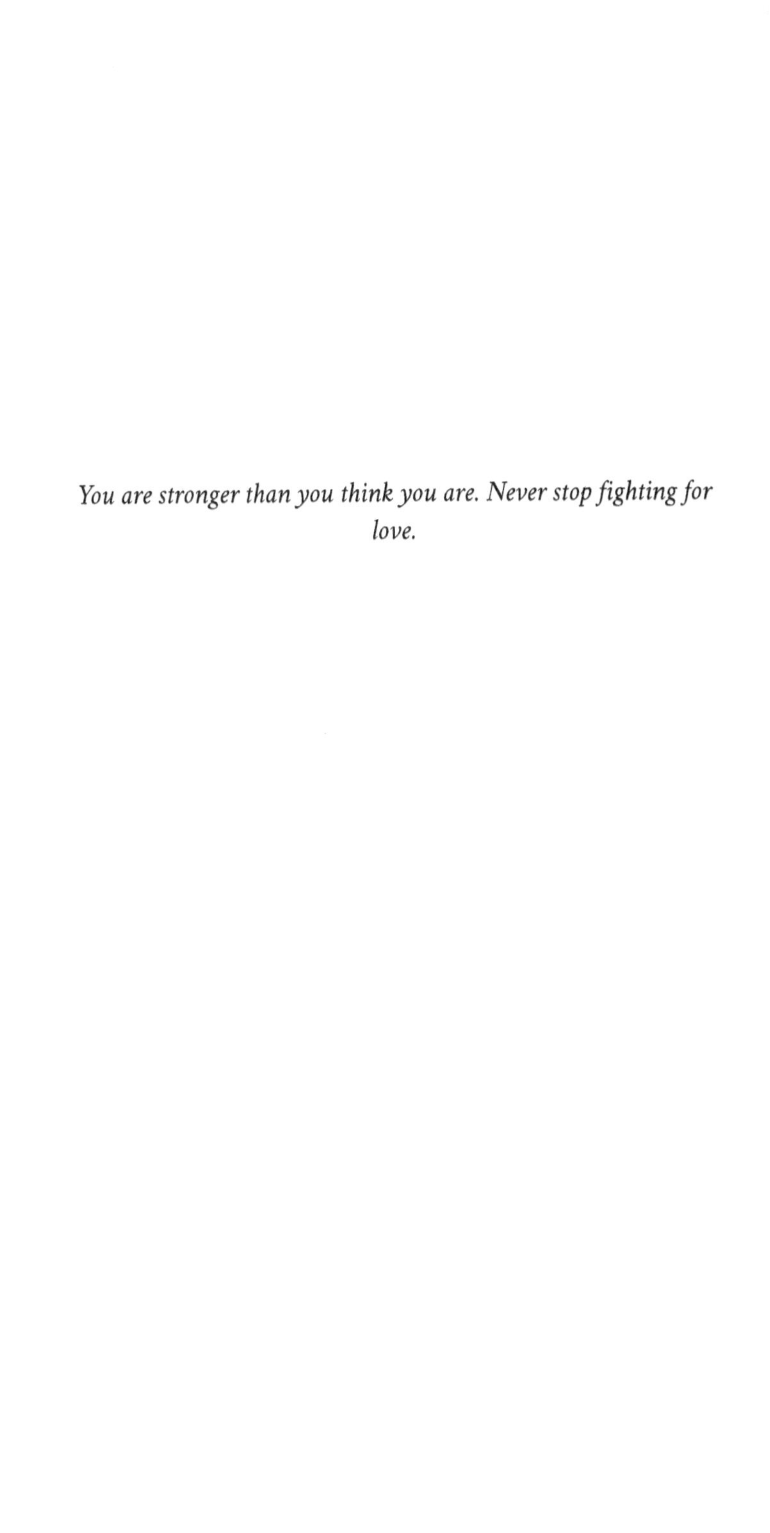

You are stronger than you think you are. Never stop fighting for love.

ELISE

It really didn't get any better than a day outside. A cool breeze, a gentle sway of the boat, birds chirping, the smell of fresh water and flowers. Summer wasn't quite here yet, but it was so close I could taste it. I was ready to shake off the winter and get back to being outside and free.

First, I had to sit through training I'd been through five other times. No one got a pass, not even if you were a lifer. Which meant I was there, again.

"Hey!" I heard from across the room. I looked up and found my friend, Ava Bailey, waving and rushing toward me. Ava and I worked together on the Tours from the Cove boat tours. She left MacKellar Cove through the winter for school, but she was back for her third summer as a guide.

"Hey," I said, hugging her when she sat down.

Ava was a hugger. She was since the day we met. She was also a college student and still all shiny and happy and the way a person was supposed to be when they were twenty-one and had their entire lives ahead of them.

"Your hair looks awesome. How was your winter?" she asked.

"Thanks," I said, touching my purple locks. It was my latest color. "Winter was good. Busy but not insane. How about you? How are classes going?"

"Great," she said with a grin. "I can't believe I only have one more year."

"Assuming you pass your exams," I teased.

Ava shoved me and grinned. "True. I'm only here for today, then will commute for a few weeks until exams are over. But hopefully I can keep doing this even after I graduate."

Ava was a secondary education major with an ELA certificate who was hoping to move full time to the area and teach middle school. If she did, she was going to continue to work summers as a tour guide to earn extra money. I hoped it worked out for her.

"Is it too early to start looking for jobs?" I asked.

Ava nodded. "A little. I have one more semester of classes and then a semester of student teaching. I'm hoping I can land a spot here and stay on after, but I don't know of any MacKellar Cove teachers looking to leave."

I grinned. "People have a tendency to stick around here forever."

"I totally get why."

Ava grew up a few hours away on the other side of the Adirondacks. MacKellar Cove sat along the St. Lawrence River, west of the mountains. A small cove separated the town from the river, giving us opportunities for swimming and fishing in a quiet area relatively untouched by the deep, powerful waters of the St. Lawrence.

It was home for me. Sanctuary in a way. It was the only place I ever wanted to live, the only place I could imagine living.

"So, what have you been up to? Meet anyone new?"

I shook my head and forced a smile. Ava was a coworker and sweet, but she didn't know me well. She didn't know that meeting someone new was not going to happen. Been there, done that, had the scars to prove I survived it.

"Nah. You know how it is here. Everyone knows everyone."

Ava nodded solemnly. "It's really the only downside to living here. But since I didn't grow up here, it's not as bad for me. There are still a lot of new men for me to discover."

I grinned. "Definitely. Hopefully you'll find a good one."

"God, I hope so. I'm sick of being single."

"You need some friends," I told her with a chuckle. If I didn't have my group of friends, I'd go nuts, but not because I was waiting for a man. Having good friends made everything better.

"I need that, too," Ava said with a laugh. She wound her long, dark ponytail around her hand and swung it over her shoulder. She was pretty with a cute nose and hazel eyes behind glasses that made her look a little nerdy. She was curvy like me, but where I could wear maternity clothes even though I'd never been pregnant, Ava looked more like Marilyn Monroe with her sexy, proportional curves.

Our boss and the owner of the company, Walter Coronado, moved to the front of the room. Everyone fell silent. Walter was a good boss and treated all his employees like family. It was why people came back year after year to work for him.

"Hello, everyone. Are you ready to get back on the water?"

We all cheered.

"Good. I'm ready, too. We're going to run through some basic stuff that most of you have heard before, then we're going to talk about the tours we're offering this summer. I'm really excited about this summer and can't wait to share it with all of you."

"Woohoo!" Ava called.

Walter smiled at her. "Glad to see you're just as excited, Ava. How was school?"

"Good," Ava said, "but I'm ready to be back here for a few months."

"We're happy you were able to come back. For those of you who are new, we have a lot of employee events so you can all get to know each other. I hope you'll participate," Walter said, meeting the gazes of the staff.

I sat back in my seat at the back of the room and surveyed the others. Most of them I knew from previous years working on the boats. A few faces were new. Every summer, the staff got younger and younger. Not the operators, but the guides. I was one of the oldest ones left, and at twenty-nine, I didn't usually think of myself as old.

I got it, though. Last summer, one of the other guides was about to get married. Another one was pregnant. One was finishing college and not coming back to the area. It was the kind of job most people didn't hang on to for a long time. But I loved it. I loved cracking jokes with the tourists and being outside and knowing I was safe because there was nowhere to hide on the boats. Nowhere to get trapped or cornered or...

I pushed the thoughts away and focused on what Walter was saying. All of us were required to having fishing licenses and CPR and lifeguard certifications. In order to drive the boat, a captain's license was required, and most of us didn't have that, but in an emergency, we all knew how to use the radio and get help if needed. Walter didn't take any chances with his customers or employees.

The safety stuff was a review for me, but I listened

anyway. When it was time for lunch, two massive sandwich platters arrived, courtesy of Walter. Ava and I grabbed food and returned to our seats.

"This is so good," she said around a mouthful. "I was starving. I didn't eat breakfast this morning."

"Why not?"

"I'm trying that intermittent fasting thing. A friend of mine lost a ton of weight doing it."

"You don't need to lose weight," I told her.

She shook her head. "Oh, I definitely do. If I could drop about forty pounds, I'd look so much better."

"You do not need to lose forty pounds!"

Ava rolled her eyes. "Yeah, I really do."

"Curves are hot, and if someone you like can't see that, then you shouldn't be with them."

Ava smiled. "I wish I had your confidence. I get overlooked all the time for the skinny girls. I'm kind of sick of it. I just want a guy to see me and have his eyes do that lazy slide up and down before he smiles and asks what my name is."

"College is not the time to judge men for the quality of their choices," I said.

She laughed. "True, but I figured I would have met someone by now. If I don't find The One this year, I worry I'm going to be single forever."

"Would that really be the worst thing in the world?" I asked.

She shrugged. "The worst thing? No. But I don't want to be single. I don't know how you've stayed single for so long."

I grinned. "Good vibrators."

Ava choked on her drink and struggled to breathe while she coughed up the water. I slapped her on the back and felt bad for scandalizing her.

"Jeez," she wheezed. "You need to warn me before you say something like that."

"Sorry," I said, grinning wryly.

"No, you're not," Ava said.

I shook my head. "No, I'm not."

We laughed.

"What did I miss?" Walter asked, turning the chair in front of our table around to face us.

Ava and I exchanged a look and broke out laughing again.

"Trust me," Ava said. "You don't want to know."

I nodded.

Walter raised a dark eyebrow at us and shook his head. "Pretend I didn't ask. How is my dream team doing this year? You ladies ready to handle the big boats?"

Ava and I exchanged a glance and nodded.

"Good. I'm going to keep you two together as much as possible. Elise, while Ava is finishing up school, I'm going to pair you up with a few of the newer guides. We need to find a third to send with you two on some of your trips. You need to let me know who works well with you."

"I'm sure anyone will be fine," I said automatically.

Walter smiled. "I'm sure they will, but I want to be positive. It won't cost anyone their job, but I trust your judgment. I know you'll find someone great to pull onto your team."

I appreciated the confidence he had in me, but I was a background kind of person. I could get up in front of guests and make them laugh, but I wasn't good when it came to getting to know my coworkers or figuring out who was the right fit with the customers and who wasn't.

The only reason Ava and I were friends was because she didn't give up on getting to know me. She was always nice, but she was the one who made the effort over the last few years.

"She'll find someone awesome, won't you?" Ava asked with far more confidence than I felt.

I nodded. "Yep."

Walter held my gaze for another minute, then nodded and asked how we were doing.

"Good. Ready for tours to start," Ava said. "And ready for exams to be over."

Walter chuckled. "Don't rush it. College should be a fun time. A time for you to find yourself and figure out who you are. Those were some of the best years of my life. It's all downhill after college."

Walter and Ava laughed, but I had to force a smile and choke back the bile threatening to spill out. College was the worst three years of my life. So bad I left college a year early and finished my degree online. Just the fact that I was alive and surviving on my own made life after college much better than college.

The bar was low for me.

Walter stood and knocked on the table. "Back to it. Elise, we'll talk in a few weeks or so about your first instinct with some of the newbies. You guys ready for a tour?"

We nodded and cleaned up our lunch. Walter led the group outside to the boats. Tour boats couldn't dock in the Cove because of the shallow water so we were just south of town on the bank of the river. The St. Lawrence was plenty deep for the boats Walter had. All six of them.

"Ooh, I like that one," Ava said when she saw the shiny, new boat in the water at the Tours from the Cove dock.

I laughed. "Of course you do."

"Oh, come on," Ava said. "It's gorgeous."

I nodded. "It is, but I'm more of a well worn kind of girl."

Ava grinned. "Yeah, yeah, I know. It has to be broken in for you to know it's any good."

I smiled and followed her onto the deck of the first boat.

It was one of the biggest ones in the fleet. Cove 1 and Cove 2 were used for the tours that ran consistently to the local castles and other tourist attractions.

Walter went through the boat for the sake of the newbies, showing them all the little things they needed to know about it. He also reminded them that they would always work with an experienced crew member so they had plenty of chances to learn the ins and outs of each boat.

Since Cove 2 was exactly the same as Cove 1, we moved to the next dock and walked onto the smallest boat, the one used only for private tours. It didn't get used often, but it was there and it was a good boat.

The last dock held the three boats I favored, including the new one that fit in the same class size. They were the utility boats. The boats that were used for regular cruises but held about half as many people. These were the lunch cruises, the dinner cruises, and the sunset cruises. I'd driven one of them a few times on really quiet cruises. It made me think about getting my captain's license, but I hadn't made that choice yet. Especially because the big boats scared me.

When we stepped on the deck of the new boat, Ava sighed. "She's gorgeous."

I grinned. "Yes, she is."

"See, I told you you would love her."

I chuckled. We listened to Walter's spiel then filed off the boat and down the dock with the others. Walter dismissed us when we got back to the training room.

"I was hoping we'd have time to grab a drink and catch up, but I have class in the morning. Next time?" she asked. "I'll be back this weekend."

I nodded. "Sounds good. Drive safe getting back to school."

"Yes, Mom," Ava said with a smile. She hugged me again, then we walked in different directions to our vehicles.

I drove north past MacKellar Cove and thought about stopping in town, but I was ready to be home. I pulled into my neighborhood and waved at Mrs. Lockhart. Her trailer was the first one after the entrance, and she was the unofficial neighborhood watch. Nothing happened without her knowledge, or her approval sometimes. Knowing she was always watching made me feel safer and was one of the reasons I bought my home when I moved back to MacKellar Cove.

Some people looked down on trailer parks, or mobile home communities if you were upscale, but I loved where I lived. My neighbors all watched out for each other. We got together regularly for impromptu gatherings, and everyone pitched in to help each other out. And in our area of Upstate New York, there were plenty of communities like ours, full of people who owned their own home on wheels.

I backed my hatchback into the spot next to my trailer and checked my mirrors before I got out. Satisfied no one was around, I got out and locked the car then skipped up the two steps to my door. I unlocked my door and went inside, closing and locking the door behind me. I listened, even though I knew I was alone, just to make sure.

My trailer was small with an open floor plan, just how I liked it. No one could hide because my closet didn't have a door and neither did my bedroom. The only door was into the bathroom, and that was wide open with a clear shot though the see-through shower curtain.

I poured a glass of water and carried it to the couch. I turned on the TV and called my mom.

"How was it?" my mom said when she answered the phone.

"Training was good, Mom."

"Was Ava there?"

"She was. She has one more year and is still hoping to

find a teaching job here. She's also looking for a student teaching position for the second semester."

"I'll ask around," Mom said. My mom was also a teacher, but she was at MacKellar Cove High School. She said if Ava wanted to work with her, she'd take her in a heartbeat, but Ava was set on middle school.

"Thanks, Mom. How was your day?"

"Good. Dad and I got the boat out of the garage. Ian is going to take a look at it for us."

"Good. Let me know when you want me to help you get it in the water."

"If Ian says it's good, then soon. Bob and Sandy already have theirs in the water. They went out today. Said it was beautiful. A little cold, but gorgeous."

"It was definitely a nice day. Walter bought a new one for tours. Ava loved it."

"But you didn't," Mom said with a smile in her voice. "You always like the things that have the edges rubbed off."

"It's better when all the kinks are worked out."

Mom chuckled. "Well, I can't always disagree with you. Are you coming over for dinner tomorrow night? Chelsea said she might come. You should call her."

I nodded and made a mental note to check in with my cousin. We grew up like sisters, both of us the only children of sisters. Our families spent a lot of time together when we were younger. Chelsea and I drifted when I went to college, but we'd gotten closer again in the last few years being back in the same town.

"I'm planning to come. I'll talk to her. Are Aunt Cathy and Uncle Ken coming?"

"Yep. And maybe one day you two girls will bring someone over to fill in those last two spots at the table."

I made a noncommittal noise and let my mom ramble on. She knew I was in a serious relationship with Andy in college, but they never met. He never wanted to travel with me when I went home to visit my family, and eventually, I stopped visiting. For almost a year, I didn't see my parents because of him.

I know now it was one more thing he wanted control over. But he was the reason I'd never bring someone to fill up the empty seat I sat next to at the table. Maybe Chelsea would have a kid one day and she could fill both seats.

Not that I thought it would get my mother to stop talking about my need to settle down.

"...never see it happen. I just don't know about you young kids now. Waiting forever to get married and have kids. Don't you know that if you don't start having kids soon, you might not be able to? I mean, you're not that young anymore, not biologically."

"I know, Mom," I said. I'd never win the argument with her, so I agreed and blamed my lack of interest in dating on having grown up with almost all the single men in town. She told me I should broaden my horizons and date men who didn't live nearby, but I told her I wasn't driving two hours each way for a date.

And she thought my generation was crazy.

"Promise me you'll give me a grandchild one day, Elise," she begged. It was how she ended every conversation.

"I promise I'll try," I said, like I always did.

She huffed because she wanted more than that, but we both knew I got my stubbornness from her, so that was the best she could expect.

"I love you, Mom," I told her to ease some of the irritation.

"I love you, Elise. We'll talk soon. I'll ask if anyone knows any single men who aren't more than an hour away. I'll let you know."

"No, Mom—"

"Bye, darling."

"Mom..." I looked at my phone. "And she hung up on me." I shook my head. I couldn't say I blamed her. Once upon a time I wanted kids. Two, maybe three. With a big yard to play in and a husband who doted on all of us.

That dream ended the day I landed in the hospital.

2

COLIN

I stared at my phone for longer than felt sane. The text didn't change. It didn't rearrange itself into something that made sense. It just sat there, begging me to reply.

RAMSEY HOLLAND

A few of us are meeting at O'Kelley's for a drink. You should join us.

I double checked the number and wondered if I was losing it. He was my lawyer. Yeah, MacKellar Cove was a small town, but was it small enough that you socialized with your lawyer?

He seemed like a nice enough guy. I'd met his kid and wife, and they were nice. But all that was basically work. I invited him out to the farm to make sure he knew what we were fighting for. He suggested a grand opening and it was only right he was there since it was his idea. But we didn't hang out.

Hell, I didn't even know what or where O'Kelley's was.

Maybe that was a sign I needed to get out more. Or maybe it was a sign my business was going to be a success.

Then again, did socializing with my lawyer help with that?

Hell, I had no idea what I was doing. All I knew was I was exhausted and not really in the mood for small talk with a bunch of strangers.

> Thanks, but I think I'm in for the night. Next time?

Understand. Definitely.

I pocketed my phone without another glance. He was my lawyer. You didn't hang out with a guy you paid to work for you.

"What are you up to?" Nicky Holbrook asked as he set a beer on the desk for me.

I couldn't help but laugh.

He sat down and raised an eyebrow, silently asking what I found so damn funny.

I shook my head. "My lawyer just invited me out for a drink."

"So?"

I shrugged. "I said no because I don't think it's a good idea to hang out with someone you pay."

Nicky gave me a wry smile and shook his head. "Then I guess this other beer is for me, too."

I laughed and grabbed the bottle before he could take it back. Nicky worked for my grandmother for years. Forever if you believed him. They became friends, and Nicky stayed on even after she was sick and stopped maintaining the Jones Family Maple Farm. When she passed, Nicky still stayed, to make sure nothing happened. He didn't get paid. He didn't have instructions. He just stayed because he was that kind of man.

"Things here aren't the same as where you grew up, Colin. People here look out for each other. They care. And your lawyer invites you out for a drink sometimes. It doesn't mean you have to be friends, but it means you can be if you want to be."

I twisted off the bottle top and tossed it in the bin under my desk. One of the many projects I hoped to get to one day. I didn't know what I was going to do with all of the bottle tops, but eventually I'd come up with something.

"I don't have time for friends," I told Nicky. "I work eighty hours a week. When I'm done, I'm barely able to stand let alone go out and drink a beer."

"But you can stay in and drink one?"

I rolled my eyes at him.

"Listen, kid, I get it. You've only been here a few months. It's tough to meet new people. But hanging out with me all the time isn't going to be good for you. I'm old and crotchety and too damn stubborn. If you're not careful, you'll end up like me."

"I don't know if that would be so bad."

Nicky laughed, a rough, weathered laugh. He'd never been a smoker, but he sounded like it. He liked his whiskey as much as his beer, and he spent more than his fair share of hours outside in the cold. He blamed the cold instead of the whiskey for his rough sound.

"Trust me, you don't want to end up like me. Life is better when you have a woman by your side and some friends to grab a beer with once in a while."

I shook my head. "Maybe one day, but things are too busy right now. I need to focus on the farm for the first few years. Get things settled. Then I'll think about it."

Nicky shook his head. "You'll regret it. You're already getting old."

"Hey! Thirty-nine isn't old."

Nicky grinned and tipped his beer to me. "Forty is, though. You only have two months."

"Forty still isn't old. And if the woman isn't the right one, she's not worth it."

"Speaking from some experience?" Nicky asked.

I shrugged. We were still getting to know each other, and I wasn't a big talker. I didn't share a lot about my past, and especially about my past mistakes.

"I haven't been a monk for thirty-nine years."

"That either means you're too picky to be willing to let the right one in or you know exactly what you want in a woman. Or a man? I never asked."

"I know what I want in a woman. If I thought I'd met the right one, I'd let her in."

My mind went to Ramsey's friend. Elise. She was at the grand opening, but we only met for a moment. Barely a moment. She was stunning in a way that most men overlooked. I saw her from behind before I saw her face, and I admit it was an asshole move, but shit, her curves had me salivating before I walked over. When she turned and smiled at me, it was tentative, but I felt like I'd been hit with a lightning bolt.

I hadn't seen her since, but I also hadn't ventured far from the farm. I wasn't lying when I said work took up all my time.

Nicky stood and slid his empty bottle into the bin by the door. "I still think you should go meet your lawyer for a drink. Maybe he has a cute friend he can hook you up with."

I chuckled and shook my head but couldn't deny he had a point. If I wanted to meet Elise and maybe get to know her, Ramsey was a connection to her.

"Think about it. And get some sleep tonight. You don't need to be in here when I arrive in the morning."

I nodded even though we both knew it was likely I would be. Nicky knocked on the door frame and left, leaving me to my quiet, lonely office.

My grandmother worked out of the barn, but I decided I needed to spread out more. I moved the office to one of the bedrooms in the main house, and had plans to knock down the office walls in the barn so we could do more in there. It was another One Day project. I really needed to write some of them down.

I dug out my phone to look for a list app and clicked to the text app instead. It had been an hour since Ramsey texted me. How long did people hang out at a bar, if O'Kelley's was a bar?

I searched the place and found an address. It wasn't far, and while I second guessed myself again, I grabbed my sweatshirt and headed to my truck.

The town was quiet, but I didn't expect much on a Tuesday night. I listened to the directions as my phone read them to me and found the place right on the waterfront. It was definitely in a great location, and judging by the cars parked out front, it was popular.

I found a spot a block away and walked back to the bar. Inside was a little dark, but not so dark I couldn't see. I scanned the place quickly and didn't think I saw Ramsey.

The bartender met my gaze and nodded once, whether in invitation or acknowledging that he was watching me, I wasn't sure. Depending on the person, it definitely could go either way.

I walked over to the bar and took a stool in the middle.

"What can I get you?" the bartender asked.

He was a big guy, close to my height, with dark eyes and a dark beard. His baseball hat displayed the local high school logo, and his white tee stretched across his chest, making sure everyone knew he could kick their asses if they got out of line.

"A beer. Whatever you have on tap."

He gestured to the list. "I could guess for you or you could pick one. Up to you."

"Bud sounds good," I told him.

He nodded and pulled the lever. "You're Cleotha's grandson, aren't you?"

I nodded, curious that the man in front of me knew my grandmother.

"She was a damn good lady. I'm sorry for your loss."

I nodded again. "Thank you."

My grandmother was a good woman, but she was also a little of a mystery to me. My parents met on Jones Family Maple Farm, and when my mother died, my father couldn't stay in the area. It reminded him of my mother, and he chose to leave so he could focus on me instead of letting his grief drown him.

But that meant I grew up without my grandmother or my mother. My father was wonderful, and we were still close, but there was a part of me that knew I was too gruff at times.

"I'm Hudson. This is my place," the bartender said. "First drink's on me since you've never been here. Hopefully you'll come back."

"Thanks," I said. "I was actually supposed to meet someone here."

"Don't tell me it's someone from that dating app," Hudson said with a groan.

"Dating app?"

He rolled his eyes. "One of the locals is a tech genius or something and she made an app. All the women around here are going crazy for it, but since they know I won't take shit from anyone, they're meeting their dates here. Who are you supposed to meet?"

I shook my head. "No one from the app. My lawyer actually. Ramsey Holland. He suggested I stop by."

Hudson relaxed. "Sorry. You missed them by about ten minutes."

I shrugged. "Maybe next time."

Hudson nodded. "Hey, nice to meet you. If you need anything else, let me know. The kitchen closes at nine tonight, so if you're hungry, we need to get an order in soon."

I grabbed the menu and thanked him, realizing I was a little hungry. It didn't take long to decide on something to eat and put in my order. I also asked for another beer and checked out the bar around me.

There was a dance floor to the side. Bathrooms ran down the hallway. An old juke box sat in the front corner and pool tables made a square in the back. Booths lined the front and side of the space with tables scattered in the middle. Waitresses worked their way around with trays of food and drinks and smiles for all the people.

It wasn't insanely busy, but it was busier than I expected for a small town bar on a weeknight.

"Hudson, I'm getting a refill," I heard a woman shout from a few stools over.

I turned and watched as she reached over the bar and grabbed the soda gun. Her breasts flattened on the top, her ass in the air. She stuck her tongue out the side of her mouth as she watched, completely focused on the liquid filling her glass.

She stopped halfway to the top and put the soda gun back, then set the glass on the top and pushed herself off the bar.

Elise.

It made no sense that I was so mesmerized by her. She

had her purple hair up in a messy bun. A black sweatshirt hid her upper body. Jeans hugged her legs. She even had on shoes that looked like slippers. Hair slid into her face, and she blew out the side of her mouth to push it back then took a sip of her drink.

She defined cute. And with those curves, she defined sexy.

She turned her head and met my gaze. Almost as quickly as she saw me, she looked away, her eyes sliding right past mine like I was no one important. Then again, I wasn't. We met once, and it wasn't for long. She might not even remember me.

I opened my mouth to say something to her, but she hopped down and turned away. I watched her walk through the crowd, smiling at people as she moved. When she stopped, she sat at a table of other women, women I didn't know but recognized.

I guessed saying hi was out of the question. I hadn't even wanted to meet my lawyer, and I definitely wasn't intruding on a bunch of women I didn't know so I could say hello to one.

"Do you know Elise?" Hudson asked.

I hadn't heard him come back, but I wasn't surprised. He made it clear he wasn't going to let me, or anyone else, mess with his bar.

I shook my head. "Not really. She came to the grand opening and we met, but that's it. She's friends with Ramsey's wife."

Hudson nodded. "Yeah. All of them are friends."

I glanced at the table again, just in time to see Elise tip her head back and laugh at something someone said.

When I finally looked away, Hudson was gone, but I knew he noticed. I wasn't exactly being subtle. My dinner showed up, delivered by one of the servers, not Hudson. I ate and finished my beer and stuffed a few dollars into the tip jar. I nodded at Hudson and thanked him for the beer.

Just before I reached the door, Elise and one of her friends did.

"Hey, aren't you the guy from the maple farm?" her friend asked me.

I nodded. "I am. I'm Colin."

"That's right. We met at the grand opening. Nice to see you again, Colin. I'm Trinity. And this is Elise."

I shook hands with Trinity then offered my hand to Elise. She stared at it for a long moment until her friend nudged her. Elise forced a smile and stuck her hand in mine for the briefest of moments. That one quick touch was enough to send a spark through me, but Elise clearly didn't feel the same.

"We haven't seen you here before," Trinity continued.

"Oh, um, yeah, I've been working like crazy. I was actually here to meet someone. Uh, Ramsey. I think you know him."

Trinity laughed and nodded. "We do. I thought you were going to say you were meeting someone from Book Boyfriends Wanted."

"What's that?" I asked her.

"It's a dating app. No judgement if you were," Trinity said.

"No, I...quite honestly, I don't have time to date."

"Really? Well, that's a shame," Trinity said. "Maybe things will slow down for you at some point. But a lot of people are busy in the summer, right, Elise?"

She nudged Elise, and she nodded.

"Elise works for Tours from the Cove boat tours. They're starting up soon, and she's going to be crazy busy. That's what happens when you live in an area that shuts down for the winter."

I nodded and tried to figure out what was going on.

"Well, we should go," Trinity said. "It was nice seeing you again."

"You, too," I told her. I smiled at them both, but Elise barely acknowledged me. I tried to tell myself it was for the best.

I went outside behind them, but they were walking the opposite direction from where I parked my truck. I got in and turned on the heat, needing a little warmth to fight off the chill of the spring night.

On my drive home I tried to decide if Trinity was flirting with me or if she was trying to get me to ask Elise out. By the time I got home, I realized it didn't really matter because I didn't have time to date. I didn't have time to do anything.

But I did want to see Elise again.

Even though I knew better, I looked up the dating app Trinity mentioned. Before I could convince myself not to, I downloaded the app. I didn't open it, but it was there. If nothing else, maybe when I was ready to date, I could meet someone.

Maybe Elise was on it.

3

ELISE

I zipped up my jacket and tied my hair back into a ponytail. It was going to be cold on the water for my first tour, but it would be worth it to be outside in the fresh air with the wind and water whipping around me.

Tourist season wouldn't be in full swing for a few more weeks, but Walter liked to start early so we had a few runs in before things got too busy. Especially for the newbies. It was good for them to be a part of the smaller groups before we were facing groups that just about filled the boats.

The employee lot was quiet when I got there. The other tour companies weren't running boats for another week, which made it nice for us. I locked my hatchback and threw my backpack over my shoulder, shivering at the chill in the air.

"Hey, I'm Cami," a woman said, walking over to me. I recognized her from the training as one of the new hires for the summer. "You're Elise, right?"

I nodded. "I am. We're working together today. Are you ready?"

She nodded, her grin wide. She had that fresh, new look

of someone who'd never done this before. She definitely had energy, which would be a good thing when we were on our fourth trip of the day and still had two more to go. Her dark hair was tied back into a thick ponytail. She was smart and not wearing any makeup and had a pair of leggings on under her Tours from the Cove sweatshirt and jacket.

"I've always wanted to do something like this. I grew up a little north of here and worked my way through college. I still am not totally settled on what I want to do with my life, so I figured working here for a summer would be fun. Maybe longer if I like it."

I smiled. I always wondered if it was a slight when newbies talked to me about working there a few years until they decided what to do with their lives, or if they were just oblivious. Cami had an oblivious vibe to her.

And besides, it didn't matter what they thought. I loved my job. I had fun every day and I was free. No one got to tell me what I should do with myself.

"It's a great job. As long as you don't mind sun and wind and talking," I told her.

Cami chuckled. "I can handle all those. How long have you been doing this?"

"Six years," I told her, bracing for the flinch and the attempt to disguise her shock. I'd made a career out of a job most people tried for a summer or two. It didn't always matter that their opinion wasn't important. People looked down on others all the time.

"Seriously? That's awesome. That really gives me hope that this is going to be a great place to work."

"It is," I told her honestly. Well, she sure surprised the hell out of me.

"So cool. Now I really can't wait to get started."

I smiled and held the door for her. "Then let's go."

We had a short meeting with Walter, then divided into

our crews for the day. Cami stuck by my side as we headed out to our boat.

"Wow. This is gorgeous. How many people are on this one?"

"It can hold one-fifty, but we're not going to have that many today. We'll be lucky if the boats are a third full."

Cami nodded. She was looking a little green, but her color came back slightly. "That's good. I wasn't prepared for that many people."

"Do you get anxious talking in front of a large group?" I asked her.

She shook her head. "Not usually. I was a theater major, but that was playing a part. I had a role. This is me."

I shrugged and shook my head. "It doesn't have to be. You can make up the persona you want to be when you're up there."

"How? My name is right here on my shirt."

I laughed. "True, but you don't have to be you, Cami. There are other women named Cami in the world. Maybe you're Cami who's visiting the area for the summer and looking to marry a rich, older man. Or maybe you're Cami who's shy and quiet and wants to keep to herself. Or maybe you're Cami who's loud and fun and always a party. You can be anyone you want to be because the chances of you seeing most of the people on the boat again are slim to none."

She grinned and tilted her head. "I never thought of that. Wow. I love the idea. Do you do that?"

I smiled. "I'll never tell."

She laughed, not pressing for more information. Usually people took the statement as a joke. The truth was a little too close to home to tell them. Even Ava didn't know all of the real me. She knew the version I shared at work.

My friends knew more than anyone else. They knew I'd been in a bad relationship that stopped me from wanting another one ever again. They knew I wasn't okay, and likely never would be. And they knew I wanted all of them to be happy more than anything else in the world. Some of them knew most of the story, but there were things I never told anyone. Things I couldn't bring myself to admit.

"What other tips do you have for me?" Cami asked, bringing me back to our conversation.

I recommended she get to know the crew on all the boats because we were moved around a lot, and I was honest about Walter asking me to evaluate the newbies to find a third to work regularly with Ava and me.

"I would love that, but I know if you don't recommend me, there will be a good reason. Can I ask you something?"

I nodded and focused on her.

"If there's something I do that you think I could improve, will you tell me?"

I nodded again. "I would anyway. This is a great job, but ultimately, we're here for work. If there's something you or anyone else is doing that impacts our ability to earn money, I am not afraid to share that. I have a few rules personally, and fair or not, I hold everyone to those rules."

"What are they?"

I grinned. "First, no picking up passengers. This is not your dating app. Second, no language that would be inappropriate around guests of all ages. And third, don't air your dirty laundry at work, with guests or coworkers. If you're friends with someone here, that's okay, but go somewhere else to talk about personal things. Guests overhear a lot, and they don't want to be dragged into your drama."

Cami nodded. "Those sound like good rules. I can live with them."

"Good, because you're going to have to. Are you ready?"

She nodded again and followed me to the helm. Ned was

inside running through his pre-checks. We waited patiently until he finished his step and turned to us.

Ned's dark brown eyes lit up when he saw me. He set the clipboard down and scooped me up.

"Damn, is it good to see you, Elise. How was winter?"

"Good," I said, hugging Ned back. We'd worked together since I started there. He was like a father to me, always watching out for me and making sure I was okay. He requested me to work with him when I was first starting out, and we'd stayed close. "We have a newbie with us today. This is Cami. Cami, this is Ned. He's the best captain we have, so treat him well."

"It's nice to meet you," Cami said with a wide grin.

"You, too, Ms. Cami. Is this your first season with us?"

Cami nodded. "It is. I always wanted to do this, and I'm finally taking the plunge."

Ned shook his head. "No plunges on my boats. I aim to keep us above water."

Cami chuckled when Ned winked at her. "I like that plan."

"Can we help?" I asked Ned.

He shook his head again. "Nah, I got this. I took her out yesterday to make sure things were in tip-top shape. I'm just going through to make sure I didn't miss anything. I haven't been behind the bar, though."

I nodded and squeezed his arm. "We'll take care of that. Give a shout if you need us."

"Will do. Good to see you, and nice meeting you, Cami."

"You, too," she said with a smile.

We turned back toward the rear of the boat. The snack bar was always well-stocked, but being the first run, it was possible some of the items had changed or weren't in yet. Cami and I went through the list and moved things to where we wanted them behind the bar. By the time we were done, the office was calling about our list.

"Hey, Elise," Wendy said through the earpiece. "We have forty-seven checked in. Another six bought tickets, but I haven't heard from them yet. We're ready to start loading when you are."

I glanced at Cami. She raised her brows in question, and I said, "Go ask Ned if he's good to go, please."

Cami nodded and rushed toward the front where Ned was still looking around.

"We're checking with Ned, but in the back, we're good."

"Copy," Wendy said. She knew it would only take a few seconds to ask Ned and was waiting for the reply.

"He's good," Cami called out, bursting out of the helm and racing back to me.

"Calm down," I told her. "Relax and breathe. We have plenty of time and a long day. Don't wear yourself out before our first trip starts."

Cami nodded and sank onto one of the benches. I called back to Wendy and told her we were all good, and she said passengers would be heading our way.

"Time to greet our guests," I told Cami.

She followed me to the port side where guests would board. I stood on the dock, and Cami stood on the edge of the boat. We watched as our first guests of the day, and year, walked the dock toward us.

"Welcome," I said with a wide grin. "Thanks for joining us today."

"Thank you," many of them replied as they hurried past me to board.

Cami repeated the same short speech to everyone, letting them know there was seating on top or underneath and they could pick their spot and would be allowed to move during the cruise.

Guests filtered in until the dock was empty. I breathed a short sigh of relief that I didn't know anyone on the boat.

Speaking in front of acquaintances was always more difficult than speaking in front of strangers.

"The line is gone and only a few more are to come," I told Cami, "so why don't you go stand behind the bar in case anyone wants anything before we go."

She nodded and pasted on a grin before walking away.

I tilted my head back and let the sunshine warm my face. By the end of summer, I'd be sick of it, but for now, I was loving the warmth on my cool skin. I wore jeans and my Tours from the Cove shirt, but I covered it with a sweatshirt and windbreaker with the Tours from the Cove logo on it. We were required to wear branded clothes so guests knew we were the crew.

"Am I too late?" a voice asked, startling me. His footsteps were quiet on the old, wooden dock and I didn't hear him coming. He was close, and I nearly jumped, which would have sent me into the icy cold water.

Then I opened my eyes and wished I had jumped. Because that would have gotten me out of the tour.

"Um, no," I said, forcing my heart to slow and my face to turn up into a smile. "We still have a few passengers to board. There's seating on top or below deck. We have a snack bar below, also."

"Thanks. I, um…sorry, I didn't know you would be here. Hudson, the bartender at O'Kelley's, mentioned you worked for this company, so I signed up for a tour since I figured if you worked here it was good, but I didn't realize…I'm Colin. We talked the other night. At O'Kelley's. And I own Jones Family Maple Farm. We met at the grand opening. Melody introduced us."

I nodded and prayed my smile stayed in place. I knew exactly who he was. That was why I wished I was anywhere but there. Because he was the kind of man I needed to stay away from. The kind who could disarm me with a look, who could make me want him with a smile, and who scared the shit out of me because the same was true about my ex.

"Oh, um, yeah, I remember you. Nice to see you again." Thankfully, more people walked up behind him. "You should find a seat. We'll be taking off soon."

Colin nodded and walked onto the boat as though he didn't realize anything odd was happening. That was good, but it put me even more on edge. Andy used to do the same thing. He was oblivious to how I was feeling. Now I knew it wasn't oblivion, it was a lack of caring, but at the time, that was how it felt.

Another reason to stay away from Colin Jones.

I smiled and welcomed the new passengers, ticking them off on the counter in my hand. I radioed up to Wendy and confirmed the number with her. She said we were all set to go. I relayed the message to Ned, then checked in with Cami. She was good behind the snack bar and wanted to watch me work for a few days before she tried to lead a tour. I didn't tell her that was policy anyway, but I'd fill her in another time. She seemed like she could be a good fit, and I wanted to help her.

I grabbed the headset and secured it around my neck. I positioned the mic and tried to glance around without it being too obvious what I was doing. When I didn't see Colin downstairs, I closed my eyes and took a deep breath, praying I just missed him even though I knew I hadn't.

I forced myself to smile as I walked up the stairs. It was worse than I thought. Not only was he upstairs, he was in the front row, which meant there was no way to convince myself he wasn't watching my every move and hanging on my every word.

Time to bring out Confident Elise.

"Good morning, everyone!" I said brightly as I walked past the rows of benches to the front of the boat. "It's a beautiful day for our first tour of the season. I'm Elise, and I'll be your cruise director today. Go easy on me because I've never been here before. We're going to see Niagara Falls, right?"

The murmured concerns were what I was hoping for.

I chuckled and shook my head. "Just kidding. This is my sixth year as a guide for Tours from the Cove. I grew up in this area and have lived here my whole life except the few years I was in college. How many of you are here on your first trip to the Thousand Islands?"

A few hands went up.

"Good. Welcome to the most beautiful place on Earth."

There were a few snickers and a few nods.

"The Thousand Islands is a truly stunning vacation spot that attracts visitors from all over. To be counted as one of the Thousand Islands, an island must have at least one square foot above sea level year round and support a living tree. All of the islands are either in Canada or the United States. None are split between the two countries. Does anyone know how many islands make up the Thousand Islands?"

A few people raised their hands.

"One thousand?"

I shook my head. "More than that."

"Two thousand?"

"Less."

"One thousand five hundred."

I grinned. "More."

"One thousand seven hundred fifty?"

I laughed with the rest of the passengers. "I'm sensing a trend here. And more."

"Eighteen hundred."

"More."

"Nineteen hundred."

"Less.

"Eighteen fifty."

"More."

"Eighteen seventy-five."

"Less."

"Eighteen sixty?"

"Getting close, but more." I held up two fingers close together.

Together, the passengers counted up until they said eighteen sixty-four.

"Finally!" I called. "Correct! There are one-thousand-eight-hundred-sixty-four islands. And now that we've all learned about that, we're out in the water where we can start to see some of them." I pointed toward the Canadian side of the river. "To my right, is Canada. As you all know, to the left is the United States. The St. Lawrence River splits the two countries. Many of the islands are private islands owned by one person or family. If you're in the market for a home, the island coming up on our left is currently for sale. The home sits on a private island in the US. It's a nice home at twenty-four hundred square feet. The sellers have included the boats and all the furniture in the home with the very reasonable list price of two-point-three million."

The chuckles and gasps mixed together.

I grinned. "If that's a little on the low side for you, I'll show you another one that's three times the size and only double the price. While we're out here house hunting, make sure you leave your phone number with me if you have any sons. I'm looking for a house, too."

That got a lot of laughs. I carefully avoided looking at Colin. We weren't dating. We weren't anything. And I was playing my part. But having him sitting there was the reason I didn't like having acquaintances on the boat. It unnerved me.

I glanced around, checking to see where we were, and pointed out some of the landmarks. Just Room Enough

Island, the smallest inhabited island in the United States, was big enough for a home and a small dry area next to it. Tourists loved seeing the island with its house that almost appeared to float at times.

We kept going down the river, looking at other notable homes. I shared the rich history of the area and the pirates who once lived there. It was only when I started telling the story of George Boldt and his wife, Louise, that I looked at Colin.

Then I couldn't look away.

4

---

*C*olin stared at me instead of Boldt Castle as we approached. His gaze watched me, hanging on my every word. I kept talking, telling him about the love George Boldt had for his wife and the devastation that losing her caused. He abandoned the property, never to return, and halted all work after learning of her death. It sat for seventy-three years as a monument to their love while the harsh winters and waters of the St. Lawrence took their toll. A beacon of love lost for nearly a century.

"The Thousand Islands Bridge Authority bought the property for one dollar and have worked to restore the castle to its original beauty. There is still work to be done and parts of Heart Island to restore, but the beauty of Boldt Castle and Heart Island is apparent. As we approach, you can see the castle from the front. To the side is the power house. We will go around back and dock, and you are welcome to tour the island for as long as you'd like. George and Louise would have welcomed guests with doors opened wide on a day like today. They would have smiled and waved you in and shared their love with you. I hope you feel a little of their magic today."

I finished with a smile, but my heart was pounding. I always said something similar, making sure guests knew they weren't going to a museum, but to a home. A place where a family was supposed to be. A place where parties and births and weddings would have taken place if tragedy hadn't struck.

George and Louise were real to me. I wanted them to be real for everyone else. But when I wished magic for everyone with Colin's eyes locked on mine, I thought maybe I found a little of that magic myself.

As soon as we docked, I was off the boat. It was my job, but I made sure I did it well so I didn't risk getting caught with Colin. I even pulled aside an older couple who were staring at a brochure to ask if they needed help or advice on anything. While I answered their questions, Colin stood to the side.

Cami, thank God for Cami, asked him if he needed anything. He said he didn't and finally headed toward the castle with the rest of the group.

If Cami picked up on anything, she didn't mention it. Once the boat was clear, we worked together to pick up random things guests left behind. We collected the lost items in a box behind the bar and tossed the trash. After that, we went back to the dock to check for passengers who didn't want to stay on the island and look at the castle. Later in the day, once a few tours had run, we'd fill up for our trip back to the docks, but being our first run of the day, the boat was empty as we set off again.

For the rest of the day, I was on edge. I waited for Colin to step back onto our boat, but he never did. I silently thanked whatever power kept him off my radar the rest of the day.

"Today was fun," Cami said as we cleaned up and finished our paperwork for the day.

I nodded. "It was. You were good to work with. Have you figured out who your characters are going to be?"

She shrugged. "A few, I think. I really like the idea of adding a little humor in with the stories. And making sure people know the history. You've clearly got all of it down."

"You'll get it, too. It's good to know about our area and what happened here. And what I've found is if you know five to ten really good stories and can recite them without thinking about it, you'll be through the trip before you even realize it."

"That's all?"

I nodded. "It sounds crazy, right? But yeah. The tours we did today were ninety minutes. On each trip, I told them about Boldt Castle, which we always do, a few of the private residences for sale, some of the most popular homes, and the pirates. I also talked about the area in general and shared a small bit about me. People don't need you to talk constantly."

Cami thought about it for a minute then chuckled. "Wow. I never picked up on that, and I've been listening to you all day. It's amazing."

I grinned. "It's years of practice."

Cami laughed. We walked to the parking lot together and I asked about her as a person. She shared that she has a boyfriend but doesn't think it's going to work out. She has two siblings. Her parents are still together. And she has no idea what she wants to do with her life long term.

I resisted telling her my only goal in life was to survive it on my own terms.

"Thanks for giving me so much advice today," she said when we parted ways in the lot. "I really appreciate all the help."

I nodded. "Any time. I'll see you soon."

"Bye!"

I couldn't complain. Aside from Colin showing up, it was a great first day.

No one else I knew showed up on my trips the next few days, and on Sunday night when I walked into girls' night, I was feeling good.

"How's the water?" Karissa asked me with a knowing grin.

"Wonderful," I said. "I finally feel like myself again."

Karissa laughed. "Sometimes I wonder how we're friends. I only feel that way when I'm cooped up inside and working on a new app."

I smiled. "It doesn't matter what helps you feel that way, it's something we should never let go of."

Karissa nodded, her smile understanding and sympathetic. Her brown eyes were kind, always, but when I made any mention to my past, she looked as though she understood just a little more than our other friends. Not that she'd been through the same thing, and not that she had to, but she'd experienced loss like the rest of us hadn't. Losing her mom was hard on all of us, but Georgia was Karissa's best friend her whole life. That was the kind of thing you never got over.

"My mom always said the same thing. That's why she worked at Cracked for so long. She loved it. The early hours and the busyness of it would have driven me crazy, but she thrived there."

Karissa shared her mom's positive outlook on life. Georgia always encouraged her to do something she loved. She encouraged all of us to love our lives. She was the one who told me to be a tour guide. I was feeling lost, and I mentioned one day that I hadn't spent enough time outdoors lately, and she said I should be a guide. I didn't listen right away, but she kept pushing me to try new things and eventually, I went out on a tour. I was hooked from the first trip.

"She had a way with people," I said with a sad smile. "Everything was easier with her around. She could see things the rest of us couldn't."

"Like what?" Trinity asked. Trinity and Georgia shared a birthday, but they'd only met once. Georgia convinced Trinity to move to MacKellar Cove, but when she did, Georgia was already gone. We brought her into our little group because we knew if Ms. Georgia loved her, we would, too.

"She always knew when someone needed advice, even if they didn't," Karissa said with a smile.

I nodded. "And she knew what would make you talk. She coerced me with French toast. Whenever she put it down in front of me, I knew I was in trouble because she'd get me to spill everything."

"Bacon for me," Finley said.

"I was sourdough toast," Melody admitted. "She was a little scary. I didn't like going to Cracked because she saw way too much."

"Mom was amazing," Karissa said, reaching out to grab Melody's hand. "She loved all of us so much. Even you."

Melody chuckled. "I think I was one of those problem children. She had to chase me down."

"She loved doing it. She loved all of it. I think that was what she hated the most at the end. The treatments and getting sicker and sicker were horrible, but she thrived with people, and she couldn't be around people as much," Karissa said sadly. She sniffed and wiped her eyes.

"I still remember the last day she came in," Blake said. "We were all shocked she was there, but she said she wanted to see everyone and wanted to be home for a little while. Eddie brought her in and sat with her at that back table." Blake smiled like she was seeing it all over again. "Everyone who came in went to her. Some sat and talked to her for a while and some just said hello, but everyone went to see Ms. Georgia that day. I swear she left looking like her old self."

"She felt like it, too," Karissa said. "She told me about it. She was so happy. She decided that day she was going to go back at least once a week, but she didn't make it to the following week."

We were all quiet for a long moment. Ms. Georgia was the heart of us. She brought us together like she did so many others. She was a matchmaker, not just for couples, but for friends. There was no one else like her.

"I wish I'd gotten to know her better," Trinity said.

"Me, too," Melody agreed.

We all nodded.

Finley grabbed her cake and lifted it. "To Ms. Georgia."

We followed suit and toasted Ms. Georgia with our cakes, laughing and shaking our heads. She would have loved it.

"Okay, I need to talk about something else," Karissa said. "Who has news?"

"I'm trying out some new designs," Trinity said, showing off her bracelet. "I am also thinking about expanding my website and selling more on my own. I love working with Olive, but I need to make more money if I'm going to keep doing this full time."

"I can help you with your website," Karissa offered. "And I can design an app for you. That would be really fun."

"Do I really need an app?" Trinity asked.

Karissa shrugged. "Doesn't everyone?"

We laughed.

"We have an app for boat tours," I said. "It really does come in handy. It was new last year so we're still getting used to it, but it helps us with a lot. There's a user section for people to book tours, and an employee part for us to manage things like who is working which tour and ordering supplies. It's nice to be able to do that on the fly."

Trinity nodded cautiously. "I'll think about it. For now, I think I need to focus on my website."

"I'll wear you down," Karissa said with a smile.

"I heard Colin went on one of your tours," Melody said, catching my eye.

To say I was shocked was an understatement. "How do you know that?"

"He told Ramsey. He thinks he upset you."

I shook my head, trying to come up with an answer, but Laura did it for me.

"Elise doesn't like anyone she knows to be on her tours. I went on one shortly after I got here because I wanted to see the area. I found out which one she'd be working because we'd met a few times and I thought it would be fun to see her in action. She was uncomfortable. Of course, she didn't tell me that until a while later, but Elise is a bit of a control freak. She likes to be the one who calls the shots."

I smiled at Laura, silently thanking her for saying what I couldn't say. She winked back.

"I don't think he asked for you," Melody said. "But he did know you worked there. Hudson told him."

I nodded. "I know. He mentioned it. He introduced himself and asked if I remembered him. I kind of froze."

"Why?" Finley asked.

I shrugged.

"Are you okay? Did something happen?" Blake asked.

I shook my head. "No. Just…I don't know."

"I'll tell Ramsey to tell him to back off," Melody said.

I gave her a tentative grin. "Thanks, but he's fine." I probably should have let her do it, but it didn't completely sit right with me. If he backed off, I wouldn't have to tell him no, and if I didn't have to tell him no, I wouldn't worry about the way he'd respond. But if he didn't go there to see me specifically, then I was overreacting and being crazy.

WHEN I GOT HOME LATER that night, I was still thinking about Colin. I wasn't sure if I judged him too harsh. He seemed like a nice guy, but nice guys weren't always nice.

God, I was so messed up. The only time I interacted with men was if they were involved with a friend of mine, customers on the boat, or hook-ups from one of the dating apps. I couldn't just have a conversation with a random guy without worrying about how he'd treat me if we were alone. And then I get scared and have to be a bitch to get him to go away.

It was a painful cycle. There were times, about once every two to three months, that I missed being with someone. Not the bad days, but the good days. The mornings waking up next to someone and feeling cared for. The evenings when I would come home and he cooked dinner.

Every day with Andy wasn't bad. That was part of what made our relationship so painful for me. He was sweet a lot of the time. He took care of me. He paid for everything, and he actually cared about me. For a while, at least.

It was the jealousy and the control that made what we had ugly. He wanted all of me, and he wasn't willing to share me. Not with my family or friends or classmates. It was a long time before I realized everything he was doing, and by then, I didn't have anywhere to go. He was the only person left in my world. Leaving him meant leaving my life behind.

But doing it meant I could live.

And I did. I created a life in MacKellar Cove that was

better than I ever imagined. I always loved it, but it truly became home for me when I stood on my own two feet. I was free from Andy and from the restrictions he placed on me. No one told me what to do.

I still missed having a partner. I considered moving in with one of my friends, but we were all single at the time. And moving in with someone meant giving them full access to my home, and allowing people they knew into it. I couldn't handle that kind of stress.

There was a knock on my door that made me jump. I clapped my hand over my chest and felt my heart pounding against my ribs. I closed my eyes and counted to five, then opened them again.

I installed one of those video doorbells as soon as they came out. I pulled it up on my phone and sighed when I saw Mrs. Carter with a pie.

I set the phone down and went to open the door. Mrs. Carter took a step back so I could open the screen and let her in.

"Did you make me a treat?" I asked her with a wide grin.

Mrs. Carter lived next door to me. Her husband died the year before. She had one son, but he lived in New Jersey. She'd adopted me as her family the day I moved in, and she hadn't stopped treating me like family the entire time I lived next to her.

"I did," she said with a grin. She climbed the two steps into my trailer and stopped to kiss my cheek. "I know you just had cake, but I was hoping you wouldn't mind pie also."

I rubbed my stomach and said, "There's always room for pie."

She laughed and headed for my kitchen. She set the pie on the counter and grabbed a knife from the block next to my stove. I liked having easy access to knives, just in case.

Mrs. Carter cut two large slices of pie, the dark red cherries bursting from the exposed crust. She went into my fridge and grabbed the can of whipped cream, adding a healthy dollop to both slices, then carried the pie to my table.

She lifted her fork and tapped mine. "Enjoy."

I grinned and watched as she took a bite and groaned. Mrs. Carter was one of those people who enjoyed everything life had to offer. She loved sharing her gifts with others, and she reveled in them herself.

I speared a bite, the flaky crust resisting my fork long enough to squish more cherries out of the side of the pie. Once I had a piece broken off, I scooped it up, snagging the runaway cherries and a bit of the whipped cream.

I groaned and closed my eyes, too. "This is so good," I said around my mouthful.

Mrs. Carter nodded. "It is. Cherries are good. They're not local yet, but they're still delicious."

"Yes, they are. I wish I could bake like this."

"You make that amazing cake," she said kindly.

I did enjoy baking cakes. For some reason, pies never came together for me, but cakes I could handle. "This crust is delicious. It's perfect."

"It was my grandmother's recipe. I'll share it with you. You should come over sometime so we can bake a pie."

Mrs. Carter was lonely. She'd told me a few times that it was too quiet without her husband there. She considered moving to a home for seniors, but she didn't want to be limited. She was still capable of living on her own.

"That sounds like fun. I'm off a few days this week," I told her.

She grinned. "Excellent. I'll get all the ingredients."

"Why don't we go together so you can show me how to pick out the good stuff?"

She nodded enthusiastically. "That's a great idea. Now, what kind do you want to make?"

We talked about pies and flavors and all the different pies we were going to make through the summer. Mrs. Carter stayed a couple of hours, and when she was ready to go home, I walked her back so I knew she was okay.

I smiled when I walked back into my home. She was the reason I lived there. Mrs. Carter and all the other neighbors who watched out for each other. Mrs. Carter was rarely alone. Someone checked in on her regularly. Just like someone checked in on Mr. Robinson and his kids, and Ms. Goldman and her cats, and me. We all looked out for each other, and that made all the difference in the world. I knew I was safe, and I knew I was cared for, and whenever I started to think I needed something else, they reminded me I had it really good exactly where I was.

5

—————

COLIN

*N*icky tipped the bucket over, spilling the sap into the gathering tank. The work was backbreaking, but it was necessary.

"Last one," he said with a groan. He set the bucket back on the spile and stretched. "We should really look into connecting all these to the tubing. I'm too old for this."

I chuckled and nodded. "I am, too." I rubbed my own sore back. We took turns emptying the buckets. My grandmother wanted some of the farm to stay the way it was historically with buckets hanging on trees and sap collected by hand daily. Modern farms invested in tube systems that collected the sap and vacuumed it directly to the sugarhouse. Over time, she was transitioning the farm to that, but she still held on to tradition.

"Cleotha loved to get out here and look around, but the hills are much easier to manage," Nicky said.

I chuckled. "That's because all we do is drive through there."

He nodded. "Exactly."

I shook my head. "I'm hoping we have the money to

45

convert the rest of the farm within a couple of years, but since we haven't made anything for a few years, I don't know what surprises we're going to face. I know this sucks, but we're almost done for this season."

Nicky nodded. "I get it, kid. I'm just messing with you."

I rolled my eyes and grinned. I definitely didn't feel like a kid, but Nicky saw me as Cleotha's grandson, and I had a feeling he always would.

"Let's get this back to the sugarhouse and start working on the next batch," I said.

Nicky jumped into the truck and closed the door. The drive back to the sugarhouse was short, but we took it slowly. April was a busy time of the year for us, and it brought out a lot of wildlife so everything went a little slowly.

I was almost sad to see the trees giving us less sap day after day. The routine had become familiar and relaxing to me over the last six weeks. I started my day early, checking on the sugarhouse and the sap that was starting to flow as the sun came up. We headed out to the field to check the bucket sections, then went back to the sugarhouse and spent the rest of the day turning the sap into syrup. The reverse osmosis machine did most of the work, but we stayed close by in case there was an issue.

The evaporation cloud typically brought customers to the farm. Sometimes it was tourists visiting the area, and sometimes it was families looking for something to do on a spring afternoon. Whoever showed up, we treated them with fresh syrup samples and maple flavored treats.

When we pulled up to the sugarhouse, Nicky jerked his head toward the barn and the car parked out front. "I'll head in. You go see who's come to visit you today."

He walked away chuckling, but I didn't find his jokes nearly as funny as he did. After families and tourists, the other group of visitors we had regularly were single women who apparently thought I was fresh meat.

Ramsey tried to warn me, but I thought he was kidding when he said there would be some local women who pounced as soon as they knew where to find me. Since so many people in the area were born and raised there, many of them had exhausted all the possibilities for dates. And a new person in town was prey until one of them caught him.

According to Ramsey.

I didn't want to be prey.

"Good afternoon," I said with a smile when I walked into the barn.

Two women stood to the side, looking at the maple products we had. The barn was equipped with a state of the art security system with cameras pointing at everything. Nicky recommended I hire someone to watch the barn when we were out on the farm. I put him off on that the same way I put him off about the tubes. Something was going to break, or die, or happen that was going to require money. I had a little savings, and I had the operating money from the farm, but depending on how bad the disaster was, it wouldn't be enough. And until I knew I could hire someone and not have to fire them almost immediately, I wasn't asking for any help.

"Hi," one of the women said. "We heard you have some great stuff here."

The sex in her voice did nothing for me. I liked a woman who was more subtle. One who didn't feel the need to flaunt herself in order to get attention. One who knew she was beautiful, or one who didn't think she was anything special, but she was.

One like the woman I hadn't been able to stop thinking about since she told me about George Boldt and how much he loved his wife.

"We do," I said, forcing a smile for the women in front of

me. "We carry a lot of items made by locals. We have some stuff you can only get here. Our goodies section is especially popular."

"Are you in it?" the other one asked, chewing on her nail.

I smiled and shook my head. "Uh, sorry ladies, but no."

Their faces sank. "You're taken? We heard you were single."

I considered lying, but it wasn't in my nature to do so, even if it was in my best interest. I shook my head. "I'm not taken, but I'm also not looking for anything serious right now."

"We don't have to get serious," the first one said. Her friend followed right behind her. "We could all just have a little fun together."

Her friend nodded when I looked at her. Was she seriously…No. It wasn't possible.

"We don't mind sharing. Especially a guy like you. I'm sure you could make both of us very, very satisfied," the second one said. She slid her hand up my chest.

I backed up and found myself against the table. A part of me, the primal male part, said to stay put and enjoy whatever they wanted to do, but the decent part said it wasn't fair. Not to them and not to me. I didn't care if people wanted more than one lover, but it wasn't me. I was a one-woman kind of man, and even considering something else went counter to who I was.

"I'm sorry, ladies, but I don't have the confidence in my skills that you do. Besides, I'm out of practice. I have a feeling you'd be satisfying each other more than I would be helping out."

"We'd give you a chance," one said, pouting as I side-stepped to get away.

The other one turned her friend's face and kissed her.

They got lost in each other for a moment, forgetting entirely that I was there.

The first one broke away from the kiss and smirked at me. The second one kept her focus on her friend.

"How about now?" one said.

The other one finally pulled her adoring gaze from her friend. She found me watching her. Her eyes widened with realization that I knew what she was thinking. She jerked her jaw upward and snapped her gaze away from mine.

"Let's go, Kris. He's not worth it."

"But…" Kris protested.

I smiled at her as her friend dragged her away. I hoped one day Kris would realize how much her friend loved her and give her a chance.

I closed my eyes once they left and drew in a breath. Maybe I did need to hire someone. Soon.

I went back to the sugarhouse and found Nicky unloading the gathering tank from the farm into the storage tank. He drove a forklift like it was an extension of himself. It probably was after all the years he'd been driving the same truck.

He set the tank on the ground and turned off the forklift. He got out with a wide grin that said he knew exactly what happened in the barn.

"How many?" he asked.

"How many what?" I replied.

"How many women were in the barn waiting for you."

"They weren't waiting for me."

"Did they buy anything?"

I shook my head.

"Did they try to leave with something?"

I chuckled at his thinly veiled innuendo.

"I knew it. Man, I tell you, if I were forty years younger, I'd be gone by now. You need to live a little."

I shook my head. "I don't think that's living. Living is enjoying life. It's doing the things you want to do. Those women were beautiful, but I'm not looking for anything right now."

"Then why did you download that dating app?"

My cheeks heated. "How did you know about that?"

He chuckled. "You just told me."

I groaned. I always fell for that one. "I just wanted to…I don't know."

Nicky shook his head. "There's no shame in wanting to spend your life with someone, kid. We all should have someone special. Someone who makes us happy. No one said you have to be single to take this job."

"You are," I countered.

He shrugged. "I wasn't always. I had the love of my life for many years."

"You did? You never mentioned anyone."

He smiled sadly. "We talk about her all the time."

I thought about it and couldn't come up with anyone. "We talk about work and my grandmother. That's it."

He smiled and nodded slowly.

It hit me, and I wondered why I never figured it out. "You and my grandmother. You were together?"

He nodded. "For years. I started working here after your grandfather passed. She loved him, but over time, she was lonely, too. We spent time together as friends, two lonely people who wanted someone else. Eventually, that friendship became more."

"Why didn't I know this?" I asked him.

He smiled. "No one did. We didn't want to tell anyone. What we had was between us. It didn't involve anyone else, so we kept it between us. Neither of us wanted to get married. We just wanted to love each other for as long as possible."

"Wow," I breathed. "I'm sorry, Nicky. I knew you were close, but I didn't know."

He smiled again. "I know, kid. And the only reason you know now is because Cleotha would have wanted you happy, too."

I nodded, wishing I'd known my grandmother better. We hadn't been in touch much over the years, but she always seemed kind. My father loved her, and he wished he could have handled being at the farm, but it was too painful for him.

Nicky clapped me on the shoulder and padded away. He went about his work, taking care of things like he always did. I tried to wrap my head around all of it and wondered when I'd have time for a woman in my life. And if I was willing to give up something else for one.

That answer was easy. For the right one, I would do anything.

EVERYTHING WAS BUSIER on the weekend. In my old job, I was off weekends. We would kill ourselves all week to get things done, and mostly be off for the weekend. What I never realized is the owners weren't.

Now, I was the owner.

Nicky was a huge help. He checked all the taps and made the rounds on Saturday and Sunday mornings while I focused on getting things ready for the guests who would flood in around ten.

I restocked the shelves with customer favorites like the maple candies and ice cream topping, then straightened up items that were on display. We carried a variety of things, all maple themed, from food to clothing to jewelry. Most of it was made by locals, many of them friends of my grandmother's. I wanted to carry on some of her traditions and help out locals. When you owned a farm, it only made sense to work with others who lived near you and supported your business.

The first customer slid the door open a little before ten, and when I looked up, I couldn't help but smile. Ramsey was dressed down in jeans and a dark tee and had his daughter tossed over his shoulder in a fireman's hold. With his other hand, he held his wife's.

"Morning, guys," I said as they got closer.

"Morning," they said together.

"What do we have here?"

"Someone wanted to go check on her tree. I told her she couldn't go running through the woods without an adult."

"I told Daddy you said I could go anywhere I wanted, Mr. Colin," Amber said in her sweet voice. Her red hair covered her face, even when she turned to the side.

I nodded and crossed my arms, giving Ramsey a stern look. "She's right. I said she can go anywhere she wants. She's an honorary owner because she helped me tap the first tree."

Ramsey struggled not to smile. Amber wriggled against him until he slid her down into his arms. She was extra bright in her purple leggings and hot pink sweatshirt against Ramsey's muted clothes. "Even if you're an honorary owner and can go anywhere you want, you're still too little to be running all over the place. There could be bears out there."

Amber's eyes got wide. "Really? I want to see a bear!"

I couldn't stop my chuckle. I tried to cover it with a cough, but Ramsey saw right through that.

"Amber," Ramsey began, "bears don't love it when you come into their territory. They get protective, especially if there are babies."

"Aw, babies! I want to see a baby bear."

"Let me take her," Melody said, letting go of Ramsey's hand and reaching for their daughter. "You're just making it worse." She mock-glared at her husband. "Amber, let's see what's over here."

Amber went with Melody, and Ramsey watched them walk to the far side of the barn. The love in his eyes was much better than the pain I saw there when we first met. Day one he told me they were separated and probably headed for divorce. I was more than a little happy they worked it all out.

"She's a handful," Ramsey said with a shake of his head.

"Yeah, but you wouldn't trade her," I replied.

He chuckled and nodded. "Very true."

"So, to what do I owe this honor?" I asked. It had been a while since they'd been out to the farm.

"Melody thought I should check on you," Ramsey said.

I was taken aback a little. "Why?"

Ramsey shook his head and smiled. "She thinks you're interested in her friend, and she wants me to find out. Checking on you is just a cover for acting like high schoolers."

I snorted. "She's funny."

Ramsey stole a glance at his wife. "She is, but she's also rarely wrong. Are you after Elise?"

I shook my head, forcing my body not to react. "No."

"But you think she's hot?"

"I do. I won't lie about thinking a woman is attractive. That doesn't mean I'm after her."

"Melody seems to think Elise is interested, but I am already too much in the middle of all this. We need to grab a beer and talk about sports or something."

I chuckled and agreed. "That's more my speed, too."

"Good. Next time?"

I nodded. "I did head over there last week. Hudson?"

Ramsey nodded.

"He said you guys left just a little while before I showed up."

Ramsey nodded again. "Yeah, he told me. Sorry I missed you."

I shrugged. "My fault. I'm still getting used to the small town life and everything."

"Like your lawyer inviting you out for a drink?" he said with a grin.

I laughed. "Yeah, pretty much."

He shrugged. "You'll learn that everyone here is friends with everyone else. MacKellar Cove is pretty tiny, and we all know each other. If you don't know someone, chances are you know their family. We don't have lines between us like a lot of places do. We all look out for each other."

I grinned. "I think that's my favorite part about living here. It's still going to take some getting used to."

Ramsey clapped me on the back as new customers walked in. "That's okay. We'll wear you down eventually."

I laughed. They already were.

Ramsey rejoined his family, and I greeted the new guests. They looked around and by the time they approached the register, more customers were milling about inside.

It wasn't long before people were spilling out into the farm. Ramsey and Melody took Amber to see her tree, and stopped by the barn on their way out. The day was busy, but not so busy that I didn't notice that Elise wasn't there.

Not that I expected her to be, but wishful thinking never killed anyone.

6

ELISE

I couldn't shake the uneasy feeling I had. It had been building for a while. I knew what it was and I resisted it as long as possible, but I had to accept the fact that I just needed some sex.

Most of the time I could get rid of the urge with one of my vibrators, but this was one of those times when I needed physical contact with the orgasm. But it also made me uneasy because I had to maintain control. Not dominatrix kind of control, but the kind of control where if the guy was a creep, I could get away without worrying about becoming a horror story kids whispered about one day.

My imagination was a scary damn place.

I searched Book Boyfriends Wanted, knowing I needed to find a temporary guy to scratch an itch. A long-term kind of guy was out of the question, but one of those guys who was interested in seeing where thing could go or who was new to the site were usually good bets that they were looking for sex and not anything longer than a night. Once in a while they wanted more, but I'd picked through enough dating profiles to have an idea of the kind of guy I was looking for.

The one called SweetStuff caught my eye. He was new to the site, which was good. He was funny, which I always found attractive, and he admitted he was a little bit of a workaholic. It was the kind of trifecta I would have bet on.

I sent him a message, just a hi, and asked how he was doing. I wasn't sure if he'd reply, and set my phone down so I could fix dinner.

After I ate, I noticed a message from him.

SWEETSTUFF

Hi, Captain. I'm good. How are you?

Yes, my screen name was Captain. I figured it told them off the bat I was in charge. If they didn't like it, they didn't have to reply.

CAPTAIN

Good. Saw your profile. It looks like you're a busy guy.

SWEETSTUFF

Too busy, unfortunately. I don't get to have enough fun.

CAPTAIN

Want to have some fun with me?

SWEETSTUFF

What kind of fun?

CAPTAIN

How about you meet me at O'Kelley's in MacKellar Cove and find out? Do you know where it is?

SWEETSTUFF

I do. Be there in 30?

CAPTAIN

I'll be the one in the yellow sweater at the bar.

SWEETSTUFF

I'll find you.

I grinned and signed off. Hudson was going to be pissed I was meeting a hookup at O'Kelley's, but he would get over it. He talked big, but he was like a big brother to all of us. He was a protector, and he would make sure nothing bad happened to anyone.

I considered changing into something nicer than my leggings, but decided against it. Leggings were good for casual hookups because they said I was laidback and easy going and not trying to impress the guy.

I pulled my yellow sweater over my head and headed out the door. I wanted to be there early and maybe scope the guy out before he saw me, if I could figure out who he was. I also liked to have a drink in my hand before meeting a stranger so he didn't offer to buy me something and add a little extra something to it.

I parked on the street in front of O'Kelley's and walked in. Hudson was behind the bar and nodded when he saw me walk in. I went right to him and ordered a tonic water with a twist of lime.

"Are you kidding me?" he asked, scowling.

"What?"

"I told you not to meet any more random men from that dating thing here. It's bad for business."

"It's great for business. I tell random people to come here, and they show up and buy drinks," I argued.

"And if you get attacked?"

The fear that word carried with it slithered down my spine. I had to freeze before the feeling made me shudder. If Hudson had any idea how terrifying it was to imagine anything like that ever happening again, he wouldn't joke.

Not that he was kidding. He was worried about me. But that was exactly why I went there.

"You'll be here," I said when I could finally speak. "I know you'll never let anything happen to me. You hate it, but would you rather I meet some random guy at my house?"

"Fuck, Elise, don't ever tell a stranger where you live."

"I don't. That's why I meet them here, and if they aren't too creepy, I go to their house. Once I get a copy of their driver's license and text it to a friend."

Hudson barked a laugh. "Only you."

I shook my head. "No. All smart women should do things like that. People hide all sorts of things about themselves. There is no way of knowing everything about a person, even a person you've known for years. I sure as hell am not going to trust someone I just met."

"Good. So, who's the guy tonight?"

I shrugged. "I don't know. He should be here in about five minutes. I told him I'd be wearing my yellow sweater, so when a guy walks up, he's probably the one."

Hudson raised his eyebrows and chuckled. "Dating sure has changed since the last time I went out with someone."

I nodded. "Yeah, but this isn't really dating. This is fucking. That's all it is. I'm going to meet this guy, we're going to go back to his place for an hour or so, and then I'm never going to see him again."

Hudson shook his head. "I'm definitely not cut out for this. I'm glad I already had a wife. She was it for me. All this is too much."

"It's not that bad," I said, taking a sip of my drink. It was fizzy so people thought it was something fancy, but I never ordered anything with alcohol when I was going home with someone. I needed a clear head, both to make sure I was alert and to make sure I remembered the night. It would be a while before I was brave enough to find someone else.

When I first moved back after college, I slept around a lot. I felt the need to reclaim myself, and I started by doing what I could to erase Andy from my sexual past. If he was one of many, he would be less important than if he was one of two or three.

One night, I went out with a guy who put his hands around my throat. It wasn't an attempt to choke me, but no one else had touched my throat. The memories came back full force and I had a panic attack. The guy had to call Laura to get me to come out of the bathroom. He felt horrible, but I couldn't even look at him. Laura told him to lose my number, and I never saw him again.

But it scared the hell out of me. I'd been much more careful since then, and much less brave.

"Are you Captain?" a man said from over my left shoulder.

I pasted a grin on my face and turned around. My eyes widened and my smile fell. I shook my head before I even processed what I was doing.

"No. No. You can't be SweetStuff," I told Colin.

He rocked back on his heels. The man was potent. Just being that close to him set off every hormone in my body. I wanted to press my nose to his throat and get a good whiff of the scent that was teasing me. I wanted to run my fingers up his chest and learn the contours of those muscles under his shirt. I wanted to go up on my tiptoes and seal my lips to his and find out what he tasted like.

But I couldn't do any of it. Not with him. He was too tempting. He was too close, too attractive, too everything. He was the man I'd lose myself in and forget why I put up all the walls I did. He would destroy me, if I let him.

"I am," he said after a minute. "I didn't know that was you."

"That's the point," I said flatly. "Karissa designed the app to eliminate the things that most people looked for. No photos, no identifying details, no judgement. You meet someone who truly likes the same things you do, and you decide if there is more to it after you get to know each other."

"We didn't get to know each other yet. Are you sure—"

"I'm sure," I said firmly. "This isn't going to work."

"But—"

"No, I'm sorry. I wasted your time." I turned my back on him, hoping he'd get the point and leave.

He didn't.

He took the stool next to mine and turned toward me. "Why do you hate me? Did I do something? Because if I did, I'm sorry."

I sighed. On top of everything else, he was kind. Men who looked like him weren't supposed to be nice guys. They were supposed to be first class assholes so when you rejected them, they got all pissed off and said they were too good for you anyway.

It wouldn't have been the first time a hot guy said he was only asking the fat chick out to make her feel good. I'd gotten over the idea of simply being 'the fat chick' with them, but with Colin, he wanted to know why.

I sipped my drink and studied him out of the corner of my eye. He didn't press for me to answer him right away, but I knew he was waiting for me to say something. He held himself upright with one arm stretched across the bar. He kept his distance from me, not crowding me, but making it clear to anyone who glanced our way that we were talking.

His dark eyes slid down my body, making me even hotter. When they skidded back up, they collided with mine. He showed up looking for sex with a stranger, and he was leaving without it. I waited for his eyes to tell me he was angry, but he was more concerned than anything else.

I turned my head to look at him and said, "You didn't do

anything. I'm sorry I asked you to meet me here. When I meet guys online, it's for one night only. I'm not interested in anything longer than that."

"Okay?"

"We know each other. We've met before. You're too close."

"And that makes it worse, not better?" he asked.

I chuckled. "How would it make it better?"

He shrugged. "You know I'm not going to hurt you."

"What?" I breathed.

"You're safe. Your friends know who I am, we have friends in common, and if anything happened, Ramsey would kick my ass, and I'm pretty sure Hudson would help him."

"Damn right," Hudson said from a few feet away, clearly eavesdropping on our conversation.

"So, doesn't it make more sense?"

I opened my mouth to argue and found that I couldn't. He made sense. Everything he said made sense. And if he was anyone else, I'd probably seriously consider it, but he wasn't. He was the man I'd woken up in a tangle of sheets dreaming about. He was the man who made me forget who I was. He was the man who had the same easy charm as my ex.

"We just can't," I said.

Instead of letting him argue some more, I got up. I considered, for about half a second, picking up someone else in the bar, but the mood was gone. The desire passed. I just wanted to go home, crawl into my bed, and pretend I never met Colin Jones.

7

COLIN

I watched Elise race out of O'Kelley's like her ass was on fire. I checked, and it wasn't, but she was acting like it was.

I sighed and shook my head. Hudson was watching me, so I figured I'd ask him what I did. After all, he heard our entire conversation.

"Did I screw that up?"

He shook his head. "No. She's cautious. Anonymity is good for her, and you're not anonymous."

"But she knows she can trust me."

He chuckled. "No, she doesn't. To a logical brain like yours, it might make sense. Even if she calms down, it might make sense. But you're not who she expected. She expected a random guy she'd never seen before that she would never see again. She expected a guy she could give a fake name to if she wanted. She expected a guy who would enjoy whatever she gave him and not ask for more. And when you walked up, every possibility of logic disappeared. And with that, any chance that she might trust you."

I groaned and closed my eyes. God, she was fucking beautiful. When she said yellow sweater, I was picturing a hideous knitted sweater the color of the sun in a child's drawing. Hers was more of a copper or a golden yellow. It hugged her every curve and hid the roundness of her ass. Damn, did I want to get a better view of her ass. Those leggings were doing amazing things for her legs, and that sweater…fuck me. There would be no getting her off my mind when I went home. A thousand cold showers wouldn't do a damn thing. I was already planning to take myself into my own hand and alleviate the pulsing behind my zipper.

But first, I needed to know something.

"Does she meet up with guys here a lot?"

Hudson stared at me for a long moment before answering. Finally, he sighed and shook his head. "No. She has in the past, but recently, no."

I wasn't sure if that made me feel better or worse.

"Do you want a drink?" Hudson asked, still standing in front of me.

I nodded and asked for two fingers of whiskey. I could sip it slow and watch the people in the bar.

I thought about what Hudson said as I sipped my whiskey. It burned as it went down, but the realization that he was right burned even hotter. Elise wasn't looking for me, or for anything. She was looking for a release.

If I was being honest, I was, too. I didn't agree to meet up with her because it was her. I agreed to meet up because I thought it would be a good chance to decompress.

And doing that told her I wasn't the kind of guy she should get involved with.

The shit part of all this was I wanted to see her. I wanted to meet up with her. She was the woman I was thinking about when I agreed to meet Captain. I wasn't sure if that made it better or worse. Probably worse. It wouldn't have been fair if another woman showed up and we slept together. It would have been even worse if I pictured Elise while I was inside someone else.

I needed to get my head on straight. And that meant I needed to get back to work and forget about Elise, and all other women.

I THREW myself into work over the next week. It had always been my go-to, and it never let me down.

But at night…that was a different story.

I worked myself to exhaustion during the day so I would sleep through the night. But at night, my dreams made it impossible to stay asleep. I woke with my hand around my cock, pumping furiously as I called out Elise's name.

The dreams grew more and more graphic as the week went on. I thought they'd stop eventually, but they didn't. They kept coming, and so did I.

But it wasn't just the sex fantasy that was keeping me up at night. I started seeing her every time I went into town. She was driving by when I went to get supplies from the hardware store. She was walking down the street when I went to pick up groceries. She was at a table when I walked in to have lunch.

I was losing my fucking mind.

Wherever I saw her, Elise had a smile on her face. She was a happy person. I saw something behind her smile, but her smile was there. And it was telling me more about her every day. Sometimes her smile was for another person, one that said she was kind. Sometimes her smile was a secret thought, which told me she had a sense of humor. And sometimes her smile was for herself. Those were my favorite ones. The ones when she walked by a window and grinned at her reflection. Or when she picked up her cheeseburger and smiled before she took a bite.

She was the kind of woman who loved herself, and that was the sexiest woman on earth. A woman who wasn't ashamed of who she was. It didn't matter if she was thin or curvy, if she was short or tall, if she had dark hair or light, if she loved herself, she was the kind of woman I wanted in my life.

And all that made it impossible to resist her, and impossible to stop wanting her.

I wasn't sure I believed in fate, but something put us together again. Maybe it was fate, or maybe it was the blessing of living in a small town where you could only avoid people for so long, but whatever it was, it brought us together.

"Order for Elise," she said, stepping up next to me and smiling at the woman behind the counter.

When I walked into the burger place, I didn't think anything about sitting at the counter and eating. I was trying to do the small town thing and get to know people. Luck was definitely on my side.

"Hey," I said when she glanced my way.

She jumped and froze, then plastered on a smile that was as fake as her recently pink hair. "Oh, um, hey."

"I guess this place is pretty good if you're here," I said.

She smiled and nodded, avoiding looking at me again.

"The sky is a pretty blue today," I said, just to see if she would keep ignoring me.

She nodded again, staring toward the back and tapping her card on the counter.

"Your ass looks fantastic in those pants," I said.

"What?" she blurted, finally looking at me.

I grinned. "I wanted to know if you would ever look at me."

She rolled her eyes and looked away again.

"Why don't you sit and eat with me?"

She shook her head. "I can't. I have to go."

"Because you have something to do or because you don't want to sit with me?"

She glanced at me and chewed on the inside of her lip.

"Because of me," I answered for her.

She sighed and turned toward me. "It isn't you—"

I laughed and shook my head. "Let me guess. It's not me, it's you?"

She twisted her mouth and sighed again. "I don't do relationships."

"Okay?"

"You have relationship written all over you."

I barked a laugh. "Really? What makes you say that?"

She raised an eyebrow. "For starters, you're a lot older than me."

"Wow. I did not expect you to make me feel like a dirty old man."

"I didn't say that," she protested.

"You didn't have to."

She smirked then tried to hide it. "You're not dirty. I just know older guys are usually ready to settle down."

"And you're not?"

She shook her head. "No. I'm not interested in settling down. Ever. I tried, and it wasn't right for me."

"Maybe he wasn't right for you."

"What?" she breathed.

I shrugged. "Maybe it wasn't the settling down that was the problem, but the person you were settling down with. Maybe it was him."

She chuckled. "It definitely was him. And because of him, I'll never try again."

"You won't even give me a chance? One date?"

She shook her head. "I don't date."

"One night?"

She shook her head again. "I don't stay overnight."

"One hour?"

Her eyes slid down my body and back up again. "I don't know if you could handle it."

I clutched my heart and leaned against the counter. "You wounded the old man," I teased her.

She laughed, and the sound went straight through me. I wanted to hear it over and over again.

"I'm not sure I'll ever recover," I continued.

She shook her head. "I'm sure you will."

I groaned. "I think you should let me buy you lunch to make up for it."

She hesitated, then saw the woman coming back with her food. When she handed it over, Elise nodded to me and said, "He's buying my lunch."

The woman looked at me and raised her eyebrows. I nodded in agreement and handed her cash to cover the bill.

"Thanks," Elise said, grabbing her bag and heading for the door.

"Wait a minute," I said. "I thought you were going to eat with me."

She shrugged. "You said you wanted to buy me lunch, not that I had to have lunch with you."

I opened my mouth to argue, but all I could do was laugh.

"Thanks for lunch," she said, pushing through the glass door. She jogged across the parking lot and disappeared when another vehicle drove by. When it cleared, she was already pulling out of her parking space and leaving.

"Here's your change," the woman behind the counter said. "Sorry."

I shook my head. "I'm not. That was the most we've ever spoken. It was worth every penny."

And just that fast, my commitment to stay away from her was crushed.

I SAT on my decision to pursue Elise for a day then decided I couldn't wait for her to realize she should give me a chance. I pulled up the conversation we had the night we met at O'Kelley's and started a new message.

> **SWEETSTUFF**
> How was your lunch yesterday?

CAPTAIN
Delicious.

> **SWEETSTUFF**
> Glad I could be of service.

CAPTAIN
LOL. Me too.

> **SWEETSTUFF**
> Are you going to let me buy you dinner next time?

CAPTAIN
I don't know. Are you going to say something dumb again?

I laughed out loud and shook my head.

> **SWEETSTUFF**
> If memory serves, I was the one being wounded. Maybe you should buy me dinner.

CAPTAIN

Something tells me your ego could take it.

SWEETSTUFF

I think it's my age. I'm more sophisticated and able to accept when someone is trying to be funny but missing the mark.

CAPTAIN

I don't think I missed. Everything I said was the truth.

I laughed again.

SWEETSTUFF

You sure know how to hurt a guy. How old do you think I am anyway?

CAPTAIN

How old are you?

SWEETSTUFF

No cheating.

CAPTAIN

Fine. If I had to guess, I'd say in your 40's.

SWEETSTUFF

I'm not sure if I should be offended or not. Upper or low 40's?

CAPTAIN

I'd say mid. Maybe 44?

SWEETSTUFF

You're off by 5 years.

CAPTAIN

Wow. I really didn't think you were 49.

"What!" I shouted to myself.

SWEETSTUFF

I'm 39, not 49. Wow. Now I think I am offended.

CAPTAIN

J/k. And sorry. I didn't mean to actually offend you. I was just kidding.

SWEETSTUFF

Me too. Age doesn't matter to me. When I was in my 20's, I felt much older because I wasn't doing things a lot of people I knew were doing. Now that I'm almost 40 and not married and don't have kids, I feel younger.

CAPTAIN

I get that. I'm 29, and I've always felt older. I had some wild years, but I bought my own place a while ago and like my life. I'm starting to feel old at work lately. Some of the people starting there this summer weren't even in high school when I graduated college. It's making me feel old.

SWEETSTUFF

You're still a baby.

CAPTAIN

LOL. Cami, the other girl on the cruise? She's 22. Some of her friends are only 21. I'll be 30 in October. They're going out after working all day and I'm wondering how quickly I can get home so I can watch Netflix and go to bed early.

SWEETSTUFF

See? We would be good together. That's a good day for me, too.

I added a winky face when she didn't reply after a minute. I knew pushing too hard wouldn't be good, but I didn't want her to think I was just chatting. I wanted to see her again.

SWEETSTUFF

And now I've scared you off. I know you don't date, or don't like to, or something, but I want to get to know you.

CAPTAIN

Why?

SWEETSTUFF

Because you smile at everyone you talk to, and I think we all need someone like you in our lives.

CAPTAIN

I'll think about it.

SWEETSTUFF

Saturday at two. I'm going for a hike on the farm. Fresh air, should be a nice day. If you want to join me, I'll meet you in the barn.

CAPTAIN

I'll think about it.

SWEETSTUFF

See you then.

CAPTAIN

You're persistent.

SWEETSTUFF

Only when I know I'm missing out on something great.

CAPTAIN

I'll think about it.

SWEETSTUFF

I guess I have to take that answer.

CAPTAIN

Yep.

SWEETSTUFF

> Have a good night. And thanks for not unmatching me.

CAPTAIN

> Good night.

I closed the app and set my phone down. She was going to show up. I could feel it. And it was going to be a great date. It had to be.

I TRIED NOT to be too confident on Saturday, but I was. I knew Elise was going to show up. I woke up in a good mood, and I couldn't stop smiling all through the morning, even when a kid got away from his parents and crashed into a display. Thankfully, it was a display of books by local authors and not anything breakable, and the kid wasn't hurt, but it was a pain for me to pick up. And the parents barely acknowledged that their kid was to blame.

Just before two, I walked outside to wait for Elise. I considered packing a lunch or a blanket or something, but I was going to be casual about the whole thing. It wasn't a date, not really, although I was hoping it would feel like a date and she'd be willing to go out again.

I walked around, greeting new people as they walked up and thanking others as they left. I forced myself not to check the time or wonder where she was. She was coming.

I went back inside and looked around to make sure I didn't miss her, but she wasn't there. Not many people were. It was a beautiful day, and people didn't want to be cooped up inside. They were grabbing the items they came for and heading out.

When the last customer left, I had to admit to myself that she wasn't coming. I finally gave in and looked at my phone. It was almost three o'clock. She wasn't coming.

I closed up the barn and slid the lock into place. Nicky cocked his head at me and asked what was going on.

"I was hoping someone would show up today," I said.

"A special someone?"

I nodded. "She could be. I wanted to get to know her."

"Maybe something came up?"

I shrugged. "Maybe. Or maybe she isn't as interested as I am."

"What are you going to do about it?"

I chuckled. "What can I do? I'm not going to force a woman to go out with me. If she's not interested, she's not interested. End of story."

"And what if she shows up late and has a good excuse."

"Like what?" I asked.

He shrugged. "Why don't you ask her." He nodded behind me.

I turned and saw Elise sitting in the parking lot watching us. I didn't know how long she'd been there, but I was sure she wasn't there when I was outside earlier.

Did it matter? She was there now. And I still wanted to spend time with her.

"Have you ever been to the swimming hole?" Nicky asked.

I tore my gaze from Elise and shook my head. "Not in years. I vaguely remember it from when I was a kid. I'd forgotten about it."

"It's on the north end of the property. About a thirty minute hike from here. Quiet and peaceful. Might be a good place to take your woman, especially since she looks like she might be afraid to get out of that car of hers."

I glanced back at Elise. She was holding the steering wheel firmly in both hands. I wondered if she was going to drive off. It looked like a real possibility.

"Good luck," Nicky said with a smile. He waved at Elise, and she took one hand off the wheel to wave back. That had to be a good sign, right?

I approached her car slowly. She watched me the entire way. I waved when I got close to her door. She waved back. It was like we were playing cat and mouse, but I wasn't sure which of us was the cat.

She was afraid of getting out, and I was afraid she would stay in. We were in a standoff, but she had all the control.

"Do you want to come out?" I asked through the rolled up window.

Her chest rose with her deep breath, then she nodded and turned off her car. She grabbed the handle and the door released. I pulled it the rest of the way open and offered her my hand.

"I'm sorry I'm late," she said before she took my hand.

I shrugged. "I figured you'd show up when you could."

She looked up at me. "Are you upset?"

I smiled. "I was disappointed when I thought you stood me up. But once Nicky pointed you out, the only thing that mattered was you're here."

"Even though I'm a wreck?"

I took her hand and pulled her out of her car. I wanted to yank her into my arms and tell her she wasn't a wreck, but I had a feeling that would send her right back into her car. Instead, I held her hand for a second and squeezed her fingers. "You're the only one who thinks there's anything wrong with you."

She laughed. "That's because I know me best."

I nodded. "Yeah, but you're also your own worst critic.

We all are. And being cautious is never a bad thing when it comes to meeting new people."

"So, you don't think I'm crazy?"

I shrugged. "Not yet. I'm sure you can change my mind today, though."

She laughed and finally closed the door. It was small, but it felt like a huge victory. One I'd happily take.

8

ELISE

I didn't know how he did it, but Colin had an ability to put me at ease. Andy…well, at first I wanted to impress him. He was older, but he was also one of my teaching assistants. He had power over me from the beginning. For him, his age and position were things he used to convince me to do things. For Colin, his age was something that gave him an ability to read people.

"Where are we going?" I asked him as we walked deeper into the woods. When he asked if I wanted to take a walk, I was excited about the idea. As we went farther and farther from the barn and the world I knew, I grew uneasy. Was I foolish for thinking I could trust him?

"Nicky gave me the idea. He mentioned a secret place that I forgot about. I haven't been there since I was a kid. Do you want me to send you a pin? Then you can send it to a friend so someone knows where we'll be?"

I looked at him from the side, wondering why he would ask. "Should I be worried?"

He glanced over at me and caught me watching him. "About me? No. But you don't know that yet. A woman needs to be smart. Men do, too, but I'm bigger than you. I'm taller and I weigh more. I could overpower you. You would have to catch me by surprise, which is possible, but if you would rather share your location with a friend, I get it. You just need to give me your number."

He handed me his phone with a smile. "Was all this a rouse to get my phone number?"

He shrugged. "Just a convenient way to get it."

I rolled my eyes and added myself to his contacts. I may have also scrolled through to see how many women he had in there. Not many.

"If you want to keep searching my phone, you can, but I need it to send you the pin."

My cheeks burned at being caught, and I handed his phone over without a word. My phone buzzed in my pocket, and I snatched it. I forwarded the location to Laura with a note that I was off on a walk with a random stranger and that if she didn't hear from me within a few hours to send help.

She replied back almost immediately.

> What? Why? Where did you meet him? I'm coming to get you right now!

> Relax. He's not random. It's Colin from Jones Family Maple Farm. We're somewhere on the property, but he thought I'd feel better if someone knew where we were headed.

> Seriously? He knows?

> No. He just understands somehow.

> I didn't tell anyone anything.

> I know. I never thought you did.

So, is this a date?

I don't know. Maybe. He's…a lot of things. Which partially terrifies me. He seems perfect, which is never a good thing.

Sometimes you find someone who is perfect…for you. Be happy. Don't wait for the bad to come.

The bad always comes. It's just if I saw it coming or not.

Where is he now?

I glanced over at Colin. He was walking beside me, enjoying the walk.

He's right next to me.

You're with him now? Why are you texting me?

So you know where I am!

Jeez, go have fun. I'll send a search party if I don't hear from you. Be careful.

I always am.

I locked my phone and slid it back into my pocket. Colin didn't say anything.

"Sorry," I said after a minute.

"About what?"

"Texting my friend."

"You don't need to be sorry. Friends are important, and so is your safety. I'd rather you're cautious than hurt."

"Are you for real?" I asked him.

"What do you mean?"

"Are you for real? I've never known a man like you."

"Maybe you just haven't known the right kind of man."

"That's definitely true."

He breathed a laugh but didn't say anything else. Instead, he handed me his phone again. "Did you want to look for anything else?"

I hesitated then shook my head. "No. I'm sorry I violated your privacy."

He shrugged. "I don't believe in secrets. Keeping things from the people we care about doesn't help anyone."

"I think you might be a unicorn."

"A unicorn?"

I nodded. "Fictional being that everyone wishes was real but isn't."

"You think I'm fictional."

I nodded again. "It's the only explanation. No man is as perfect as you."

He chuckled. "I'm nowhere near perfect."

"You seem like you are."

"Trust me, I'm not."

The tone of his voice sent a shiver down my spine. Not the bad kind of shiver. The good kind. The kind that said he had all sorts of dirty things on his mind. The kind of things that would make a woman beg for more. The kind that was making me reconsider the promise I made myself to keep my clothes on.

"We're here," he said, a smile curling his lips up.

I followed the direction of his gaze and knew, without a doubt, I'd be breaking that promise. My clothes were definitely coming off.

"Wow," I breathed. The pond was relatively small, but the stream that fed it poured down a short waterfall. At the far end, it narrowed and disappeared again. The section we stood in front of was clear all the way to the bottom and so inviting.

"Beautiful, isn't it?"

I nodded, unable to tear my eyes from it. "I never knew this was here."

"Not a lot of people do. It's so far from the barn that no one would venture all the way out here. It's completely on the Farm, so it's private. It's a perfect cure for a warm spring day."

Colin took a few more steps forward and grabbed the edge of his shirt. He yanked it over his head with unintentional flourish. He mouth went dry at the sight of his bare back. Dark, smooth skin covered thick muscles. Two dimples were just above his waistband. His short hair glistened with his sweat. The walk was not bad, but the spring sun was warm. I was sweating, too.

Even more with his shirt off.

Sweet baby Jesus, he unzipped his jeans and dropped those, too.

My pulse thundered in my ears and my heart throbbed in my chest. I didn't want to stare at Colin, but he was even better than the view.

He unlaced his boots then toed them off and left his jeans on top of them. He finally turned back to look at me and raised an eyebrow. "Are you coming in?"

I opened my mouth and snapped it closed again.

He smirked. "Chicken." Then he ran to the water and jumped in.

"Woohoo!" he shouted as he came up for air. "Damn, that feels good. Come on, Elise. You know you want to join me."

The water looked refreshing. I knew it would be cold, but I didn't really care. What I did care about was taking off my clothes in front of him.

"Turn around."

He did as I asked, treading water. I watched his back the entire time to make sure he didn't peek. When he didn't, I started stripping off my clothes. My boots and socks went first. He still didn't turn. My leggings followed. He didn't turn. Finally, I dropped my sweatshirt and pulled my tee off. When it cleared my head, he wasn't looking at me.

A tiny part of me was disappointed. Maybe he wasn't interested. He didn't try to look at me, and he hadn't touched me since he helped me out of my car.

That should be a good thing, but it wasn't, and I hated it.

I tied my hair up in a ponytail and tiptoed over the cold grass to the edge of the water. There was a drop off just beyond the rocks that lined the pond. I didn't know how far down the water went, but it looked deep enough that I could dive or jump in and not worry about hitting the bottom.

I stood on one of the rocks and took a deep breath. If I felt the water first, I'd chicken out, so I just jumped.

The cold water wrapped around my body instantly, startling the breath from me. I fought the urge to suck fresh air back in and kicked to the surface. When I came up, Colin was grinning at me.

"Feels good, doesn't it?" he asked.

"That's fucking freezing."

He threw his head back and laughed. "Yeah, that, too."

"You could have warned me."

He chuckled. "I thought you grew up here. The water won't be warm until August, if we're lucky."

"You still could have warned me," I said.

He shrugged. "I wanted you to join me. I figured you wouldn't if you knew how cold it is."

I licked my lips and tugged the bottom one between my teeth. He was giving me that look again, the one that said he was thinking dirty things.

I swam closer to him. He reached for me but stopped

before he touched me. I swam a little closer, close enough that I could feel the heat from his body in the water. Our feet brushed as we kicked to stay afloat.

"I'm not going to lie and say I don't want you, Elise, but that's not why I brought you here. I just wanted to share something with you."

"Thank you," I said softly.

"Can I kiss you?"

I didn't have to think about it. I nodded and let him pull me into his arms. One hand warmed my back while the other helped keep us above water. I expected his kiss to come all at once, hands, lips, bodies colliding without a second thought. But Colin was proving to me over and over again that he wasn't who I thought he was.

He stared at me, the distance between us barely enough to lock eyes. His were dark brown, almost black when we were this close. His lashes were short but perfect on him.

His hand branded me, telling me I was his even though I wasn't. Not yet. I couldn't deny the urge to let him claim me was there, but I wasn't ready for that.

Every so often, our legs would brush, but just as quickly, we separated, both of us fighting to stay above the water. I let my hands float on the surface, but I wanted to touch his skin. To feel his body under my palms.

He finally moved closer, his chest bumping mine. My bra and panties didn't do much to shield me from him and I found myself aching for more. Aching before I'd even gotten a taste of him.

I'd never known desire like that. Wanting something without even knowing if I would enjoy it. But I knew I'd enjoy Colin. I knew I'd lose myself in him. I knew I'd drown in him and never think twice about coming up for air.

"You could put your arms around me," he said.

"We'll both go under."

He shook his head. "I won't let anything happen to you."

I trusted him. I didn't want to think too hard about why it was so easy to do. I slid one hand around his neck and let the other drift over his chest. Tight curls abraded my hands as I touched him.

"We're at the side, Elise," Colin said softly. "So I can hold on."

I turned and saw the rocks looming above us. A flash of panic told me to run, but I looked back at Colin and all of it disappeared again.

I wanted him weeks ago, when we were matched on Book Boyfriends Wanted. I wanted him months ago, when we first met. And I wanted him in that moment, and I couldn't say no.

I wrapped both arms around his neck and pulled him to me. He groaned as our lips touched, but he didn't take over. He let me lead, let me choose how our kiss was supposed to happen.

I parted my lips and brushed over the seam of his. He opened and licked my tongue. I tightened my hold on him and plunged my tongue into his mouth. His hand eased farther around my back, bringing more of our bodies into contact.

I spread my legs and wrapped them around his waist. His hand fell to my thigh then slid up. Both his hands circled my waist...

And we went under.

He pushed me up, his firm hands shoving me out of the water. I grabbed at him to come up, and he let go of me to swim.

I coughed up icy cold water, holding on to the rocks so I didn't go under again. Colin did the same next to me.

"Sorry," he finally choked out. "I got lost in you and forgot we were in the water. Are you okay?"

I nodded and tried not to laugh, but it was just too funny. Colin choked and coughed, and I laughed then choked. And we floated on the side of the pond alternating between choking and laughing.

"Why are we laughing?" Colin finally asked.

"Because we almost drowned trying to make out."

Colin chuckled and shook his head. "I'm glad you're amused. I feel like an ass."

I shook my head. "It's a good story for our first kiss."

"First kiss? That makes it sound like there will be more than one."

I shrugged. "As long as you don't try to drown me again, I think we can talk about it."

"Dry land," he said.

I laughed. "Yeah, dry land is a good idea. But I'm not ready for dry land just yet."

I laid back in the water and closed my eyes. It was peaceful, and I couldn't resist it.

After a minute, Colin's hands brushed mine. He hooked his fingers into mine and floated with me.

I don't know how long we laid there, the sound of the water lapping and the cool breeze drifting over us. I almost fell asleep. It was relaxing and peaceful. Two things I hadn't felt when I was alone with a man in many, many years.

"You're shivering," Colin said, squeezing my fingers.

I opened my eyes and found him treading water next to me. His eyes were locked on mine, but the ticking in his jaw said he was trying his best to keep them there. I kicked so I was upright and remembered I was wearing a pink bra and panties. I thought they were cute when I put them on and they gave me a little bit of confidence, but I had no doubt they were completely see-through when wet.

I pulled my hand from his and crossed my arm over my chest. "Sorry."

He shook his head. "You don't have to say sorry all the time. There's nothing for you to be sorry about right now."

"I feel like I'm being a tease right now."

"Why?"

I glanced down and saw my nipples through the fabric of my bra. "Um, because I'm practically naked."

"You didn't know we were going to come here. I didn't tell you to bring a bathing suit. And I have no expectations from you. Hell, I'm so unprepared, I don't even have towels for us to dry off."

I laughed with him. "We're kind of a mess."

He shrugged. "A beautiful mess." He smiled. "Your lips are turning blue, though. We should probably try to dry off a little. The sun is still warm."

I nodded. "I am kind of cold. Maybe I should just get dressed, though."

"It's up to you. I won't look. Too much."

A surprised laugh bubbled out of me.

Colin grinned and winked at me. "Come on, let's get you warmed up."

We swam to the side and climbed out. I shivered without the water to keep the breeze off me and wrapped my arms around myself. Colin hoisted himself up and out of the water easily. He walked over to me and rubbed his hands up and down my arms.

The friction warmed me and the heat between us almost made me want to jump back in the water. He took a step closer, and I tilted my head back to look up at him. He leaned down, silently asking my permission. I lifted up on my toes and met him halfway.

I felt the effort he made to hold back, to let me be in control. I wanted to explore him, to learn things about him. I didn't kiss my one-night-stands very often. If I did, they were sloppy kisses that led to panting. It had been a long time since I'd simply kissed a man. I missed it even more than I missed companionship.

I built our kiss slowly this time, keeping my lips closed for a few seconds before I nipped the underside of his jaw. He groaned and tightened his hold on me, loosening it almost immediately.

I stepped closer and pressed my body to his. My curves fit him perfectly, like every inch of him was made to cradle me. I'd never known what people meant when they said they fit with another person. It was as frightening as it was exciting to feel like we matched.

I lifted my lips to his again and ran my tongue over his lips. His tongue darted out and slicked against mine. I sucked his tongue into my mouth and pulled him closer to me. My pulse kicked up, and my breath turned to pants. His erection twitched against my stomach. He didn't push against me or push me, he simply stood there and let me lead.

And that was a heady feeling.

I dragged my nails over his chest, brushing them over his nipples. He groaned again, but he still didn't take over. I tilted my head the other direction and thrust my tongue into his mouth over and over, but he didn't try to control me.

When I finally pulled back, he kept his eyes closed for a long moment. I studied him, from the dark freckles on his cheeks to the small scar by his right ear to the way his pulse beat in his throat. He was just as crazy as I was, but he was able to hold it in.

"Are you warm yet?" he asked when he opened his eyes.

I nodded.

"I'm about to catch on fire."

I laughed, and he pulled me in close and pressed his nose to my neck.

"You smell amazing."

"I smell like a pond."

"I like ponds. And I like you."

I smiled. I liked him, too.

We dressed in silence, and when he reached for my hand to walk back, I let him take it without thinking. When we got back to the barn, he walked me to my car and thanked me for coming over.

"I had a lot of fun," I admitted, almost surprised that it was true.

"Does that mean I might get a second date?"

I grinned. "Maybe. If you ask nicely."

He chuckled. "I'll see you soon, Elise."

"Bye, Colin."

9

———

I didn't want to tell anyone about my date with Colin, but I forgot to call Laura later that night, so she decided to make me pay for it at girls' night out the next day.

"Elise had a date yesterday. With a certain sexy syrup maker," Laura said as she cut herself a piece of cake.

It was rainbow cheesecake, something Trinity wanted to try out. I was a sucker for cheesecake, which was good because I could stuff my face and pretend I couldn't talk.

Unfortunately, Laura was free to talk for me.

"She texted me her location yesterday, just in case, and then forgot to tell me he didn't kill her and bury her body in the woods. I freaked out when I didn't hear from her and went to her place last night. But she was completely fine," Laura continued.

"Nothing happened," I said around my cheesecake. I couldn't meet the gawking stares of my friends.

"She said that, too, but I don't believe her. Her hair was wet and her clothes were damp, like she was wearing a bathing suit underneath. She kept saying nothing happened, though," Laura said.

"You and Colin?" Melody asked. "I knew you two would be good together. When I introduced you, I thought I was going to get burned from all that heat."

"I remember that," Trinity said. "It was the same when we saw him at O'Kelley's a few weeks ago. Colin is seriously cute, but he barely even glanced at me. He was too busy eye-fucking you."

"He was not," I argued.

Trinity snorted. "Uh, yeah. He was. He was totally into you. And I'm pretty sure the feeling was mutual. Still is from what Laura is saying."

"Nothing happened," I said again. I wasn't ready to admit it all yet. Not even to my best friends. It was too soon, too much.

"Should we be worried?" Finley asked softly.

My gaze snapped to hers. The depth of her fear was right there in her eyes, and I felt guilty for it. I knew what she was asking.

"No. He was sweet. Too sweet. It scares me how much I like him. In some ways he reminds me of Andy, but the more time I spend with him, the more I wonder if he's for real," I said.

"Who's Andy?" Melody asked after a few seconds.

Everyone else went still. They all knew who Andy was. Even Trinity, who didn't know the whole story, knew who Andy was. I'd gotten used to everyone understanding that he was bad news and that it was a painful part of my past that I didn't like to talk about.

But Melody hadn't been around us for long. Blake brought her into our group of friends, and a few months wasn't nearly long enough for her to know everything that happened to all of us forever. So, she asked questions.

"Andy was my college boyfriend," I said.

"Things ended badly?" she asked. If it was anyone else, I wouldn't have said much, but it was Melody. She wasn't being nosy or argumentative. She was trying to learn more about me, about all of us.

"Andy was a TA for one of my classes. I went to him for help about some assignments and he ended up asking me out. We started dating after the class was over, and eventually moved in together. He convinced me to stop talking to everyone I knew at college and to distance myself from my family. Once he isolated me, he became physically abusive. I left him, and school, after he almost killed me one night," I explained.

Years of therapy taught me to give details when talking about Andy. Telling someone new was always hard, but giving details and not sharing emotions allowed me to almost pretend it happened to someone else.

I rubbed my throat subconsciously, not realizing I was doing it until Melody asked, "Are you okay?"

I forced a smile and sat back. I nodded and said, "Yep. I'm free, and he'll never come near me again. I make my own rules and live my life for myself. Which means not getting involved with men anymore. Not serious, at least. Once in a while, I get...lonely. But I find someone and get it out of my system, then I'm good again."

"Colin is a good guy," Melody said. "He's not like that."

I smiled at her. "No one believed me when I admitted what Andy did. They all said the same thing about him. It wasn't until another student came forward and said the same thing happened to her that anyone trusted my story. People aren't always who they seem. And some people are particularly good at hiding their true selves."

Melody opened her mouth to say something, but Laura

shook her head. When Trinity leaned forward, we all turned to her.

"My mom was in an abusive relationship. Not with my dad, but with one of her boyfriends after my dad died. She tried to hide it from me, but I was old enough to know things weren't okay. I called the cops on him one night. She was scared to do it herself, but she was really grateful I did. He was a powerful man, and she didn't think people would believe her. We moved in with my grandmother after that, and my mom hasn't dated since. It's not easy. Even good relationships aren't easy. I give you a lot of credit for going out with Colin." Trinity's smile was sad and understanding. I hated that she knew any part of what I'd been through. I wouldn't wish abuse on anyone, as the victim or as someone who loved the victim.

"I'm sorry," Laura said. "I shouldn't have told everyone about Colin."

I smiled at her and shook my head. "It's not your fault. I should have told everyone. I'm just all messed up. Right after Andy, I wanted to reclaim myself, so I erased him with other men. When I stopped that, a part of me feels like I stopped living. I've let fear control everything for a long time. I lost so much of who I was when I was with Andy, and it's hard to bring it all back."

"It won't all come back at once," Trinity said. "There are pieces of my mom that will never come back. But there are pieces of her that are. You have to decide what you can handle, and if you aren't ready to date, then don't. If you only want casual things, do that. And if you want to tell us all the dirty details about what happened with Colin, we're all ready to listen."

A surprised laugh burst out of me. I shook my head, but the expectant faces around me said I could trust them. They weren't going anywhere. I'd never get into a situation like I did with Andy because the amazing women surrounding me would be there every step of the way to pull me back if anything happened.

I had love in my life, the kind of love that everyone wanted. Love that was unconditional and forever. Because I had the best friends in the world.

So I told them all the not-so-dirty details about Colin. And I knew it was the right decision.

TRINITY WALKED out with me at the end of the night. She asked if I was okay.

I nodded. "I'm good. How are you?" The response was automatic.

She studied me closely. Her brown eyes felt like they could see inside me. I focused on the rest of her so I didn't have to meet her gaze. Her dark ringlets that framed her face. The light blush on her cheeks. The pink lip stain she wore most of the time. Her yellow top.

"You know that's not what I meant," she said, drawing my attention. "How long ago were you with Andy?"

"A long time. College. I left him when I was twenty-one. Eight years ago."

"Time can only heal so much. My mom's ex went to jail when I was a teenager. It's been more than fifteen years, and my mom still has no interest in dating."

I sighed. "I don't know if I'll ever fully trust a man again."

"You trusted Colin enough to go out with him alone. Be vulnerable."

I nodded and tucked my hair behind my ear. "I wasn't sure I could, but yeah."

"I didn't date for a long time after it," Trinity admitted.

We kept walking past our cars until we made it to Catherine Park, what we all called the square. It was quiet for late on a Sunday, but quiet was good.

"Did he ever…?"

Trinity shook her head. "No. I think my mom would have killed him if he tried to lay a hand on me, in any way. He kept his distance from me."

"It still messed you up, though."

Trinity nodded. "It did. Knowing what she went through, even though I'm sure I still don't know all of it, it really bothered me. When we moved in with my grandmother, my mom retreated into herself for a while. She barely left the house. My grandmother was the one who taught me how to make jewelry. We became really close."

"It's good you two had each other. And that you were both there for your mom."

"Did you have anyone?" Trinity asked.

I hesitated for a second, then shook my head. "He made sure I was alone. My cousin and I were really close, but he made her feel really uncomfortable when she came to visit. When she questioned me about it, I took his side. We haven't been close since."

"Did you ever tell her?"

I chuckled. "No. No one in my family knows."

"But you told all of us?"

I nodded. "Laura was the first to find out. I started seeing a therapist right away, and she always told me I needed to talk to people, but until I freaked out during sex one night, I thought I was okay. Laura had to come get me, and after that I realized I needed to talk to people. I think they all knew, but no one asked questions."

"It's like that a lot."

I nodded. "True. It took me a long time to admit I was ashamed of it. I told myself it wasn't anyone else's business, but I blamed myself for not being stronger. I thought I should have seen it coming or stopped it or left him sooner. I told myself I was to blame."

"And now you're telling yourself the only way to stop it from happening again is to not get involved."

"Bingo."

Trinity grabbed my hand and squeezed. "I get it. But I hate the idea of anyone missing out on something amazing because of someone else. My mom's ex stole a piece of her. I don't think she's ever going to get it back. But she tells me she had her one great love. She had my dad. He died in a car accident when I was thirteen, and it destroyed my mom. But she loved him. She doesn't feel like she's missing anything because she knows what love is. But you…"

"I've never truly known love," I finished for her.

Trinity shrugged. "Only you know if that's true. And only you know if you want love. I think it all starts with liking someone and giving them a chance. You did that with Colin, so maybe there's more there."

"Or maybe he's going to be a story one day."

Trinity smiled. "A great story."

"Or not."

"But you won't know until you give him a chance."

I groaned. "Why does dating have to be so hard?"

"Because nothing worthwhile is ever easy."

"True."

Trinity and I stood and walked back to where we parked. We hugged and said goodnight and I promised her I'd think about seeing Colin again.

Growing up, I believed in love. That it was something everyone could have. My parents were still crazy in love, and I thought love was just something that happened one day. When I met Andy, I thought he was it for me.

But after Andy, I saw love more like Gone With The

Wind. It was one of my mom's favorite movies. She watched it all the time when I was a kid, and she said she knew Rhett and Scarlett got together eventually. I hated the movie. I saw a toxic relationship from the beginning, one that left both of them miserable and hurt. But after Andy, I told myself that was what love was really like. For some people, it was beautiful and magical, and for others, it was painful and tragic.

I was definitely in the second category. And I wasn't sure I was meant to be in the first.

Life after Andy meant taking care of myself. It meant trying to reclaim who I was and who I was meant to be. It meant accepting my fate as a single woman forever. I was okay with it. I enjoyed sex, and I had it when I wanted it, but I was okay with not having anything more than that. I'd gotten good at pushing aside the desire for something else, and even though it snuck out once in a while, I could squash it with sex and move on.

But Colin…Colin was a danger to that. I stripped down to my underwear with him. I went swimming in a deserted area with him. I kissed him. He took care of me. He made me feel safe. He scared the hell out of me.

I didn't know how I was going to handle things with him. I liked him, but I was broken. Broken people couldn't fall in love. My heart was damaged beyond repair, and if I tried to love someone, my fractured heart was just going to let all the love slip out through the cracks.

So it was better if I didn't try. It was better if whatever was happening between us was casual. Maybe we could have a casual thing for a little while. Or just once. We did match, and that had to mean something. Right?

MY PARENTS WANTED to do another family dinner that week, so I drove straight there after work on Tuesday. I was tired, but Chelsea wasn't available the last time my parents had us for dinner, so we were doing it again.

My mom and Aunt Cathy were best friends growing up. They were only two years apart, and while they had their share of fights, they always had each other. Chelsea and I were similar. We were close, and I hated when Andy ran her off. She was my best friend at one point. We were working on getting back to that, but it wasn't easy. Chelsea kept her distance at times. I understood. I never explained to her why I took Andy's side in their fight. I wasn't sure I ever would.

Everyone was there when I arrived. I let myself in and followed my nose to the kitchen. My mom always loved to cook. She had the look of a chef, plump and round with a perpetual smile on her face. My dad wasn't a thin man either. He had a belly and cheeks that would make a baby jealous.

Growing up, they were simply my parents. I never saw them as overweight. They were just who they were. I looked like them with my round belly and large breasts. I had my dad's chubby cheeks and my mom's chubby everything else. I loved that I looked like them.

Until I got to high school. Kids were mean in high school. I was called names and criticized for the way I looked. I tried to diet and look like the skinny girls, but it never worked because I enjoyed food too much.

In college, I tried harder to diet since I was away from my mom's cooking. I lost a bunch of weight, but I was miserable. To keep the weight off, I had to count calories and exercise a lot. After Andy, I moved back home and put most of the weight back on. I was never skinny, but once I gained weight again, I was happier.

Walking into the kitchen with my family all around, I felt like the person I was supposed to be. All of us were a little too round and a little too loud. We were made to be that way, and I loved it. I was comfortable in my body again. And I loved that I could eat my mother's cooking without feeling guilty because life was better when you enjoyed it.

"Hey, Ma," I said, walking over to give my mom a hug.

"Oh, Elise, you have to hear this. Cathy was just telling us about the new maple farm. It sounds wonderful. You should go out there," Mom said. She brushed my hair back and tucked it behind my ear and smiled at me.

I smiled back. "I've been. It's beautiful."

"When did you go? I was there Saturday," Aunt Cathy said.

"I was, too, but late. And I was there for the grand re-opening. The new owner is a friend of a friend," I explained. I went past my mom to hug Aunt Cathy, then worked my way around until I was next to Chelsea. "Hey, cuz."

"Hey," Chelsea said. "How are you?"

"Good. Busy. You know how it is."

Chelsea was a hair stylist. She wanted to stay in MacKellar Cove so she took a job with Debby, the resident stylist. Debby had been in the same shop forever. Her styles were outdated and so was the decor of the shop, but Debby was an institution in MacKellar Cove. I think she was around when the town was founded.

"Things are busy. Debby isn't thrilled with my work because I'm trying to do things people in this century want. I wish I could just open my own shop."

"Why can't you?" I asked.

"I'm already working too many hours. And I'd feel guilty putting her out of business," Chelsea said. Chelsea's brown hair was in a thick braid down the center of her back. She kept it tied up when she was working, but when she let it down, it fell in loose waves that I'd been jealous of my whole life.

"What did you think about the farm?" Aunt Cathy asked, bringing the conversation back to where it started.

"It's beautiful. I'm glad Colin reopened it. He's doing a great job," I said.

My mother stopped stirring the sauce and stared at me with her mouth wide open.

"What?"

"Elise McKenna Webber. Do you have a crush on that man?"

I rolled my eyes and laughed, praying the burning on my cheeks wasn't visible. "Of course not. I barely know him."

Mom narrowed her eyes at me. "You sound like you know him fairly well."

I chuckled. "Mom, your grandmother biological clock is getting too loud. You're not hearing properly. I've only met Colin a few times."

"And yet you're on a first name basis with him?" Aunt Cathy chimed in.

I looked to Chelsea for help but she just shrugged. "I told you. He's a friend of a friend. Am I supposed to call him Mr. Jones? He's ten years older than me, not thirty."

"How do you know how old he is?" Mom asked.

"I, um, well, I asked him," I confessed.

"You asked him? That definitely sounds like you know him better than just a friend of a friend. Are you keeping something from me? Are you dating that man?"

"No," I said firmly.

"Oh, Elise, you should have invited him over for dinner. We could have set another place setting. Why don't you call him right now?"

"No, Mom. I'm not calling him because we're not dating. We're talking, but we barely know each other," I explained.

As soon as the words were out, I knew they were a mistake. She jumped on them and asked me everything she wanted to know about Colin, and us. Aunt Cathy joined in, too.

It didn't matter how many times I told them we didn't know each other well, they were convinced I was going to marry him and have his children.

I was so screwed.

COLIN

Socializing was never my strong suit. I always felt too old, and that meant I couldn't relate to people my own age. As I stared down forty, I felt like I was too young. Not that I was young, but the people my age had kids approaching the teen years, and I was still single with no kids.

I was not a catch. I was the guy that had everyone wondering what was wrong with me.

Most of the time it didn't bother me, but when I was sitting on a bar stool at O'Kelley's with Ramsey and his friends, talking about their lives, I found myself wondering what was wrong with me.

"Amber is so ready for summer to be here. I don't think she realizes it, but I think she missed Melody all year," Ramsey said.

Ian, a boat builder and fiancé to one of Melody, and Elise's, friends, said, "I bet Melody missed her, too."

Ramsey nodded. "She's staying busy with her new business, though. She loves creating party packs for busy parents. She got so excited last week because she got an order from

Wyoming. It's the farthest away she's had to ship a box so far."

"Very cool," Ian said. "It's exciting to know you're reaching new people."

"How about you?" Ramsey asked, turning to me. "How are things going with you?"

"Good," I said. "Everything's good."

Ramsey narrowed his eyes. "What's going on?"

"Nothing, why?"

"Because you sound weird."

"He's chasing Elise," Hudson said, notching his hip on the other side of the bar. "I'm guessing he doesn't want you guys to know about it."

"Melody was right about you two?" Ramsey asked, trading a look with Hudson, then Ian.

"We're just talking."

"They got paired up on that app," Hudson provided.

"Dude, do you have to tell them everything?" I asked.

He shrugged and shook his head. "Not if you want to."

Ramsey snorted. "Hud, leave him alone. If he doesn't want our help, he doesn't need to take it."

"Help with what?"

"With Elise," Ian said. "She's a tough one."

"What makes you say that?"

Ian shrugged. "She's always watching things, taking in the world around her. It's not bad, but she rarely gets too involved. She'd rather be on the outside."

"Really?"

"Yep," Hudson said. "She finds her happy where she can, but if you're not it, back off. I've seen her take down a few men."

"But she's a good person, right?"

"Without a doubt," Ramsey said. "She's loyal and kind and

protective. I also think she's scared and wounded. Approach with caution."

"I've already learned that lesson," I said.

"Did she kick your ass?" Hudson asked.

I shook my head. "We went swimming."

Ramsey, Ian, and Hudson all traded dirty smiles. "Nice."

"Shut up," I said, trying to hide my grin. "Nothing happened."

"Aw, look. He's blushing. It's so cute," Ramsey said.

"Fuck you," I said, my cheeks burning hotter.

"He's adorable," Ian added.

I shook my head. Anything I said was going to make things worse.

"Seriously," Hudson said, "be careful with her. You fuck her up, we'll fuck you up."

I looked the three men around me in the eyes and nodded. "I'd expect nothing less."

They all nodded back.

"So, you like her?" Ian asked.

I shrugged. "What I know of her, yeah. She's beautiful. And funny and smart. And when she smiles, the whole world is a little better."

"Damn," Ian said. "He's gone."

"Yep," Ramsey agreed, lifting his beer in a toast. "Welcome to the club."

"I'm out," Hudson said, walking away.

"What club?" I asked.

"Do I even want to know what kind of club you have?" another guy asked from next to me. He slid onto the stool to my right and extended his hand. "I'm James."

"Colin."

"What kind of club is this?"

"The kind where the only men allowed are the ones who are whipped," Hudson said, sliding a beer in front of James.

"Oh, screw that. I'm not getting tied down. Single is so much better. Right, Hud?"

Hudson glared at James for a minute, then walked away. Ramsey reached behind me and slapped James on the back of the head.

"Ow, dammit. I didn't mean it like that," James said.

"Then how did you mean it?" Ian asked.

"I'm just a dumbass," James said, shaking his head.

I looked at Ramsey for clarification. "Hudson's wife died a few years back."

"Damn." I turned to James. "Ouch."

James winced and nodded. "Yeah, I'm an ass."

"Thoughtless," Ramsey said. "You owe him an apology. You know how he is."

James grumbled but slid off his stool and followed Hudson through the back hallway with his shoulders slumped.

"James is a cop. He and Hudson are good friends. Hudson knows he wasn't intentionally being an ass, but Hud's also touchy about Hillary," Ramsey provided.

"I can understand that. I've never been married, but I'd like to think if I was, I'd feel the same if she died," I said.

My dad certainly felt the same way. It killed him when we lost my mom. He could barely function at the beginning. It was only when we moved away from MacKellar Cove that Dad started to become himself again.

"I can't even think about losing Blake," Ian said. He shook his head. "I waited too long to be with her. Losing her isn't an option."

"It's never an option," Ramsey said. "I've had years with Melody and losing her for a few months was the worst thing I've ever been through in my life. I'm never going to let anything like that happen again."

I listened to them talk about the women they loved and

wondered if I'd ever feel that way. The women I dated in the past were women I cared about, but none of them sparked that same passion. When things ended, they just ended. We didn't go back and forth, debating if it was right. We were done. Even the relationships that were more serious just ended, and we both walked away.

With Elise, I wasn't there. Yeah, I liked her. And I hoped we got to know each other better, but I would move on if nothing came out of it.

But my chest ached at the thought. I didn't want to move on yet. I wanted to know if something could happen between us. I wanted…her. It was as simple as that. I wanted Elise.

And I was pretty damn sure she wanted me, too.

I'D JUST SAT down for a lonely dinner the next night when my phone rang. Since I only knew one person who called instead of texted, I picked it up without looking.

"Hey, Dad," I said.

"Colin!" my dad's voice boomed through the phone. "How are you?"

"I'm good. Busy, but good. How are you?"

"About the same. You know how it goes. How's the farm?"

I smiled. Dad always asked about the farm. I knew he missed it. Leaving was a tough decision, one that he always second guessed.

"The farm is good. Sap is done since the nights aren't dropping to freezing. We're processing everything. The store is doing well. All's good," I told him.

My dad was a business guy. He liked to talk about business. Emotions were an option, too, but he preferred to talk about things that wouldn't tug too hard at him.

"That's good. It sounds like you're on the right track."

I nodded. "I hope so. Nicky's been a huge help. I don't think I could have done all this without him."

"He was always like that. I still remember when he first started out there. He was funny and he loved my mother so much. I was happy when they finally got together."

"You knew about that?" I blurted.

Dad laughed. "I did. I never told them I knew, though. Ma wanted to keep their relationship a secret. It wasn't up to me why. I always thought love should be celebrated. That's what your mother showed me. But not everyone sees love the same way. Some see it as a trap instead of a place where you can be free to be yourself. If you don't feel that way when you're with the person you love, I don't think it's really love."

I nodded. I'd been getting a lot of unintentional relationship advice lately. I weighed all of it against Elise, which probably wasn't fair to her. We'd only had one date. It was a great date, but it was only one. We weren't in a relationship. We were barely even dating. But I thought of her first when I thought of someone I wanted to spend time with.

"Hey, Dad, do you want to come visit me sometime? Come up to the farm, maybe stay a little while."

He sucked in a sharp breath. "Oh, uh, I don't know, son. I loved that place, but my memories are so muddled at this point. Everything I remember about the farm is tied to your mother. And without her, or your grandmother, there, I don't know if I can do it."

"It's fine," I said, even though I was disappointed. I understood. But I'd hoped he would come.

Dad sighed. "I'll think about it."

"No, Dad, I get it. It's too painful to come here."

"It would be, but I've been hiding from that pain for years. Maybe it's time to stop hiding and feel it. I loved your mother, and I still do. She was my world. And when she died,

I knew I'd never be the same. I've tried my best to be a good father for you, but I'm failing you right now."

"No, you're not. You're taking care of yourself. I understand, Dad. You need to take care of yourself."

"Not at the expense of you. Leaving the farm was a hard decision for me because I knew you loved it. Ma told me taking you away would be bad, but she didn't understand. I was losing pieces of myself every day. Your mother was there, in every inch of that place. I saw her everywhere I went. And staying there made me feel like I was losing her every minute of every day. It hurt to be there. I put myself over you then, and I'm still doing it."

"It's fine, Dad. Really. I just thought you might want to see the place."

"Have you been out to the old swimming hole?" Dad asked.

I was startled by the subject change but went with it. "Uh, yeah. I was there over the weekend."

"That's where I fell in love with your mother. I took her there on a date, and we floated in the water and talked. It always felt like we could say or do anything when we were there. That was where we decided we wanted to get married and start a family. It was where we talked about everything."

My throat swelled at the raw emotion in his voice. I wanted that. Not the pain that came with loss, but the joy that came with love.

I thought about Elise again and the time we spent at the pond. The place really was magical. We didn't talk much, but we also didn't keep our distance. The water let us relax and be ourselves.

She was beautiful floating in the pond. Her hair spread out around her like a pink crown. Her eyes closed and all of her relaxed. Her body tempted me and made it hard for me to breathe. Her hard nipples pressed against the see-through fabric of her bra and begged me to touch her.

But I couldn't. I wanted to, but I wouldn't violate her trust. I didn't know what happened in her past, but she was definitely not a person who trusted easily. She needed reassurances.

"I think I want to go back to the pond," Dad said after a minute. "Just thinking about it makes me want to go there. I feel like your mother is there."

I hope not, I thought. If she was, she got a show last weekend.

"You should come, Dad. Anytime you want."

"I will," he said. "I'll look at my schedule and let you know soon. And maybe when I'm there, you can introduce me to the woman you're thinking about right now."

"What?" I blurted, knowing the shocked word was all the confirmation Dad needed.

He chuckled. "Yeah, I could hear it in your voice. You started falling in love at the pond, too. Or maybe it was just lust. Whatever it was, if you took her there, I know she's special."

"Yeah, she is," I admitted.

"Good. Now I have two reasons to visit."

I shook my head. He always had the ability to know what I was thinking. When I was a teenager, it was decidedly frustrating, but as an adult, I just wished I had the same ability.

We talked a few more minutes then hung up. I reheated my dinner and sat back down. I found a movie I'd been wanting to see and let myself get lost in the story. Before I knew it, the movie was over, dinner was gone, and I was falling asleep.

A FEW DAYS went by and I didn't hear from Elise. I wasn't sure if she would reach out, but I wanted to see her again. I was too old for games, and I'd learned being direct was always the best way to be with people.

SWEETSTUFF

Thought anymore about letting me buy you dinner?

The app notified you when there was a message waiting, so I hoped Elise would see it and reply, but I didn't expect it to be quick.

My phone pinged a minute later with a notification from Book Boyfriends Wanted, and I grinned.

CAPTAIN

I am a little hungry.

SWEETSTUFF

Got any ideas?

CAPTAIN

I was planning to stay home tonight.

I was more than a little disappointed, but I understood.

SWEETSTUFF

Maybe next time?

CAPTAIN

Giving up so easily?

SWEETSTUFF

Not at all. But not willing to change your plans.

CAPTAIN

Tell me something no one else knows.

SWEETSTUFF

You have a huge heart.

CAPTAIN

I meant about you.

I laughed. I could almost hear her roll her eyes.

SWEETSTUFF

I can't stop thinking about you. My dad
wants to meet you.

CAPTAIN

You told your dad about me?

SWEETSTUFF

We were talking and he picked up on
something.

CAPTAIN

What did you say?

SWEETSTUFF

I told him we were getting to know each
other.

CAPTAIN

That's it? What did he pick up on?

I took a breath and reminded myself women were
supposed to be cautious. If they weren't, I'd be disappointed.
Not every man was a good man, and a woman needed to
know she was okay.

SWEETSTUFF

I invited him to the farm. He hasn't been here
since I was a kid. He asked me about the
pond, where we went, and when we were
talking, I was thinking about you. He noticed.
He's very perceptive.

CAPTAIN

What did you tell him about me?

SWEETSTUFF

That I want to marry you and move you onto the farm immediately so I can get you pregnant as quickly as possible.

I grinned as soon as I hit send, then started typing again.

SWEETSTUFF

J/k. I told him we were getting to know each other and you are special. I'm not the kind of person who rushes into things.

CAPTAIN

I'm sorry. I shouldn't be so freaked out by this. My family knows about you.

SWEETSTUFF

Oh, really? You're talking about me?

CAPTAIN

No, but it seems my mother has the same powers of perception as your father. My aunt mentioned your farm, and I told my mother I'd been there. She pressed me for information and figured out I wasn't just a customer.

I grinned as I read her last line. No, she definitely wasn't just a customer. Not to me.

CAPTAIN

I didn't mean that how it sounded. I am a customer, but we're talking. Do you know what I mean?

SWEETSTUFF

Absolutely. You mean you want to see me naked.

CAPTAIN

I never said that!

SWEETSTUFF

Didn't have to. I have the same power of
perception. You're dying to see me naked.

CAPTAIN

OMG, I never said that.

SWEETSTUFF

Maybe, but you were thinking it. It's okay. I
know I'm impossible to resist.

CAPTAIN

And so humble.

SWEETSTUFF

But I made you laugh. God, I wish I could
hear your laugh right now.

I was still staring at my phone when it rang. Elise's name was on the screen. I'd forgotten she saved her number in my phone.

"Hello?"

"You're incorrigible," she said with a chuckle.

I laughed and settled back in my chair. "I am, but you find it sweet."

"I don't know about that," she said.

"Oh, I think you do know. I think you find me adorable and sweet and you can't get enough."

"Wow. You continue to amaze me."

"My dazzling wit?"

"No, I was thinking about your shameless confidence."

I barked a laugh and shook my head. "If you only knew how not confident I felt talking to you, you wouldn't say that."

"Why?" she asked, her voice changing, dropping.

I matched my tone to hers. "I haven't dated much. A few women, but I'm not a serial dater. Most of the women I've been involved with haven't understood the demands my schedule places on my time. And I know that's mostly my fault. I haven't ever made any of them a priority."

"Why not?"

I shrugged. "I knew it wouldn't last. With all of them, I knew it would end at some point, and I wasn't willing to give up what I loved for a woman who wouldn't be there forever."

"You've never been in love?" she asked quietly.

"Nope. Not in the truest sense. I've thought I was. I've wanted to be. I've said the words. But in all those situations, work came first in the end. If any of those women were the right ones, that wouldn't have been the case."

"That seems very insightful."

I breathed a laugh. "My parents loved each other. So much that when my mom died, my dad left the only home he'd ever known because it was too painful to be reminded of her every day. He never dated again. He still loves my mom. They had the kind of love people only dream about, the kind of love most of us don't think exists because it's rare. Maybe it would have changed if my mom hadn't died, but that wasn't what was meant to be. My dad told me recently that love should allow you to be the truest version of yourself. That if you can't be who you want to be with the person you love, then you don't really love them. I always tried to be someone else with the women I dated. That's how I know it wasn't real love."

"That's both the most beautiful thing and the saddest thing I've ever heard."

I chuckled. "Yeah, it really is."

We kept talking for hours, sharing stories about our families and growing up. We talked about work and friends and life in general. And when we finally hung up, I realized I didn't hold anything back from her. I was just me talking to Elise.

But I wasn't willing to admit what that meant yet.

113

11

ELISE

I was almost out the door when Walter asked if he could talk to me. He was talking to someone else, so I waited to the side and tried not to eavesdrop on his conversation.

"Thanks, Elise," he said when he joined me. "You came in at noon today, right?"

I nodded. "Yeah, why? Do you need me to stay?"

He sighed. "I do. If you can. If you have something going on, I can ask someone else, but—"

"It's fine," I said. "I don't have any plans."

Plans didn't include checking my phone and hoping I had a new message from Colin. It had been two days since we talked, and I had to admit I was hoping to hear from him since then.

Working a few extra hours would take my mind off Colin and would help me to remember that I was a strong woman and I didn't need a man to reach out first. I just had to find the guts to contact him.

"Thank you," Walter breathed. "I really appreciate it. This will be a huge help. We had a last minute booking for a private dinner cruise. I'm working out all the details for it, but the guy wants to propose."

I stifled my groan and forced a smile. I hated engagement cruises. Not that I didn't want people to be happy, but I hated witnessing love that intensely. It was like intruding on a personal moment for some, and for others, it just reminded me that I'd never have what they had.

"What time?" I asked.

"Push off at seven. It's a two hour cruise. Are you sure you can do it?"

I nodded. "Of course. I'm going to grab some dinner first, though. That way I'm not stealing food off their plates when they aren't looking."

Walter chuckled and dug into his pocket. He pulled out his wallet and opened it. "Since I'm making you work, let me buy you dinner."

I shook my head and grinned. "It's fine. I think I know where I can get a free dinner."

Walter gave me a look but didn't press. He waved as I rushed off, pulling out my phone as I walked to my car.

CAPTAIN

Still want to buy me dinner?

His reply was almost immediate.

SWEETSTUFF

Absolutely.

CAPTAIN

Good. I'm starving and in a hurry. Meet me at O'Kelley's?

SWEETSTUFF

I'll be there in ten.

CAPTAIN

> I'll order without you. Want me to get something for you?

SWEETSTUFF

> Sure, whatever you're having is fine. Thanks.
> On my way.

CAPTAIN

See you soon.

I tucked my phone away and smiled. He didn't say no, and he didn't say he was busy. He told me the other night that his previous relationships ended because he was more interested in work than the woman he was seeing. He hadn't done that with me yet.

I drove to MacKellar Cove and found a spot right outside O'Kelley's. I knew Hudson would put an order in for me right away so I could make it back to the boat in time, but it was also my safe space. I didn't worry about anything when I was there.

Hudson was behind the bar as always. He waited until I sat down to ask what I was drinking.

"Just a water," I said. "But I need food, too. Two burgers, loaded up. Two orders of fries. And do you have any dessert?"

He gave me a look that said I already knew the answer to that.

I shrugged. "Maybe if I keep asking, you'll add it to the menu."

"And maybe I'll sprout wings and learn to fly. Who's on the way?"

"Colin," I said without thinking.

Hudson grinned. "The syrup guy? The one you blew off a few weeks ago? You're giving him another chance?"

I sighed and tilted my head at him. "I didn't blow him off.

116

I just…"

"Walked out on him?"

"It's complicated."

"It always is with you. Want to uncomplicate it?" he asked with a gleam that made me think he knew more than he was letting on.

I shook my head. "Not until you put that order in. I need to be back at the docks in thirty minutes, and I'm starving."

Hudson held my gaze for another few seconds. I gave him a dazzling smile until he turned and walked away. With any luck, Colin would show up before Hudson got back and I wouldn't have to explain anything to him.

Luck was definitely on my side. Colin slid onto the stool next to me as soon as Hudson disappeared from view.

"Hey," he said.

"Hey." I waited for him to lean in and try to kiss me or something, but he didn't. I didn't think we were there yet, but I was a little disappointed he didn't.

"Are you going back to work after this?"

I nodded. "We have a sunset engagement cruise at seven. It was booked at the last minute, and my boss asked me to handle it."

"That should be fun."

I snorted.

"Uh, or not?"

I chuckled. "It's fine. I'm just…I'm cynical."

"You? No. I never would have guessed that."

I laughed with him. "I don't have the best track record with relationships."

"How many have you had?" he asked.

I hesitated telling him anything, but I started the conversation. "One serious relationship. It wasn't a good one."

"That's why," Colin said simply. "Only one relationship

has crappy odds of being good. You can't expect to get it right the first time. Almost no one does."

I smiled and nodded, hoping he wouldn't ask another question about my past relationship.

"Colin," Hudson said, reaching across to shake his hand. "Good to see you."

"You, too. Elise, did you order?" Colin asked.

"She did. It should be out in a few minutes. Can I get you a drink?"

"Water for me," Colin said. "It's been a long day."

"Sorry I pulled you away from work," I said.

He looked at me and grinned. "I didn't mind at all. Dinner with you is better than work any day."

His words warmed me more than a half-assed attempt at a kiss would have. I knew what he was saying, and I liked it. A lot.

"Thank you."

Colin grinned and held my gaze for a long moment. Hudson and the rest of the bar faded away.

"How late do you have to work tonight?" Colin asked.

"We should be done around nine. Maybe a little later."

"Make sure someone walks with you to the parking lot," Colin said. His voice was tense and tight.

I nodded. "I always do. There are three of us on trips like this, and we watch out for each other. I know MacKellar Cove is a small town, but we need to be careful."

"Good. I'd hate for anything to happen to you."

I smiled and looked away. If he only knew.

"When are you going to let me take you out and not have to run off after I buy you a meal?" Colin asked, a teasing note to his voice.

I shrugged. "I don't know. The free meals are pretty handy."

"Uh huh. I think I enjoyed swimming more. And talking on the phone."

Did I imagine his voice dipping low like that? Did he lean in closer? Or did I?

I cleared my throat. "Um, yeah. I did, too."

Colin grinned. "Of course, I'll take any opportunity to spend time with you, even if it's only so you can get a free meal."

I laughed. We both knew it wasn't just about the free food. There was so much more to it than that. He was the first and only person I called.

"Hey," someone said from right behind me.

I turned. Finley. "Hey, Fin. What are you doing here?"

"I was going to ask you the same. Rissa and I were going to grab some dinner. I told her I'd meet her here. I didn't know you would be here. Want to join us?"

I glanced back at Colin. He was sipping his water like he didn't have a care in the world. The way he looked, it was as though we hadn't just been in the middle of a conversation. We were just two people who happened to be sitting next to each other.

He was leaving it up to me to say something to my friend. Wow.

"Actually, I'm here with Colin. I don't know if you've met, but Finley, this is Colin Jones. Colin, Finley Jameson. She owns Book Boyfriends Unlimited."

"The app designer?" Colin asked.

Finley shook her head. "No, I own the bookstore. The app was developed by my roommate. She's the tech genius."

"Oh, I'm sorry. I didn't realize," Colin said, extending his hand to Finley. "It's nice to meet you."

"You, too, Colin."

Hudson walked over with our food, distracting Colin for a few seconds. Finley grinned and gave me a wide-eyed look that said she definitely approved. I rolled my eyes in response, but she batted her lashes at me.

"Oh, I see Karissa," Finley said. "I'm going to join her. It was so nice to finally meet you, Colin. I look forward to getting to know you better."

"Uh, you, too, Finley," Colin said. His brows pulled together in a question. He tilted his head at me and raised one brow.

"Fine, my friends all know about you."

He tried to stifle a grin and failed.

I grabbed the ketchup from in front of him and squeezed some onto my plate. I swiped a fry through it and popped it into my mouth.

Colin just watched me.

"When we went swimming, I forgot to tell Laura I was okay. She freaked out and came over, then told everyone. She…they…I'm sorry."

He leaned back. "Sorry? About what?"

"Telling everyone. I probably shouldn't have."

Colin shook his head. "First of all, they're your friends. They should know what you want them to know. Second, I'm a little jealous. I don't have people like that in my life. I have my dad, and Nicky, but otherwise, I'm pretty much a loner. I always have been. But that doesn't mean I don't get that people need people."

I looked at him. "I really think you are a unicorn. I'd wonder if you were a figment of my imagination if other people didn't talk to you also."

He chuckled and shook his head. "I'm just a regular guy."

I shook my head. "No, you're really not. But the fact that you think you are makes you that much more of a unicorn."

Colin laughed and dug into his food. We bumped arms and legs as we ate. When we finished, I offered to buy my dinner, but Colin insisted it was his treat and walked outside with me.

The night was warm, finally letting us know spring was definitely here and summer was on the way. I loved it.

"It's a beautiful night," Colin said.

I nodded. "It is. It'll be good for a cruise."

"Maybe this one won't be so bad."

I laughed. "I'm sure it will be, but that's okay."

He reached for my hand and held it lightly when we stopped in front of my car. "Can I kiss you before you go?"

"Well, you did buy me dinner," I teased.

Colin stepped back. "This isn't quid pro quo, Elise. I don't want you to kiss me because I paid for your food."

"I know," I said quickly. "It was just a bad joke."

He stepped closer again and tucked the hair behind my ear. "I just want you to know I'll never expect anything of you. Or demand. Anything that ever happens between us will only happen if we're both completely sure it's what we want."

"Anything?" I breathed.

He pulled me into his arms and whispered, "Anything, Elise. And everything."

He pulse kicked up. He pressed his nose to my neck. My breath hitched in my throat. He kissed my cheek, then stepped back.

"Have a good cruise," he said.

"That's it?" I asked after a second.

He grinned. "I want you to be sure, Elise. And unless you are, I'm not. Call me when you get home tonight."

"Why?"

"Because I want to hear your voice before I go to sleep."

My heart melted. "Okay."

"Be safe. We'll talk later."

He turned to walk away.

"Hey, Colin?"

He stopped. "Yeah?"

"I am sure."

He grinned. "Good." He turned again.

"Really?" I said.

He chuckled and walked back. He was in front of me before I could take another breath. He swooped me up into his arms and cupped my jaw. It all happened so fast, my head spun. But he didn't kiss me.

He smiled and held my gaze. Every cell in my body begged him to close the distance between us and kiss me. But he just looked at me.

I waited, the only sound our breath. I didn't want to walk away without kissing him. I didn't want him to walk away. I wanted to breathe him in and carry him with me.

I shifted, readying to move closer, and he responded to it. He closed the distance between us, pressing his lips hard to mine. His tongue danced between my lips, opening me up to him. I let him control the kiss, to lead us where he wanted us to go. I hadn't let another person have that much control over me in years, but I knew I could trust him. I knew Colin would keep me safe.

His erection grew against my stomach, but again, he didn't grind it against me. He ignored it and focused every-thing on driving me crazy with his kiss.

And boy, did he know how to do that.

He alternated between tender pecks and pulsing demands. He held me close the entire time, his arms shielding me from everything else. He tilted his head to the other side and devoured me all over again.

And when he finally pulled back, I wasn't sure the world would ever be the same again.

He panted right along with me, his breath pulsing in and out of him in the same rhythm as mine. We stood there and held each other, neither of us able to let go. My feet barely reached the ground.

He finally opened his eyes and our gazes collided. Everything I felt was reflected back in his eyes. We didn't go into this expecting things to be the way they were, but neither of us could deny that when we didn't hold back, sparks flew.

"Thank you," I said, feeling foolish for saying something so insufficient, but knowing it was the only thing I could say.

He kissed my forehead and said, "Thank you."

He opened my car door and stepped back for me to get in. He closed it and waved when I drove off. I watched him from my mirror until I turned the corner and couldn't see him anymore.

Of all the times I told myself I wasn't going to get involved again, I knew Colin was the one who was going to be impossible to resist. He was proving it to be true on every level. Even a level I long thought no longer existed. Because I wanted Colin Jones. And it wasn't just because I was lonely or because I wanted sex. It was because I wanted *him*.

And that was the hardest thing in the world to admit.

12

The sunset cruise was underway, and I wasn't hating it as much as I thought I would. The couple were really sweet. He was about to finish law school, and she was graduating from undergrad. They had plans to move to New York City together, where he had a job lined up in a small firm. She wasn't sure what she was going to do yet, but she was applying to jobs regularly.

And yes, they both liked to talk.

I pointed out a lot of the popular landmarks as we floated around the area. For the sunset cruises, we didn't stop at Boldt Castle or anywhere else. They were just boat tours where we told people about the history of the area. I'd learned to share the romantic history when I was talking to couples.

"Did George really never come back?" Amy asked.

I nodded. "That's the story that's been told. He immediately stopped all construction and told the workers to leave. The castle was for Louise. He was creating it for her, on Heart Island, where they planned to live the rest of their lives. When she died, he couldn't take it."

"That's so heartbreaking," Amy said, taking her boyfriend's hand. "I get it, though. If something happened to you, I wouldn't be able to come back here, or go anyplace where we spent a lot of time. I totally understand walking away from the place you built for the person you love."

"True," Mike agreed. "But I'm not going anywhere. We're young and healthy and we're just starting our lives together."

"Yeah, but you never know," Amy said. "Things happen all the time. Just because we're young doesn't mean we're guaranteed tomorrow."

I saw it in his eyes when she said the words. His breath hitched, and he slid his hand beneath the table they were sitting at.

I quietly stepped back, not wanting to be in the middle of their moment. I pulled out my phone to record it so they would have the memory forever. Amy stared at the castle, oblivious to Mike's movements.

"Amy," he said softly.

She looked at him.

"Amy, I love you."

"I love you, Mike."

"I never want to be without you. You're right. We aren't guaranteed tomorrow. We aren't guaranteed anything. All we have is right now and a hope for the future. My hope for our future is a home, a family. My hope is that you're with me forever. Because I can't imagine one minute of my life without you in it."

He slid from his seat and dropped to one knee in front of her. She finally realized what he was doing. Her hands clapped over her mouth. Tears filled her eyes.

"All that starts with you becoming my wife, Amy. Please, will you marry me?"

Amy nodded as tears streamed down her cheeks. She reached for him, pulling him into her arms and kissing him.

They broke apart after a minute, and Mike slid the ring on her finger. He kissed the ring and said, "I love you, Amy."

"I love you, Mike. And I can't believe you did this. I had no idea."

Mike nodded to me. "Thankfully, Elise knew all about it."

Amy looked over at me. Her eyes widened. I waved, and she waved back. I ended the video and started laughing. "That was perfect. Congratulations."

Kimberly walked out with two glasses of champagne for them to toast. She set them on the table and we both walked away to give Amy and Mike a few minutes alone.

"That was really sweet," Kimberly whispered to me.

I nodded. "Yeah, it was."

"Do you think they're going to make it?"

I looked over at them and saw only love in their eyes. I'd watched a lot of couples get engaged, and I'd gotten fairly good at figuring out who was going to make it and who wasn't. I nodded. "They'll be fine."

Kimberly smiled and twisted the ring on her finger. "I hope so."

"When are you getting married?" I asked.

She stopped playing with her ring and shrugged. "I don't know yet."

"Have you been engaged long?"

She huffed a laugh. "Yeah. Almost a year. He's in grad school. I was going to go with him, but it's hard to do that unless we got an apartment. He's doing a work-study, so he's living in a residence hall in exchange for a reduction in tuition. It sucks not being together, but I know it's for the best."

"How much longer does he have in school?" I asked. The frustration in her voice was easy to hear, but so was the sadness.

"Two years," Kimberly said.

"Ouch, I'm sorry. But if you're working and saving money, you'll have a much better start when you get married."

"I know, and he keeps saying the same thing, but I worry things are going to change."

"Maybe the change won't be bad," I told her. "We all change, and change doesn't always mean things get worse."

Kimberly shrugged. "Yeah, but I like how things were last year. I'm ready for us to just be together. I'm living with my parents and I never see my fiancé and it's just hard."

I forced a smile and nodded. She didn't want to hear what I had to say. She was pissed, and all she cared about was venting. I hated to think it, but hers was the kind of marriage I doubted would survive. It wasn't easy to be apart, but there were always ways to make it work. Especially when it was temporary. If they weren't willing to deal with it, then maybe they weren't meant to be.

Not that I was going to tell her that.

The rest of the cruise was relatively quiet. I told Amy and Mike a few more things about the area and pointed out other landmarks for them before the sun set and we sank into an amber lit darkness.

When we got back to the dock, we said goodbye to Amy and Mike and wished them well. I stuck around to help clean up and make sure the boat was ready for the morning, then headed to my car.

The parking lot was well lit, and our town was pretty safe, but walking alone always made me anxious. The captain for the night parked the other direction, and Kimberly didn't stay, so I was alone.

I dug my phone out of my purse and called Colin. I felt stupid, but hearing his voice would make me feel better. I hoped.

"Hey, I wasn't sure you'd call," he said when he answered.

"Hey, sorry. Is it okay?"

"Of course. Are you okay?"

"Yeah, I'm just scaring myself. The other guide left and I'm walking to my car alone."

"Where are you?"

"It's fine. I'm in the parking lot. No one is around, and there are no cars here."

"Are you where guests park?" he asked.

"Yes, but by the time you could get here, I'll be home. Just talk to me, Colin. And call the police if something happens."

"Don't joke, Elise," he said. His voice was tight and serious.

"Sorry. It's my default. I know there's no reason to be scared, but I am."

"Can you see your car?"

I nodded. "Yeah, I'm almost there."

"Okay, keep talking to me. How was the tour? Did she say yes?"

I chuckled. "Yeah, she did. They were really sweet. I think they're going to be happy together."

"Good. How old are they?"

"He's twenty-five and she's twenty-two, almost twenty-three."

"That's a good age to get married." He paused, then said, "What the hell do I know? I've never been married."

I laughed with him. "It sounded good, though."

"I feel like a lot of people get married in their mid-twenties."

"Well, people in my generation are getting married older, closer to thirty."

"Ouch. You're not just telling me I'm old, you're telling me I'm from a different generation. Wow. I think you might owe me another dinner for that one."

I chuckled. "I think that can be arranged. Maybe I'll pay this time."

"You don't have to."

"Is it a problem for you?"

"Not at all. I think people are all equal, or should be. I didn't let you pay tonight because I said I would. I'm not the kind of man who goes back on his word."

"So, if I asked you to dinner, you'd let me pay?"

"Sure, why not?"

I hesitated, trying to figure out how to tell him why I wanted to know.

"Elise, are you in your car yet?"

"Oh, yeah, sorry. I forgot to tell you. I'm on my way home."

He sighed with relief. "Thank God. I was wondering why in the world you had to walk so far to get to your car."

I laughed. "Sorry."

"All that matters is you're safe."

"Thank you."

"You're welcome. Do you want to keep talking or do you want me to let you go?"

"I have you on speaker so we can keep talking if that's okay with you."

"Absolutely. Tell me more about this cruise."

I spent the rest of my drive home telling Colin all about Amy and Mike. He agreed that they sounded like the kind of couple who would make it. When I got home, I sighed with relief and started getting changed for bed.

"What are you doing now?" Colin asked.

"Oh, sorry, I was getting changed out of my work clothes."

"Can I ask you a question?"

I sat on my couch and pulled the blanket on my lap. "Sure."

"Why are you always apologizing?"

"Sorry, I don't mean to."

"I'm just wondering why you do it. You don't have to apologize to me for anything. I wasn't sure if you realized you were doing it or if you thought you were upsetting me for some reason."

"It's partly habit and partly thinking I upset you."

"I promise you, Elise, you've never done anything that's upset me. I would tell you if you had."

"You would?"

"Of course. I've already said I don't believe in secrets or keeping things from people you care about. Getting upset and holding back those feelings falls into the same category for me."

"Well, thank you. I don't know that I'll be able to do the same all the time, but I'll try."

"I think that's all I can ask for. So, can I ask you another question?"

"Sure."

"What are you wearing?"

I laughed and was relieved when he joined me.

"I had to ask since you said you were changing from work. Feel better?"

I nodded and snuggled deeper into my couch. "Yeah. I love my job, and I love being outside, but at the end of the day, there's nothing better than curling up on my couch and watching some TV."

"What are you watching?"

I laughed and told him about the movie I'd saved for that night. He started watching it with me, and we talked while the movie played on our screens. It was an even better way to end the night.

"Try this, honey."

I took the spoon from Mrs. Carter and scraped the dough from the first one. Well, dough was generous. It was still just ingredients. Hopefully it would be dough soon enough.

With the bigger spoon, it was finally coming together. I still couldn't believe the pie crust she made was so simple, but she insisted she wasn't leaving anything out.

"Okay, now we need to add the water. You're going to want to use your hands for this part."

I set the spoon in her sink and stood back while she added water to the mixture. When she stepped away from the bowl, I moved back in and kneaded it. It didn't take much for it to come together and really feel like dough.

"Wow," I breathed. "I almost think I would bake more if I knew it was this easy."

Mrs. Carter laughed. "That's why I do it. It passes the time and I enjoy it. So do my hips."

She shook her hips in a seductive way. We both laughed.

"You go, Mrs. Carter."

She smiled. "Once upon a time I could make a man do just about anything with that. Of course, the man was my husband and he loved me, but I'll take what I can get."

"Absolutely," I told her. "I've never been able to make a man do anything I wanted."

"Oh, you just haven't met the right one." She took the bowl and moved it to the table where she had a pastry mat floured and ready.

"I've been hearing that a lot lately," I admitted. "I always knew my ex was the wrong one, but I don't know if there is such a thing as a right one for me."

Mrs. Carter laughed. "Oh, there's a right one for everyone. I believe there's more than one right one, because at different times in life you need different people. Sometimes you need a man who's a little more soft and gentle, and sometimes you need a man who's going to push you. And sometimes you don't need a man at all and just need a friend. That's the stage I'm in."

I smiled at her. "You have me."

"I know, honey. And I'm happy for it. I don't know what I'd do without the people here."

"I love it here. I can't imagine living anywhere else."

"Oh, you will one day. You'll marry someone amazing and leave us."

I laughed. "I'm not so sure about that."

"Promise me something, honey."

"What's that?"

"Promise me that when you meet the person you're meant to spend your life with, you won't think twice about being happy. You've been alone and scared for far too long. It's time you let someone in and feel love."

"I'm fine being alone," I said, feeling a little defensive.

Mrs. Carter smiled at me and patted my hand. "I am, too. But it does get lonely. At my age, people are alone. But for you, you need someone who makes you feel alive."

"I do feel alive. I am alive. And I'm living on my terms."

"And you should, Elise. You've been through enough. No one should know the pain you've experienced, but you should know love. Real love."

"I..." I closed my mouth, unsure what to say. I didn't know Mrs. Carter knew anything about what I went through before I moved in next door, but there was no mistaking that she did.

"The number one secret to a great pie is an even crust. I put these little things next to the dough so I know I roll it out evenly. Why don't you try it?" she said.

It took me a few seconds to recover. She changed the subject like we were talking about nothing of any importance, and I was a little slower to catch up. I went with it and rolled out the dough, then helped her get it onto the pie plate. We added the peaches and covered it with the top crust and put it in the preheated oven.

Mrs. Carter made us tea while I cleaned up. When we were done, we sat at her table.

"I was serious, you know," she said. Her eyes locked on mine, and I couldn't breathe. She knew everything. "Mr. Carter did a search for you when you moved in. You were young, and it was unusual to have a young, single woman living here. We wanted to make sure you weren't here to ruin the neighborhood. Once we found out what happened to you, we knew you needed us."

"Does anyone else…?" Mr. Carter was a police officer so it made sense he'd found the file about Andy and me, but I couldn't bear the thought of anyone else knowing.

Mrs. Carter shook her head. "No one else knows. They asked me, but I always told everyone you were a local girl who wanted a quiet neighborhood to live on your own. No one ever asked anything else. Especially once you started letting me in."

I forced a smile but felt a little sick. I didn't want my neighbors to know about Andy, but Mrs. Carter knew all along. "Is that why you talked to me?"

Mrs. Carter shook her head. "No. I talked to you because you were new and lived next door. We don't let people be alone here, you know that. When someone new moves in, we all bring them food and invite them to our gatherings. You were the same."

"I…I don't talk about it much."

"And I don't expect you to. I only mentioned it because I want you to find someone who'll show you it isn't supposed to be like that."

"I know. I've seen friends fall in love. And my parents are happy."

"But that doesn't mean you've felt it. There's a difference between seeing love and feeling love. You have to be open to feeling it."

"I am," I lied, adding a smile to convince her.

Mrs. Carter snorted. "You're the most closed off person I've ever met. That's why we're talking. Because I want to see you open to love. Not that we need love to live, but because love makes living better."

Mrs. Carter was too smart for me. She stood and checked on the pie, leaving me to process her words. *Love makes living better.* It sounded so simple, but I'd never let those words sink in. I'd never thought about it. Because she was right, and I'd never let love in.

I tried with Andy, but he tainted everything about us, about love. He made me think love was ugly, but he was the one who made it ugly.

Love was beautiful, when it was right. When it was real. But I'd never known that kind of love.

Maybe one day.

13

"*D*o you ever feel like the world is trying to tell you something?" I asked at girls' night that weekend.

I'd been trying to understand why everyone in my life seemed to be saying the same things, and the only thing I could come up with was I was supposed to listen. I just didn't know why.

"All the time," Blake said. "I usually ignore it and regret it, but yeah, I've been there."

"Me, too," Karissa said. "But I listen. Working alone, I don't have other people to bounce ideas off of. It's not always easy, so I have to trust that when I get a signal from somewhere, it's for a reason."

"Are we talking about Colin?" Finley asked.

Everyone turned to her, then looked at me.

"She and Colin had dinner the other night. When we met at O'Kelley's?" She looked at Karissa for confirmation. "She and Colin were there together."

"Good for you," Trinity said. "He's cute. And yes, you should totally date him. Or keep dating him."

"My neighbor told me I should be open to love. She said

she knows all about Andy and wants me to be happy. And you guys keep pushing me toward Colin. And Colin…"

"You like him," Laura provided.

I nodded. "I do, I guess."

"You guess?" Karissa said.

I shrugged. "I do, but…"

"You don't want to," Finley said.

I nodded.

"Is this about Andy or Colin?" Laura asked.

"It's not about them," Melody said. "It's about her. It's about Elise trusting herself. She believed in Andy once, and he ruined that. She doesn't know if she can trust her opinions about men anymore."

Everyone looked at me to confirm Melody's assumption. She was dead-on. I nodded.

"If she was so wrong about Andy, how does she know she isn't wrong about Colin? Or the next guy? It's about learning to trust herself and listen to herself again. And that's not easy," Melody said.

"You sound like you know," Finley said.

Melody nodded. "I do. Because that's what my sister did to me. Not to the same extent, obviously, but she twisted everything for her own good and ruined what we had. Willow shut me down whenever I tried to have an opinion and blamed Ramsey for trying to change my mind all to try to split us up. When she finally admitted what she was doing, I felt broken for trusting my own sister. How do you not trust your sister?"

"Wow," Finley breathed. "I didn't know it was that bad."

Melody nodded. "It was, and it still is, but I have Ramsey. Ramsey shows me every day that love is still a possibility. He tells me he loves me. Elise doesn't have that. Elise faced the same betrayal, but she faced it from the person who was supposed to show her what love is."

"And letting go of that pain and trying again isn't easy," Laura said. "I'm sorry I've joked about this, Elise. I didn't realize how hard it was for you."

I shrugged. "Thanks. It's…I have the gift of time. It's been years since I left Andy. I'm still scared of having someone else take control of me, but I'm stronger now than I was then because I have something I didn't have when I was in college."

"What?" Finley asked.

"All of you. I know you guys won't let anything like that happen again."

"Not a chance," Karissa said.

I smiled and reached for her hand. Laura took my other hand, and we all reached for each other around the circle. I had my girls. They weren't going anywhere, and even if I gave the wrong guy a chance, they would be there for me.

"So, how are things with Colin?" Laura asked.

"I thought you weren't going to joke about that," I said.

Laura grinned. "I'm not joking. I want to know so I can live through you. I'm not getting any."

"Dr. Allison still playing hard to get?" Blake asked.

Laura shook her head. "I don't think he's playing. I just don't think he's interested."

"Sorry, Laur," I said.

"Thanks. But that means you need to tell me everything about Colin. Starting with how good of a kisser he is."

I grinned. "So good."

They all cheered, then demanded details. I didn't mind reliving those moments.

Colin asked me to meet him at the farm Saturday afternoon again. Since things were picking up with the tours, I was working, but I had the evening off. He offered to cook me dinner.

"You don't have to," I argued.

"I'd like to. I enjoy cooking for other people. And my grandmother has a great kitchen. I don't use it much because cooking for one person is tough."

"It really is," I agreed. "Are you sure you want to cook, though?"

"Absolutely. Do you have any allergies or anything you don't like?"

"Nope and nope. I'm up for pretty much anything."

"Sounds good. You know where the house is, right?"

I nodded. "I do. I'll text you when I'm leaving the docks."

"Looking forward to it."

I grinned. I was, too.

My day felt like it dragged on since I was waiting for dinner with Colin. It was better since I was working with Ava, but she picked up on my mood and asked what was going on.

"I have plans after work. I'm just anxious. Or excited. I don't know. Both, I guess."

"What kind of plans? Because I only feel like that when I have a date."

My cheeks burned, giving away my answer.

"You have a date?" Ava shouted.

"Jeez, it's not that big of a deal."

Ava shook her head and grabbed my arm. She turned me toward her and said, "Elise, I love you. You're awesome, and you should date a lot because everyone who knows you loves you. But you don't date. You hook up, but you don't date. So, yeah, this is a big deal."

I smiled and shrugged. "I like my freedom."

"I know, and that's totally cool. You shouldn't ever think you are doing something wrong. If you are happy being single, that's what matters. It is your life. I promise, I'm not judging you. I want to see you happy, and even though you're anxious, you're also excited, which makes me think this person makes you happy."

I nodded. "He does. He's…I think he's a good man. He's kind to me and to others."

"How does he treat his mom?"

"She died when he was young."

"Oh, I'm sorry."

I nodded. "I think he's okay. He lost his grandmother recently. He's fairly new to the area. But he wasn't close to his grandmother since he didn't live here. He's close to his dad, though."

"Wait, who is this?"

"His name is Colin Jones."

"From Jones Family Maple Farm?" Ava asked.

I nodded.

"He's so cute. And yeah, he seems to be a really nice guy. I've been in there a few times when women have come in to hit on him and he always lets them down easy. I've never heard of him taking a phone number or hooking up with any of them."

Unease filled me and sank in deep. I didn't like the idea of him having to turn down women at every turn. And I didn't like the idea of anyone thinking he was theirs. I wasn't the kind of woman who would fight for a guy. I didn't see the point. If a guy wasn't sure if he wanted to be with me, I didn't want to be with him. Period. Especially with my history.

Ava noticed I didn't respond and looked over at me. "Don't go there. He's not secretly sleeping with half the town or anything. He's a good guy."

"Yeah, maybe," I said, wondering if I should have stuck to my guns at the beginning and stayed away from him.

"Come on, we need to go. We'll talk about this later, but I really don't think you have anything to worry about."

I nodded and tried to believe her. I hated dating.

Ava and I traded off who gave the tours. I was distracted and off my game, so she ended up doing the last three. I felt bad, but she insisted she didn't mind.

"Don't get in your head about Colin," Ava said as we walked to the parking lot together. One of the perks of starting early was getting off at a reasonable time in the afternoon.

"I don't date because of things like this. I don't deal well with jealousy. It's a dangerous emotion that doesn't do anything except make you crazy. I don't like feeling it and I don't like being on the receiving end of it."

"But you can't stop other women from flirting. This isn't Colin trying to pick them up. It's them going after him."

"He and I matched on Book Boyfriends Wanted. We met up at O'Kelley's to hook up."

"And?"

"And how do I know he hasn't done that with other women?"

"How do you know he has? Listen, Elise, I get it. This is frightening because if you didn't like him, and I mean a lot, then you wouldn't be worried about this. You don't want things to go south with him. And since your dating history has been nonexistent, it's worse. But that doesn't mean Colin is a bad guy. It means you need to stop waiting for things to get messed up."

I sighed. "It's my default. I expect it to go bad. It always has for me."

"It does for everyone until they find the one they are meant to be with. You're not special," she said with a grin.

I laughed and shook my head. "Gee, thanks."

Ava chuckled. "All I mean is you're not alone. Now go see Colin and have fun. And if you're feeling brave, ask him how many women he's picked up from the app, or the barn, or the bar."

I snorted. Ava always made me laugh.

I took my time driving to Colin's. A part of me wanted to go home and change, but I knew if I did, I would likely stay home. Even though that was appealing, seeing Colin was a bigger draw, even when I was feeling unsure about things.

I drove up the long driveway to the farm. The barn came into view first. Aside from the day we went to the pond, I'd never been anywhere else on the farm. The house was visible from the barn, so I knew where to go, but I felt a little uneasy, like I was trespassing.

I parked next to Colin's truck and checked my reflection. My hair was a wild mess from being on the boat all day. My cheeks were pink from forgetting sunscreen. And I could use a shower, although I didn't think I smelled.

Wow, I was a catch. No wonder he had to pick women up in the barn.

I rolled my eyes at myself and dug through my purse. I found a brush and pulled my ponytail out. I brushed it, then tied it back up. I found a stick of deodorant at the bottom and put some on, just to make me feel better. There was nothing I could do about my pink cheeks, or my work clothes, but if Colin had a problem with it, we didn't need to be together.

I finally got out of my car and threw my bag across my body. I locked my car and clipped my keys to my strap so I knew where they were. I took in the house as I walked up to it. It wasn't big, but it was nice. It was an old brick and timber ranch with a front porch that ran the full length of the house. Rocking chairs were spread out across the entire porch. It looked like a home, a place where people were happy.

I stepped onto the front porch and smiled. I rang the bell and waited.

The door opened, and I took a step back when a large man filled the frame. He was older than Colin, but there was no resemblance.

I glanced around, wondering if there were two homes on the property, and if I needed to run, when the guy pushed the screen door open.

"Come on in," he said. "Colin's in the kitchen. I was on my way out and said I'd let you in."

"Oh, um, thanks," I said, trying to calm my pounding heart and sound normal at the same time.

"I'm Nicky," the man said, extending his huge hand to me. "I worked for Cleotha and stuck around to help Colin out."

"That's nice of you," I said as I shook his hand. He was a man who could overpower me without a second thought. Just shaking his hand felt dangerous. He could easily yank me inside the house and no one would ever see me again.

Nicky shrugged and quickly released my hand. "I love it here. And no one's going to hire an old fart like me anyway."

I chuckled with him, hoping I wasn't falling into his trap.

"Anyway, have a good night. Colin wouldn't let me try your dinner, but it sure does smell good."

I smiled and stepped out of the way so Nicky could walk out.

"It was nice meeting you, Elise. I'm sure I'll see you again soon."

"Good night," I said, watching him walk away. He strolled past my car and Colin's truck and kept going up the road that led past the house. I only turned when I heard a noise in the house.

I closed and locked the door, then followed my nose and ears to the kitchen. It was beautiful, like Colin said. The kitchen was open to the living and dining rooms, and the entire space was bright and airy. The kitchen was lined with maple cabinets stained a light honey color. Large black handles gave it a modern touch. Black appliances toned down the brightness and made it all look that much more homey.

Beyond the kitchen, a massive wooden table stretched out. A flower arrangement burst from a vase in the center, bringing pinks and reds and purples to the otherwise muted space.

Then there was the living room. An L-shaped couch faced both the wide sliding glass doors that lined the back of the room and a fireplace and TV on the wall to the right. A fire crackled in the fireplace, and music played from the TV.

I could live here.

The thought wandered through my mind without any warning. I didn't like it because I loved my home. It was smaller, but it was mine. This was Colin's. And we weren't anywhere near there yet.

"Hey," Colin said, drawing my attention to him. He was watching me carefully, gauging my reaction to his home.

"Hey," I said with a smile.

"How was work?"

I shrugged. "About the same as every day. I love it, though. I have a great job."

He grinned. "Good. Life's too short to be unhappy."

"It really is," I agreed. "Whatever you're cooking smells amazing."

"Thanks. Nicky tried to eat your dinner."

"He told me."

"Sorry about him."

I shrugged. "He was fine. Startled me a little when he opened the door. I thought I was at the wrong house."

Colin chuckled. "Sorry about that, too. I should have answered the door. He offered when I told him he had to leave because you were on the way. I think he just wanted to meet you."

"Does he meet all your dates?"

All humor faded from his face, and he set the spoon down. He turned to face me and wouldn't let me get away with my childish dig.

"Yes, because you're the only person I've dated since moving here."

"That's not possible," I said. "What about the app? Or the women who try to pick you up in the barn?"

Colin drew in a breath. "The app...I got it because Hudson told me you were on it. I felt guilty going to meet you that night because I was thinking about you and thought I was going to hook up with someone else."

"But you would have if it wasn't me," I said.

He shook his head. "I don't know."

I was silent for a minute, trying to process that. He broke into my thoughts.

"And the women in the barn aren't interested in me. They want someone new. I'm not interested in them either. I haven't talked to another woman, touched another woman, or kissed another woman since I met you. Honestly, since a long time before I met you. I was working like crazy the last few years, and relationships weren't a priority."

He put his hands on the counter in front of him and held my gaze.

"I don't do this, Elise. I don't play games and I don't screw around. I date one woman at a time. We've only known each other a little while, but I'm a loyal and honest guy. You can ask me anything you want, and I'll tell you the truth. But I don't appreciate you coming here and insinuating that I'm screwing around on you."

I took a breath and admitted he was right. Nothing I said was fair to either of us.

"I'm sorry," I said, meaning the words. "You're right. My ex...there were a lot of things wrong with him, but he liked to flirt with other women. He wanted to make me jealous, and it worked for a while. I couldn't trust him. He was attractive and smart and powerful, and women wanted him. He enjoyed feeling wanted. What he didn't enjoy was feeling like I was wanted, so he made me small."

"Elise," Colin said carefully.

"Andy did the same thing to me that I just did to you. He accused me of things that never happened because he wanted me to feel guilty. He wanted the power in our relationship. I never should have questioned you like I did. I was afraid you were like him. That you were making me feel special when I was really just one of many. I'm sorry I didn't trust you. And even more than that, I'm sorry I questioned who you are. I'm going to go."

I turned to leave, but Colin called out to me.

"What did he do to you?"

I looked back over my shoulder. "He destroyed me."

14

COLIN

From the first time I met Elise, I knew she was special. I could feel it when she was close. She had an ability to make people around her feel like they were important. I saw it in the eyes of her friends. They loved her, and they protected her.

The more times I saw her, and the more I got to know her, the more I realized she wasn't just special, she was a survivor. A fighter. Someone who'd seen hell and come back. I didn't know what happened to her until she said those three words.

He destroyed me.

I saw red. I wanted nothing more than to go find the man she was talking about and rip his arms off and beat him with them. I wanted to show him a fraction of the pain he inflicted on her. I wanted to ruin him.

But he wasn't the person who mattered. The person who mattered was making a break for my front door, trying to leave me.

"Please don't go," I told her when I caught up to her in the foyer.

Her hand was on the doorknob, waiting to turn it so she could leave. If she walked out that door, I knew she'd never be back. It was in her eyes. It was always in her eyes.

"I'm broken, Colin."

"We're all a little broken. That doesn't mean we can't be pasted back together."

She breathed a laugh. "I don't think there's enough paste in the world for me to be reassembled."

"Then don't start with reassembly. Start with dinner."

"What?" she asked. She released the doorknob and turned to face me. "What does that mean?"

"Food. Dinner. I cooked, and it smells good. And it tastes amazing. And I've built enough things in my life to know that putting something together doesn't work if you try to do it all at once. You need to start with one thing. My dad always said food fixes everything. It might not fix everything, but it doesn't hurt either."

She chuckled and shook her head. "I think I'd like your dad."

"I think he'd like you, too."

She smiled and reached for my hand. I stared at it for a moment. I couldn't move or breathe or even think. All I could do was feel.

And in that moment, when she put all her fears and brokenness aside and reached for my hand, I fell in love with her.

I pulled her into my arms and held her against my chest. I needed to hold her, to know she was safe. Even if it was just for a minute, and even if she pushed away, I needed it.

None of my exes shared anything like that before. None were hurt the way Elise was. And none were brave and strong like Elise was.

She rested her head on my chest and held on to me. I didn't know how long ago her relationship was or who the man was, but from the way she was holding me, she'd never allowed herself to feel safe with a man since.

So many things made sense with the new knowledge. It didn't make me think differently about her, or less of her in any way, but it helped me to understand her.

When her arms loosened around my waist, I released my hold on her. I wasn't ready, but she was, and I was following her lead.

We went back to the kitchen where, thankfully, dinner wasn't ruined. I turned the stove off before I went after Elise, so we could still eat. We worked together silently to get our food. Everything was out, which made it easier for Elise to help me.

I'd considered eating at the table, but I saw the way her eyes lingered on the fireplace when she walked in. I led her there and sat on the floor so we were close to the fire.

The home I lived in wasn't really mine yet. I felt like I was at someone else's house. Little things about it came back to me the more I explored, but it wasn't my home. Growing up, my dad created a comfortable home for us, but once I moved out, I just lived places. I didn't settle in or plan to stay. But sitting on the floor with Elise in front of the fireplace, I wanted the house we were in to be home.

For both of us, if she was willing one day.

"Are we okay?" I asked her.

She looked up at me and nodded. "I am sorry for questioning you. I shouldn't have done it. My friend Ava was talking about you today and she mentioned she overheard some women hitting on you, and I just sort of freaked out."

I drew in a breath. "The first time a random woman asked me out, I was shocked. I'd never had someone walk up to me and do that. Where I worked before, I was just an employee. I loved my job and being outside, but no one knew who I was.

It was a small community, but not as small as MacKellar Cove."

"We're special," Elise said with a grin.

"You are. And I really like it here, but I wasn't prepared for it. Nicky keeps telling me I'm fresh meat since I'm new to town. I'm not doing anything to encourage it, though. And the app…you're the only person I've talked to there. I considered deleting it, but I wanted to keep it in case you messaged me. I didn't want you to think I wasn't interested anymore."

She breathed a laugh and smiled at me. "Well, you're fresh meat, but it's not just because you're new. It's because you're hot. And thank you for not deleting the app. I probably would have thought that."

I grinned. "You think I'm hot?"

She rolled her eyes. "You know you are. When you wear those tight tees that stretch over your muscles and leave nothing to the imagination."

"Kind of like when you wear those tight yoga pants?"

Her eyes went big. Her lips curled up. "Colin!"

"You're allowed to look but I'm not? I didn't say anything about your see-through bra and panties at the pond. That about killed me."

Her cheeks reddened and she avoided my gaze.

"You're beautiful, Elise," I said. My voice was tight, my control barely restrained.

She looked up at me again, innocence and surprise in her gaze. She had no idea what she did to me.

"I…um, thank you. You're, um, not so bad yourself."

I grinned and leaned over. I kissed her, quickly, then pulled back and sat down.

"Not fair," she pouted. "I want more."

I chuckled. "Let's eat. Because when I start kissing you, I'm not going to want to stop."

Her cheeks turned red again. She nodded and picked up

her fork. She took a bite and moaned, and I swore I wasn't going to make it through dinner.

"This is so good," she said. "What is it?"

"Jambalaya. My dad and I love spicy foods. He and my mom traveled a good bit before I was born, and they really enjoyed New Orleans. Have you never had this?"

She shook her head and took another bite. "No. I always thought it would be too spicy for me, but this is amazing."

"It can be hotter, but I wasn't sure if you'd be okay with that so I toned it down a little. It has such a great flavor that it doesn't need the spice."

"It really does," Elise agreed. "I'm always starving after work, but this is delicious. Thank you for cooking for me."

"Thank you for coming over."

We ate and talked and flirted. When she laughed, my whole world felt better. She had a smile that was just for me, one with a little wrinkle of her nose and a squint of her eyes.

When we were done with dinner, she insisted on helping me clean up the kitchen. We worked together, bumping and brushing against each other the whole time. By the time we were done, I could barely control myself.

"What do you want to do?" she asked, looking up at me.

I didn't realize how small she was until we were standing in my kitchen looking at each other. I could tuck her under my chin and hold her against my chest without tilting my head out of the way. She was curvy, too, but she was small compared to me.

The fact that someone took advantage of that and hurt her pissed me off even more.

"How about a movie? You said that's what you usually do after working all day. Low key is my speed."

She laughed and nodded. "Sounds good to me."

I followed her to the living room and sat on the couch

next to her. I made sure she had space and wouldn't feel crowded by me, but she scooted closer.

"Is this okay?"

I nodded. "Hell, yes."

"Am I making you nervous?"

"Why?"

She chewed on her lip and looked away. "I've never told a guy about Andy. My friends know, but that's it. I feel like you're afraid of me or something."

I drew in a breath and told her the truth. "I don't want to scare you away. I don't want to do something that will send you running. I like you, Elise, a lot, and I guess I don't know what I can or should do right now."

"If I were any other woman and we were on a date at your home and you cooked her dinner, what would you be doing?"

"Honestly?"

She nodded.

"We'd probably be in the bedroom."

She chuckled. "My experiences with men since Andy have all been only in the bedroom. We have sex, then I leave."

"I don't want you to leave."

She smiled. "Neither do I. But I know—"

"I don't want to rush this," I told her.

She smiled and sighed. "You really are a unicorn."

I laughed. "I have the horn to prove it right now."

She gasped. "That's the first dirty thing you've said to me. Wow. I feel so much less tense now."

"You were tense?"

She nodded. "I have a bit of a dirty mind, and I've been holding back because you seem all buttoned up and proper."

I snorted. "Not even close. Trust me, I'm a fan of dirty."

"Oh, yeah?"

I scooted closer. "Yeah. Especially when it involves a beautiful woman with her own dirty mouth."

She grinned, a cheeky, tempting grin, and said, "I definitely have one of those. And I know how to use it."

My cock pulsed with her words, and I groaned. "Yeah, you're going to kill me."

She laughed. "Let's put on a movie."

I smiled and handed her the remote. I was fairly sure I didn't have enough blood in my brain to make sense of anything, so it was better she chose.

She settled back against the couch and flipped through the movie section. I watched her as she searched. She tilted her head as she considered each option, then shook it when the answer was no. Her nose wrinkled up when she passed a movie she had no interest in at all. And when she finally found one she wanted to watch, her eyes lit up and her smile made me smile.

"Have you ever seen this?" she asked when she set the remote down, next to her.

I looked at the screen and shook my head. "Nope. Is it good?"

She nodded. "One of my favorite movies."

I leaned back and watched her more than the screen. I felt like a teenager on a first date with my dad in the next room instead of a man of almost forty and my own home. Elise and I didn't touch except a few incidental brushes against each other. We didn't talk. We just sat together and watched the movie.

And the entire time, I thought about all the things I would do to her if she were any other woman. The way her skin would taste when I ran my tongue between her breasts. The way her breath would change when I slid my hand between her thighs. The way her eyes would light up when I entered her.

It was torture. I wanted all those things, but she was content to watch the movie. We would take things at her pace because I wasn't an asshole. And if I was the one who wanted to take things slowly, I knew she would be okay with it.

And I did. I wasn't interested in rushing her. I wanted her to know she could trust me and I would never push her to do something she didn't want to do.

When the movie ended, she sighed happily like she was just as invested as the characters had been. She looked over at me and asked, "Did you like it?"

"Honestly, I barely watched it."

"I'm sorry," she said. "I should have picked something you would have enjoyed. What kind of movies do you like?"

I laughed softly. "It wouldn't have mattered. I was too busy watching you."

Her entire demeanor changed. A sexy, sultry smile turned her lips up. She leaned closer. "Yeah?" she asked in a soft, timid voice.

I nodded. "Absolutely. I'm mesmerized by you."

"The feeling is pretty mutual."

I chuckled. "I doubt it. I was wondering what sounds you'd make when you came. I don't think you were thinking about that."

She shook her head. "No, I wasn't. Because I already know what sounds I make when I come."

A laugh burst free. She joined me and laid her head on my chest.

"I like you, Colin. And it scares me."

"I told you, nothing is going to happen without you wanting it to."

"Does that mean you're not going to make the first move?" she asked, lifting her head to look at me.

I drew in a breath and nodded. "It does. Because as much

as I want you, and as painful as it is to sit here, I refuse to let you feel like you have to do anything."

She pulled back a little more and shifted her weight. She lifted her leg and threw it over my lap, straddling me on the couch.

I groaned and closed my eyes to stop the onslaught of desire tearing through me. If I looked at her, I wouldn't be able to stop myself from touching her.

"Touch me, Colin," she whispered.

"Elise," I groaned.

"I want to feel your hands on me."

I opened my eyes and stared up at her. She was looking at me with so much barely restrained desire that I couldn't hold back. I cupped her ass and kneaded both cheeks with my fingers.

She groaned and slid up my thighs until her body met mine. She moaned when my cock nestled between her thighs and rubbed against her.

"I…promise me we aren't going to have sex today," she whispered. The pain and tension in her voice had me pulling away.

"I already said nothing—"

"If you touch me, I'm going to beg you for it. I want you. I want to feel you inside me. I want to scream your name and feel something. I won't be able to stop myself, but if we do…"

"We're not having sex tonight, Elise," I said firmly. "I promise you."

"Thank you," she breathed. "Now, keep touching me."

I grinned. "Gladly."

Every sound she made dragged me deeper and deeper under her spell. I couldn't get enough of her. I ached to do anything and everything she would let me, but I made her a promise, and I wasn't going to break it.

"Kiss me," she whispered.

Taking charge was new for Elise. I could sense it in the panicked way she asked if I was going to make the first move. She didn't like being the one who initiated things, but it was the only way until she felt comfortable telling me no.

I slid one hand up her back when she asked me to kiss her. My other hand stayed on her ass, keeping her body close to mine. She wiggled in place, impatient for me to do as she asked. I was going to let her decide what happened, but I was going to do it in my own damn time.

I slid my hand all the way up into her hair. The silky strands of her ponytail tangled around my fingers. I moved to brush the hair from her face and found her watching me.

"Hey," I said softly.

"Hey."

I smiled at her and couldn't resist doing exactly what

she'd asked me to do. I leaned in and pressed my lips against hers. She sighed, like she wasn't sure I'd do as she asked, and sank into me.

Trust was a powerful thing. Knowing she trusted me, not just with her words but with her body, made me feel like the biggest man on earth. Elise Webber, a woman who rarely let people in, especially men, had given me a gift few men had ever gotten.

Her tongue teased the seam of my lips, telling me she wanted more. I groaned and squeezed her cheek, drawing her body even closer to mine as I opened and let her in.

It wasn't our first kiss, not by a long shot, but it was one I would remember forever. It was one I knew was different. This wasn't a casual thing anymore, not for me. Maybe it never was, but I was able to tell myself before that it was casual. When her tongue slid against mine, her body teasing me, I knew there was no going back for me.

The urge to take over was almost as strong as the desire to let her lead. Elise wrapped her tongue around mine and teased me with every touch. She sucked hard on my tongue, and my dick pulsed like she did it to him. The woman was a fantasy in real life.

I groaned and slid my hand under her shirt. I needed to feel her bare skin. It was soft and delicate and warm. I spread my hand on her side, touching as much of her as I could. I wanted to go higher, to pull her shirt free of her body and feast my eyes on all of her, but she was still in charge.

She leaned back and tugged at the bottom of her shirt. I helped her get it up and off and froze when I got an up close and personal look at her white bra barely containing her breasts.

Being with a woman I'd already seen mostly naked was a different kind of experience. It was like doing everything with a sense of deja vu. Except it wasn't a feeling of repeat, it was a second chance.

I leaned down and rested my head on her chest. She wrapped her arms around me and held me there. Her heart pounded against my ear, the steady thump matching my own rapid heartbeat. We sat there for a minute, her holding me as I held her, not talking, just being together.

"Colin," she said softly.

I lifted my head and met her gaze. "Yeah?"

"You still haven't touched me."

I laughed. Then I held her gaze as I lifted my hands to cup her breasts. Her eyes slid closed when I stroked my thumbs over her alert nipples. I couldn't decide what I wanted to watch more…her face or her body. Her face told me what she enjoyed, but her body I couldn't get enough of.

I held her ribs still and leaned down to capture her breast in my mouth. The silky fabric of her bra wasn't as soft as her skin, but it yielded to me, soaking through almost instantly and letting me circle her nipple with my tongue. She moaned as I teased her, and her hips shifted over mine.

I bit back my groan, knowing I was going to embarrass myself in front of this woman if I didn't get a handle on it. Tonight was about her. Cooking dinner for her. Talking to her. Making her feel good. Letting her know she was safe with me. I didn't care about my own needs, not when she had unfulfilled needs.

I sucked hard on her nipple, drawing it and her bra into my mouth. Her breath hitched as she breathed my name. Her hips kept moving over me, and I wondered if she even realized she was doing it.

I released the first nipple and nearly came when I saw the outline of my mouth around her peaked nipple. It was chaste by comparison to most of the women I'd been intimate with, but it felt erotic and so personal it almost scared me.

The last woman I was involved with told me I was commitment phobic. I told her I just didn't want to commit to her. We were both right in some ways because I didn't want to commit to her, but until Elise, I wasn't sure I'd ever commit to anyone. I wanted to, and I was open to it, but there was a part of me that always held back. With Elise, I wanted to run full speed ahead until we couldn't go any further.

I moved to her other nipple, burying my face in her so I stopped dreaming about all the other things I wanted to do with her. The things that would mean she was mine forever.

She responded to me by arching her back and pressing her breast against my face. A little groan slipped past her lips. I wrapped my arms around her, her skin burning mine. I couldn't get enough of her, but just touching her was perfect. She was like the best treat on the planet. One that I wanted to both savor and devour.

"Colin," she whispered.

I looked up at her, but she wasn't looking at me. Her eyes were closed and her head thrown back. She had a look of pure bliss on her face.

I kissed my way up her chest to her neck and tasted her there. The wet rings of her nipples made me want more of her. Her neck was sweet beneath the salty taste of her sweat and the river water.

"More, Colin. Please."

"Is this the begging part?" I asked against her neck.

She nodded. "I need you."

"Anything, Elise. Tell me what you need."

"I need you, Colin."

I thrust up against her, rubbing myself on her seam. Her jeans were a hindrance, but it was the best I could do under the circumstances.

"Oh, God," she whimpered.

I did it again, kissing my way back to her nipples and pulling one into my mouth. She rode me, taking what she needed from me and letting me help her along.

Her movements were frantic, her body taking control. She whimpered, like something wasn't right.

"Colin," she moaned. "More, please. Help me."

I eased her back far enough to slide my hand between us. I looked up at her, waiting until she pried her eyes open and met my gaze. "Can I touch you, Elise?"

"Please," she begged me.

Thank God for yoga pants. They stretched away from her body when I slid my hand down the front. Curls brushed my fingers first, then slick flesh that made me groan. I kept going, dipping a finger just inside her.

She immediately starting pumping her hips again, her body drawing me in. I teased her until she let a finger slide inside and slid my thumb back up to her clit. She moaned and rode my hand.

Her fingers dug into my shoulders. Her head dropped back. I kissed her stomach and her breasts and pressed down on her clit, teasing and playing with her until her channel tugged at my fingers and her body locked up.

Then everything released.

I looked up at her, wanting to remember the look on her face as she came for the first time. Her eyes were squeezed shut, like she couldn't face what was happening. Her lips were parted in an O. Her skin was flush and damp, a flush that continued down to her breasts.

She was the most beautiful woman I'd ever seen in my life.

She shook through her orgasm, then trembled as aftershocks racked her. I did my best to stay still, but every time she shifted, my fingers rubbed against her.

"Holy shit," she breathed. "I've never come that hard."

"Ever?" I asked, slowly withdrawing my hand.

"Oh, God," she moaned, her body shaking once more. "Oh, yes."

She fell forward onto me, letting me support her weight. I wiped my hand on my jeans and held her close. Her breathing slowed and her body stopped shaking, then she tensed.

"I need to go," she said quickly, scrambling off my lap. "I, um, I…sorry."

She was up and moving away from me without her shirt on. Her movements were jerky and erratic. She hurried toward the door, looking around as if she knew she was forgetting something but didn't know what.

"Elise," I said softly.

She looked at me, and I held up her shirt. She glanced down at herself and her chest turned pink. "Uh, yeah, I guess I need that."

I waited until she came over to me then asked, "Or you could tell me what happened and we can leave it on the floor."

"I…I shouldn't have done that."

"Done what?"

She gestured to the couch. "Done…that."

"Had an orgasm?" I asked.

Her cheeks reddened. "Yeah, that. I…you felt good. And I took advantage of you."

"How do you figure you took advantage of me? Trust me when I say I enjoyed that."

"But I begged you, and I didn't give you a choice. And I made you promise we weren't going to have sex tonight."

"And we didn't."

"No, but you wanted to."

"Yes, and no. I didn't invite you over here with the hope that we'd end up in bed. I wanted to see you."

"But you touched me. I asked you to and you touched me. You gave me an orgasm and now you…"

I raised an eyebrow.

She glanced at my cock, pressed against my zipper.

I chuckled. "He'll survive."

"I should…help you. Or we can have sex."

I shook my head. "No sex, Elise. I promised you that. And no quid pro quo. That's not what this is about. Sometimes I'm going to be content with touching you and seeing you lost in your own pleasure. And sometimes you're going to do the same for me. But I am not willing to negotiate for sex."

"I really think you are a unicorn. You just…everything you say is the opposite of what I expect."

"What do you mean?"

She shrugged. "I thought you'd ask for something."

I shook my head. "I told you, I'm not going to push you to do anything you don't want to do. Ever. I want you here because you want to be here. Not because you think you have to be or you think I'll get mad if you leave or any other reason than you want to be."

"Thank you," she whispered. The war still raged in her eyes. I wanted her to stay but she wasn't going to. She was ready to leave. It didn't matter why, and I wasn't going to let her feel like she shouldn't.

I walked over to her and held her shirt up to her for her to put it on. She slid her arms through then helped me tug it over her head. She smoothed it down her front then looked up at me with regret in her eyes.

I rubbed the spot between her brows where her forehead was creased with worry.

She smiled sadly. She tipped her head back to keep her eyes locked on mine. "Are you mad?"

I shook my head and pulled her against my chest. "Not

even a little. I'm disappointed that you don't trust what I say, but I'm not mad at all. Are we going to do this again?"

"What? A date or me leaving you hanging at the end of the night?"

I chuckled. "Well, hopefully the first one, but if the second happens, too, it won't kill me."

"Men usually want sex, and if they don't get sex, they get pissed off. What's with you?"

I slid my hand down her back and breathed in her scent. "I know how to be patient. I own a maple farm, and there is not much of anything slower than maple sap dripping from a cold tree."

She laughed.

"There's no reason to rush you, Elise."

"Thank you." She took a breath. "That makes me want to jump you."

I kissed the top of her forehead. "I'm not saying it for that reason. And I think you need to know you're safe. You don't feel safe with me yet."

"We went swimming in a pond in our underwear."

I shrugged. "I guess being in my house is harder. Only you know why."

She took another deep breath, and I let go of her. It was painful, but it was the only thing I could do. She kissed me quickly, then walked to my door. Before she walked out, she said, "Thank you for tonight. Next time I won't tease you."

"Yes, you will," I joked with her. "Because just walking through that door is a tease. Breathing you in, seeing you smile, all of it is teasing me. But that only means it'll be that much better when the sap starts flowing."

She came back over and kissed me quickly, then walked out the door.

I stood there for a minute, debating what to do. The

kitchen was clean. The draw of TV wasn't there. All I wanted was Elise, but she was gone. Her scent filled me and flowed around me, and my erection pulsed with every breath. A cold shower seemed like the only option I had.

Except when I turned on the water, I made it warm. When I stepped in, I cranked it hotter. And when Elise's laugh floated into my mind, I wrapped my hand around my cock and groaned.

I let my mind replay the evening. From the second she walked in, her eyes full of wonder at the house to her opening up to me, just a little, and flirting. Then her crawling on top of me and blowing my mind with her natural sexiness.

I let the water hit my chest and slide down my body, making my cock slicker with every stroke. What started out slow became fast and almost painful. Images of Elise flooded my mind. Her in the pond. Her laughing at me. Her floating. Her cheeks red with embarrassment. Her eyes wide and joyful. Her body rocking over mine. Her chest flush with desire. Her eyes closed and mouth open.

"Elise," I grunted. My fist beat against my abdomen, squeezing the tip and retreating. Every breath was ripped out of me on need alone. Nothing in me mattered except Elise.

My body tightened. My cock pulsed. My spine tingled. I was fairly sure I was going to be sick.

Then everything released. I came with such power it blasted the wall in front of me. I slammed my free hand against the wall to keep from collapsing as I kept stroking. Every beat of my heart pushed out another squirt until I shook from exhaustion.

I released myself and pressed both hands to the wall. The water pounded on my back. I let the shower help my breathing return to normal then finished my shower and got out. I wrapped a towel around my waist and padded to my room. I flopped onto the bed and was out before I finished air drying. Dreaming of Elise.

"I heard a rumor that Trent MacKellar is moving back into the MacKellar house," Laura said once we were all eating our cake.

Trinity brought a lemon cake with a boozy rum glaze that was delicious, and much more interesting to me than another rumor about the MacKellars.

"They always say that," Karissa told her. "For years, there have been rumors about someone moving in. I've heard everything from Trent MacKellar was coming home to Trent had a wife and a bunch of kids and was going to raise them here or Trent's wife died and he was bringing his kids. I even heard they sold it once. And that Trent lost the house in a card game. None of it is true."

"Really?" Laura asked, sounding disappointed. She wrinkled her nose and shook her blonde curls back from her face.

Karissa nodded. "Yep. Trent MacKellar was ready to get the hell out of here as soon as he could. He hated living here as much as he loved it."

"What does that mean?" Blake asked. She leaned forward.

Everyone liked hearing about the MacKellars. Those who

knew Trent were almost like royalty-adjacent. The rest of us gobbled up whatever we could about the family that founded MacKellar Cove.

Karissa leaned back and tilted her head at all the faces staring back at her. "You guys didn't know him?"

We shook our heads.

"You didn't, Melody?" Karissa asked, directing her brown eyes toward Mel. Melody was a year younger than Karissa, but she was always with Ramsey and Ian, who also graduated with Trent.

Melody shook her head. "I knew who he was, but I wasn't friends with him. Neither were Ramsey or Ian. I didn't know you were."

Karissa laughed. She crossed her long legs and leaned back in her seat. She took a bite of her cake. She was one of the royal-adjacent ones. Someone who knew Trent and didn't think of him as special. The rest of us didn't share her thoughts and were desperate to know why. "I wasn't friends with Trent MacKellar. A friend of mine dated him for a few weeks, but he never stayed with anyone for long. She told me he used his name to get out of a speeding ticket one night, but he always complained that everyone only liked him because he was a MacKellar."

"Sounds like he was a tool," Trinity said, rolling her eyes. "I didn't even know there was a MacKellar that young. It had to be weird to grow up in a town named for your family."

"His mom was the one who insisted on the square. She said people should have a place to gather. It's named Catherine Park, but everyone calls it town square or just the square," Finley said, adding in the little bit of local history I knew. "I didn't know him, but I always thought it would be cool to have so many friends. We used to go to football games with Ian and he tried to point Trent out to us once. He was in the middle of a crowd. I couldn't really see him."

"Don't let the crowd fool you," Karissa said. She pursed her purple lips, the same color as her romper. "He hated the crowd as much as he hated living here. He's not coming back."

"Do you think maybe it's someone else in the family?" I asked Laura.

She shook her head. "No, I heard it was him. One of my patients told me."

"It's really a shame," I said. "The house is gorgeous, but left empty for so long, it can't be in good shape."

"They have staff taking care of it," Karissa said. "They'd never let their possessions be anything less than stellar. Trent scratched his car junior year, and his dad bought him another one that weekend instead of just getting it fixed."

"Seriously?" Blake asked.

Karissa laughed and finished her cake. She cut another piece and nodded. "Yep. That's how they were. All about appearances."

"I couldn't live like that," Finley said. "It would drive me crazy to worry so much about what other people think."

I nodded, although I kind of got it. I never told my family about Andy because I was worried they would think less of me. It was the same with a lot of people I knew or had met since I left him. Being a victim made me feel weak, even though so many people said I was strong to walk away. Admitting how long I stayed, even though it was bad, made me feel weak. If leaving was strong, then staying was weak.

I knew that wasn't true, not entirely, but it was how I felt. He made me believe no one would trust me, and years later, I was still letting his words dictate my life.

"Crap," I breathed, realizing what he dictated most recently.

"What?" Trinity asked. She was sitting next to me and the

only one who heard my barely uttered word. She leaned closer. "Are you okay?"

I started to nod, then shook my head. I wasn't. Not even a little. I walked away from Colin because I was afraid. I didn't give him a chance. And yeah, we barely knew each other, and no, I wasn't ready for sex with him, but I made him the bad guy in my head. Again.

"I…I'm so messed up."

"About what?" Trinity asked.

"Colin. We had a date last night and I got all weird and left, even though everything was going really good."

"How good?" Finley asked. "Help a girl out."

I snorted. "Not that good, but screaming O for me kind of good. He got nothing."

"That's more good than I've had all year," Trinity said. "I clearly don't know how to pick the right ones because the ones I've met are not worth a second run between the sheets."

"That's because you're looking for a connection instead of just sex," Laura said. "Men don't want relationships. They want casual hook-ups. And if the casual hook-up is good enough, then maybe they'll want something more."

"You sound like you're speaking from experience," Karissa said. "Did something happen with Dr. Allison?"

Laura rolled her eyes and shook her head. "No, not with me. But one of the other nurses said he has a regular booty call in another town."

"Is this the same person that told you Trent MacKellar is moving back?" Karissa asked with a wry look.

Laura shook her head. "Nope. It's a nurse who's been working for him longer than me. She would know. And she doesn't usually gossip."

"So, how did that conversation come up?" Blake asked.

"I don't know. It doesn't matter. Weren't we talking about Elise?" Laura said.

I shook my head. "Nope, we can dissect your relationship with your boss instead."

"No, I think the fact that you actually have a relationship makes yours a lot more interesting," Laura countered with a smile.

"She's right," Trinity said. "Sorry, Laura."

Laura shrugged.

"You're not sorry to me?"

Trinity shook her head, sending her ringlets flying. "Not even a little. Because you need help if you're going to keep that man in your life."

"Why do I need a man?" I asked.

"You don't," Karissa said. "And this is coming from the woman who created a dating app. But if you want a man in your life, that's different. You're a nurturer, Elise. You create a family and draw people to you. You're not a loner."

"What are you talking about? I live alone," I argued.

"In a community that is so up in each other's business that you can leave your doors unlocked and know that no one will ever step foot inside," Karissa argued.

"I like that," I said. "I feel safe there."

"And that's a good thing," Finley said. "But what Rissa is saying is that you're not the kind of person who will be alone forever. You're the kind of person who wants a relationship and someone to share her life with."

"But I haven't been in a relationship since Andy."

"Because you're scared," Laura said. "And you have every right to be. But that doesn't mean you want to be alone. I think your fear of being alone is starting to outweigh your fear of letting someone else in."

"I don't have a fear of being alone." I pouted as they snickered and snorted at me.

"Elise, we love you," Blake said. "You know we'll always be here for you. Like Rissa said, you've created a home right here with us. You want people to share your life with. I don't blame you. Life is better with Ian than I ever thought it could be. I was content to be alone forever, but now I can't imagine life without him in it."

"I'm not in love with Colin," I said.

"Funny how none of us said that but that's your argument," Karissa said. "I think you might have more feelings for him than you're willing to admit, maybe even to yourself."

"I like him, but that's it. He's a nice guy. He's gorgeous and sweet and smart and funny. He has a dirty side to him that shocks you when you hear it. And he's a hell of a cook."

I stopped talking and looked up at them. They were all watching me with matching smirks.

"I'm not in love with him," I argued.

"Okay, you're not in love with him," Trinity said, "but you like him. What's the problem?"

I sighed. "I don't know. I just…"

"You don't want to want him," Laura said.

I nodded. "Yeah."

"God, do I ever know that feeling. It sucks. But at least in your case you know he wants you, too," Laura said with a sad smile.

"I'm sorry, Laura."

She shrugged. "It's a good thing, Elise. Don't feel bad for me. Be happy that there is a sweet, kind, amazing guy who likes to cook and is gorgeous and good with his hands who wants you. I'd take that."

I smiled at her, hating that she and Dr. Allison weren't together. He was smart, but man was he dumb for not seeing her.

"Do you want sex or a relationship?" Finley asked.

"I…" I closed my mouth when I realized my normal

answer of sex wasn't accurate. I wanted to get to know Colin. I liked him, and I wanted to spend time with him. He made me laugh, and he made me feel safe.

"Both is an acceptable answer," Blake said. She twisted her engagement ring around her finger and smiled.

"I haven't wanted a relationship in eight years. That's a long time for me to be alone," I said.

"You haven't been alone. You have us and you have your family and you have your community," Karissa said. "You haven't had a man share your bed, but that doesn't mean you've been alone."

"It's not scary to be with you guys. You know me and you don't judge me," I admitted.

"Do you think Colin would?" Melody asked.

I shook my head. "I told him about it last night. About Andy. Not details, but he understood that my only other relationship ended very badly."

"You what?" Karissa blurted.

I froze, looking around the room at my shocked friends. "What?"

"You told him?" Karissa asked.

I nodded, my cheeks burning and my chest tightening. I didn't know why I wasn't supposed to, but it scared me that I did and I shouldn't have. "Why shouldn't I?"

"It's not that," Laura said. "It's that you didn't tell us anything for a long time. You've known Colin, what, a few weeks?"

"Should I not have told him?" I asked. My body heated up as I panicked.

"It's not that at all," Trinity said. "We're surprised because you don't talk about. Not even casually or a little bit. I get that, you know I do, but if you felt comfortable enough with him to share anything, it means you trust him. A lot."

"I do, I guess. I can talk to him and spend time with him,

but I freaked out when…I told him he had to stop us if I begged him for sex," I confessed.

"You did what now?" Karissa asked.

I covered my face with my hands. "It's dumb, but I knew if I started kissing him, I'd end up wanting to have sex. It's all I've done. I haven't had sex with someone I've made out with. It's all been quick and dirty and, quite honestly, not that great. But everything with Colin has been so good. And I…"

"Wanted to have sex with him," Melody said. "Which moved him from the safe friendly zone to the risky sexy zone. And you haven't had anyone cross over since your ex."

I nodded, surprised at her insight.

"When Ramsey asked me for a divorce, I went on some dates. I hated it, but it was kind of the same. Another parent asked me out and we went out. It was fine, but when I saw him at school again it was weird. It was like we could get along when we were at school, and we had an okay date, but once we went on a date, seeing him at school was awkward and uncomfortable," Melody explained.

"Exactly," I said. "But that's seriously messed up, right?"

"Ian was one of my closest friends for years," Blake said. "When we first kissed, it threw me off big time. He was Ian. He wasn't supposed to be interested in me. But he wanted more and more, and it was flattering, to say the least, that he wanted me. But it still messed with my head."

"You were all sorts of screwed up over him," Finley said with a grin.

"I really was," Blake said with a chuckle. "I'm like you, Elise. I didn't really want to be alone, but I convinced myself I did. I wasn't happy, but I wasn't hurt. I wasn't scared that I would lose myself like my mom did so many times. Letting Ian in was not easy, but I am so much happier for it."

"I just don't know if I can do it. I…"

"My mom never did," Trinity said. "It's been more than

fifteen years and she's still not willing to date. It's a choice you have to make, but if you trusted him to tell him about Andy, and you trusted him to go skinny dipping—"

"We did not go skinny dipping!"

"You went swimming in a pond in your bra and panties. Trust me when I tell you those did nothing to hide anything. And I'd be willing to bet whatever briefs or boxers he was wearing didn't hide anything either," Trinity argued with a quirk of her eyebrow.

My smirk and warm cheeks were all the answer she needed.

"Like I said, if you can trust him with all this…" She trailed off, letting me interpret her words.

I should be able to trust him with all of me.

"I really hate it when you guys are right."

Karissa grinned. "And we hate it when you hold back details about a good make-out session. Now spill."

I grinned and told them all about it. And my only regret was that I didn't have more to share with my friends about the man who made me want to abandon all my fears.

17

When I got home from girls' night, I sent Colin a message in Book Boyfriends Wanted about coming over sometime. I had never invited someone to my home, but I wanted him there. I wanted him in my space where I was more comfortable.

He said he was free Tuesday, and we set a date. I was big and bold all the way up until I got off work Tuesday afternoon and Ava wished me luck.

Then I started to freak out.

There was a reason I didn't invite men to my place. My neighbors for one. They would interrogate him until he made it to my trailer. And then when he got there, I wouldn't be able to walk out and go home if the date didn't go well. And if anything did happen, my neighbors would probably know because they would watch my trailer and see when he left, and probably harass him on the way out of the neighborhood.

Maybe I shouldn't have invited him over.

When I got home, I saw a message waiting for me on

Book Boyfriends Wanted. I opened it and laughed when I saw it was from Colin.

SWEETSTUFF

I grabbed a maple cream pie for dessert tonight if that's okay. Also wanted to make sure we're still on.

CAPTAIN

We're still on. I'll try not to leave you unsatisfied again. The pie sounds amazing.

SWEETSTUFF

The pie is amazing. I've had it before and it's become another of my weaknesses. And trust me, I was plenty satisfied the other night. Watching you was…there are no words.

CAPTAIN

I'm sure that's not true but thank you.

SWEETSTUFF

It's definitely true. You gave me a lot to fantasize about over the last few days.

CAPTAIN

Dirty. Old. Man.

SWEETSTUFF

You wound me. I'm not that old.

CAPTAIN

But you are dirty?

SWEETSTUFF

You bring it out in me.

CAPTAIN

LOL. I need to shower. See you soon.

SWEETSTUFF

And my pie. Tease.

CAPTAIN

That's who I was really talking to.

SWEETSTUFF

LOL. Now I know my place.

I chuckled and put my phone down. It was all going to be okay.

I raced into the bathroom and took a quick shower to wash off the day. I dressed in soft and comfortable clothes because even though it was a date, it was a date at home. And Colin had seen me in worse. I tied my hair back into a loose ponytail and started on dinner. It wouldn't take long to cook the rice since everything else was already done. I found a recipe online for pot roast and made it the day before. It was pretty easy, but I didn't have all the right ingredients. It was fine, though. It was impossible to mess up pot roast. That's what my mom said.

I heated up the pot roast, and the kitchen smelled delicious. I figured that was a good sign and happily got out everything we needed to eat.

About fifteen minutes after I expected Colin, I checked my phone. I didn't have any missed messages from him. I wasn't sure what happened until I heard voices outside.

My neighbors.

I rushed out and found Mrs. Carter talking to Colin outside my trailer. She was asking him who he was and why he was there.

"I'm a friend of Elise's. She invited me over for dinner. The pie is for her," Colin said.

"Elise likes pie. She's good at baking them, too. She came over and baked a pie with me not long ago. She's a good girl. Are you a good boy?"

"Yes, ma'am," Colin said automatically.

"I'll be watching you," Mrs. Carter said. "I'm not going to let anyone hurt Elise."

"She's lucky to have you in her life," Colin said with a smile.

"Hi, Mrs. Carter," I called out.

"Hi, Elise," she replied with a wide grin. "Did you invite him over?"

I nodded. "I did. He's going to have dinner with me and watch a movie."

"Did you cook?" Mrs. Carter asked.

I nodded. "I did."

Her smile fell. "Should I call Steve?"

I scowled at her. Steve was a friend of her son's and owned one of the local pizzerias. Mrs. Carter gave me his number the first time we cooked dinner together. I liked to bake, but cooking wasn't always as much of a success. "No, Mrs. Carter. I'm sure dinner is fine. Have a good night."

She waved and went back around her trailer. Colin finally got out of his truck, like it was safe without the attack dogs around.

"Your neighbors are intense. I didn't think the lady at the front was going to let me in," Colin said, glancing around.

"Mrs. Lockhart is better than a cop at figuring things out. She's lived here her whole life and protects us like we're all her own children."

"She almost fell off her porch when I said I was here to see you. She told me there was no way and that you never have visitors. Especially not men," Colin said as he made it to my door.

He looked good. Jeans hung low on his hips and his green tee was just loose enough to give a hint at the muscles I knew were beneath. He smelled good, too. Like he'd just taken a shower. Fresh and clean but manly in a spicy way.

But all of that wasn't enough to distract me from my embarrassment that he knew I didn't ever have people over.

"Um, yeah, well, I…"

"Thank you for inviting me," he said softly, reaching up and stroking my cheek.

All of a sudden that heat from my embarrassment turned to a totally different kind of heat. The kind of heat that had me wanting to drag him inside and do anything other than feed him dinner.

A knock drew my attention to Mrs. Carter's window, where she was watching us. I pulled back from Colin and waved at Mrs. Carter. She waved back.

I backed up so Colin and I could go inside. He glanced back and smiled at Mrs. Carter, then followed me in. I closed and locked my door while he looked at my home. It was small, but I kept it neat and clean. We walked right into my living room. A soft couch that wrapped around you when you sat and welcomed you as part of it filled most of the space. I had end tables and a TV but no other furniture since I never had more than one or two other people over. And always my friends. To one side was my bed and to the other was my kitchen. Both were visible from the front door.

"This is all you in here. I really like it," Colin said.

"It's small. I like that it's small, but it's small."

"There's nothing wrong with that. People don't need big homes or lots of stuff to be happy. You have people who clearly care about you here. That wouldn't be as likely if you all had big homes and were miles away from each other."

"That was one of the reasons I moved here. I liked knowing there were people close. It hadn't been long after Andy that I bought this place, and I wanted to know no one could hide here and that people were close if I ever needed anything."

"I'm sure if I wasn't a threat, they would be very nice people."

"You're not a threat," I said with a laugh.

He shook his head. "They don't know that. All they know is I showed up to see you, and that's not normal."

"It's fine. It's no big deal."

Colin didn't say anything, but I could see in his eyes that he wanted to. We both let it go. Talking about it was only going to make me feel awkward. Somehow, he always picked up on things like that.

"Should we have dinner? This dessert smells amazing, but whatever you cooked smells even better," Colin said.

I nodded. "Yeah, we should. Um, I don't have a dining room table. I always just eat on the couch."

He grinned. "I usually do the same."

He followed me to the kitchen and put the pie he brought in the fridge. Colin stayed back so I could dish out our meals since the kitchen was so small. It was funny because it never seemed small when Laura or Blake or Karissa were over. Only when Colin showed up did my home feel like it couldn't contain all of him.

I handed him a bowl of food and made my own. We both poured glasses of water and went to the couch. Colin sat down and groaned. "This might be the most comfortable couch I've ever sat on."

I chuckled. "I know, right? When I found it in the store, I had to buy it."

"I don't blame you. I think I'd sleep on this if I owned it. Wow."

I giggled and picked up the remote. "Do you want to watch something?"

He nodded. "Sure, sounds good."

I watched out of the corner of my eye as he stirred his pot

roast around and mixed the rice into the stew. He took a bite and chewed, then froze.

Oh, no. It smelled amazing. There was no way it was bad. I tried it. I knew I did. Didn't I? I had to have.

Colin finished chewing and swallowed. He stirred his food again but didn't go in for another bite. I had to know how bad it was.

I mixed mine up and took a bite. I almost spit it out. It tasted salty and sweet at the same time. Too salty and too sweet. The meat was undercooked and tough. Or maybe it was overcooked. It was not good. At all. And I'd fixed and eaten some pretty bad stuff in my life.

"Holy crap. Why is that so bad?" I blurted.

"It's not that bad," Colin said.

I glared at him. "I thought you were an honest kind of guy."

He barked a laugh and shook his head. "You're right, it's horrible. Did you follow a recipe?"

I nodded. "I did. Mostly. I don't know what happened."

"I think you might have mixed up the salt and sugar."

"How could I possibly mix those up? They're in different containers and I did them at different times. And it tastes both salty and sweet. And the meat is tough. What the hell?"

"Um, do you have Steve's number?"

I tried to glare at him but ended up bursting out laughing. "Steve is on speed dial."

Colin reached for my bowl and carried them to the kitchen while I called Steve. I ordered a large pizza and some wings and garlic bread. Steve said he'd have the order to me soon.

"I'm sorry," I told Colin when he sat down again.

He shrugged. "There's nothing to be sorry for. Sometimes recipes don't quite work out."

"Mine never seem to work out. It sounded so easy,

though. I really thought this one would be okay. And I wanted to apologize."

"For what? Cooking?"

I tried not to laugh. "No. For being crazy."

"You are not crazy. And nothing that happened made me think you were. You're cautious and careful. That's not crazy."

"But I climbed on top of you and rode you until I came, then ran away before you had a chance to do the same. That's a little crazy."

Colin shook his head. "Sex is different than intimacy. I get it. Sometimes you can separate the two and have sex with zero feelings. You can let it be physical, not emotional. That's okay. But when it's emotional from the beginning, sex can't be just physical. You get attached, even if you don't intend to."

I nodded. "I'm being a tease."

"Are you doing it to be a tease?"

I shook my head.

"Then you're not being a tease. Listen, Elise, I'm almost forty. I'm not a young man who thinks sex is the only thing that matters in life. Trust me, I had those years, but I've spent enough time wondering if I'd ever find someone I could share my life with to know that not everything in a relationship is going to be easy. You're not teasing me, you're just working through your own thoughts and fears."

"Thank you for being so understanding."

He smiled. "You're welcome." He held my gaze for a long minute. "I really want to kiss you right now, but I don't want to do something you don't want me to do."

"You can kiss me," I said softly.

Colin leaned toward me, his body getting closer and closer. He scooted over on the couch. His leg brushed against mine first, then his hand reached up and cupped my jaw. He leaned in, like everything was in slow motion, and pressed his lips to mine.

He kissed me softly, barely a kiss before he pulled back and kissed me again. He tilted his head and kissed another part of my lips. He parted his lips and licked mine. I darted my tongue out to catch his, and he pulled me toward him.

One kiss and I was gone. I didn't care about dinner or tomorrow or Andy or anything else in the world. All I cared about was Colin and getting more of him.

He pressed against me, his body partly covering mine. Fear threatened to well up inside me, but before it could, he leaned back and brought me with him. He pulled my body over his so I was the one pressing him against the couch.

His hand slid lower and squeezed my waist. I was in charge again. He was letting me lead. He wanted me to feel safe. Always.

Before I could do anything else, the shrill sound of my doorbell startled me off of Colin. Feeling like a teenager caught by her parents, I jumped off the couch and smoothed down my hair and clothes. I raced to answer the door before Colin got up.

"Hey, Steve," I said when I opened the door.

Steve was a little older than me with dark hair and eyes. He seemed like a nice guy, but he never did anything for me. And looking at him after I was practically on top of Colin a few seconds ago, there was no comparison. Not for me.

"Hey, Elise. How are you?"

"Good. I made the mistake of trying to cook again. Mrs. Carter threatened to call you when she heard I cooked."

Steve laughed. "Did you get a new car? I don't recognize that one."

"Oh, no. I have a friend over."

"Oh, sorry. I didn't realize," Steve said. His eyes drifted behind me and widened.

"Hey, how are ya?" Colin said.

"Ah, good. I'm the pizza guy."

Colin nodded. "Nice to meet you, Steve. Why don't I take that?"

Steve fumbled with the boxes as Colin reached for them. Colin handed him a fifty and told him to keep the change once the boxes were in his hands.

"I was going to buy the pizza," I told him. "I was the one who screwed up dinner."

Colin shook his head. "You don't have to. Or you can get dinner next time."

"Next time?" Steve asked.

I'd forgotten for a second that he was there. When I looked at him, I felt guilty. Steve had the look of a heart-broken man. "Steve."

He smiled. "Enjoy the pizza, Elise. Have a great night."

"Steve," I said again, but he was already gone.

I closed the door and turned back to Colin. He was in my kitchen, opening cabinets and looking for plates. He pulled out two and put slices of pizza on each with wings and garlic bread. He was halfway back to the couch before he met my gaze.

"Everything okay?"

"I didn't know he liked me."

Colin smiled. "There's a lot to like about you, Elise."

"Why did you pay?"

"I had cash on hand, and it was no big deal. My father taught me to pay for dinner every chance I had. He said a man should take care of the person he loves."

"Even if she can take care of herself."

Colin nodded. "Yes, because some people take care of others with money, some take care of others with their sympathy, some clean, some cook. Everyone has a talent, a way of showing that they care. My mother was the kind of woman who would cook. Whenever someone in our area had a baby or went to the hospital, my mother would cook. She would bring them food that lasted for days so they didn't have to worry about it. My grandmother was the kind of person who would clean. She set my father up with a cleaning service when we got our first house. My dad always gave me money when I was in college and whenever he saw me. All of it was because of love."

"I never thought of it that way. Andy used to pay for everything because he wanted me to feel indebted to him."

Colin froze. "I promise, I didn't intend it to be that way. I'm sorry, Elise. I never considered that side of things."

"It's okay," I said. "What you did was the kind of thing he would have done. Made it clear to the other guy that I was with you and gave him a big tip and paid so I knew he was in charge."

Colin closed his eyes and shook his head. "I didn't mean any of that, Elise. I gave him the only cash I had in my wallet and told him to keep the change because it's not easy being out delivering pizzas. I've done that job and I know not everyone tips, so I like to tip people well. And I didn't mean to imply anything to him about us. That isn't my place to do, ever. Who you tell about us is your business, not mine. And being in charge…I told you before you're calling the shots, and I meant it. I'm in this, Elise. I'm here because I like you, a lot. But everything that happens is your choice."

I don't think his answer could have been any closer to perfect.

18

"Thank you," was all I could think to say to him. "That...thank you."

"I'm sorry I remind you of your ex."

"Andy was abusive. Not at first, but after a while. He was older than me, like you are. He was the kind of man who everyone liked, again like you. He was charming and friendly and easy to be around. But he was only like that to get what he wanted."

"Elise, you don't have to tell me anything you don't want to."

"When we started dating," I continued, "we kept it quiet because he was in grad school and I was an undergrad. After a while, we moved in together because he said we didn't see each other enough. I wasn't taking his class, so it wasn't a big deal, but it was just one move he made to control me."

I took a breath and went to the couch. I pulled a pillow onto my lap and hugged it tight. Colin set the food on the end table and sat down, facing me but not touching me.

"Slowly, he isolated me from my friends and family. He didn't want to come here to meet my parents. My cousin came to visit, and he made her so uncomfortable that she and I had a fight. I took his side. It wasn't long after that when he hit me the first time."

Colin sucked in a breath and closed his eyes. I kept talking. I felt like I had to tell him. If I didn't say all of it, I knew I never would.

"It started as a slap, on my ass or my back. A punishment. He tried to tell me other girls liked being punished like that, but it only scared me. He grabbed my arm once when I tried to walk out. We were fighting, and I got mad. He grabbed my arm to keep me there. I had a bruise that lasted weeks. He always said he was sorry and that I just made him so mad. I started to make myself small so I could be the woman he wanted me to be."

Colin reached over and grabbed my hand. He didn't interrupt me, but he held my hand and gave me the strength to finish talking.

"He would go weeks without hitting me, but when he did, it got worse and worse. He saw me in class one day working on a project with a partner. The partner was a guy, and when I got home that night, Andy freaked out on me. He told me I belonged to him and that I was lucky he was still with me since I'd put on weight. He told me no one would ever love me like he did. And then he hit me. I locked myself in the bedroom and refused to come out. He finally gave up, and I ended up falling asleep. I woke up with his hands around my throat. I fought him off, but he was stronger than me. I only got away because our mail was delivered to a neighbor who heard us up and knocked on the door to return it. While Andy was talking to her, I snuck out the window and went to the hospital. I had a broken rib and my airway was bruised. The ER doctor called the police, and I filed a report."

"Did he go to jail?" Colin asked, his voice tight.

I shook my head. "Not at first. He turned it all around

and said I was lying. He even had the neighbor who delivered the mail say I wasn't home when she was there. Rumors about me started. I had nowhere to live, so I stayed in a motel for a few weeks. Another student came forward and reported Andy. Said he'd done the same thing to her when she refused to sleep with him for a grade the previous semester. When it was no longer my word against his, the police arrested him."

"How long will he be in jail?"

I shrugged. "I don't know, and I don't care. I have a restraining order against him, and if he ever gets out, I'll be notified and someone will be watching him. I'm not letting him take anything else from me. He took enough."

Colin squeezed my hand and offered me a tentative smile. "Can I hold you?"

I nodded and wrapped my arms around him. He held me against his chest, and I hugged him the way I had been hugging my pillow.

After a few minutes, he pulled back. "Thank you for telling me. I'm sorry you went through that."

I nodded. "Me, too. And I'm sorry it's still messing with my head and messing with us."

He brushed my hair back. "It's not messing with us. He has no power over us. Thank you for trusting me."

I smiled. "I feel like I can trust you. I don't know why, but you feel like someone I'm supposed to trust. Someone I should let in."

"Good."

He held up a plate, and I took it. We settled on the couch side-by-side and picked a movie to watch. I watched him while I watched the movie, wondering how in the world I found a guy like him.

After Andy, I never considered getting into another relationship. It didn't feel possible for me. A relationship meant being vulnerable, and I'd been vulnerable enough to last a lifetime.

When I met Colin, he reminded me of Andy. His easy charm and the way he talked to people were just like Andy. Everyone loved him. That was why women flirted with him. But that wasn't who he really was. The charm wasn't an act like it had been with my ex. It wasn't something Colin did to make people like him. He was just a nice person. The kind of guy you wanted to be around. The kind of guy everyone wanted to be around.

And he was in my living room, watching a movie on my couch, eating pizza he bought because my attempt to cook for him was abysmal.

He was definitely a unicorn.

And I was done waiting around to see if he was going to turn into a dragon.

I carried our plates into the kitchen and gave myself a pep talk. I had never seduced a man before. Since Andy, all the men I'd been with were sure things. It had never been a question if we were going to end up naked. But with Colin, we hadn't taken that step. He was careful to let me lead. I was ready to lead.

I pulled my hair loose from my ponytail and shook it out. I checked my reflection in the toaster and figured it was going to have to be good enough.

When I turned around, Colin was watching me with a grin. "What are you doing?"

"Um, nothing?"

"Really?"

I nodded and walked over to him. He watched me, his head tilting back and resting on the couch when I stood in front of him. I stripped my shirt off, and he hissed in a breath. His hands went to my hips to help guide me onto his lap.

He kept watching me, letting me decide what was going to happen. I wanted him to touch me, but he wouldn't unless I told him. "Put your hands on my breasts," I said quietly.

He didn't hesitate to follow my orders. He cupped them and rolled my nipples between his fingers. I moaned and let my eyes fall closed. He pinched one nipple hard, and my eyes flew open.

"Watch us, Elise. I want you to know who I am."

I knew what he was asking. I nodded and looked down. Colin's brown hands held me. They looked nothing like Andy's hands, and that helped remind me who I was with. Colin squeezed and caressed me until it wasn't enough. I needed more.

I reached back and unhooked my bra. Colin met my gaze as I drew the straps down my arms and tugged the fabric away from my body. He groaned and licked his lips.

"Please," I whispered.

He buried his face between my breasts and pressed kisses to the sides of each of them. He kissed his way to one nipple and slicked a circle around it, then kissed to the other and did the same. I held on to his head, moaning at the feel of his tongue on my bare skin.

"You taste so good," he whispered against me. "Perfect."

"You feel good. Oh, God."

He licked my nipple and sucked it into his mouth, rolling it gently along the roof of his mouth. He nipped softly and licked again to soothe the sting. It was perfect and not enough at the same time.

"Take off your shirt," I told him.

He rushed to do as I asked and tossed his shirt to the floor. I leaned back to get a good look at him. I'd seen him without a shirt before, but once was definitely not enough. A faint scar sliced below his collarbone. Another one was on his abdomen. "What happened?" I asked, running my fingers over each.

"Bicycle when I was seven," he said, pointing to the first one. "I hit a rock and went over the handlebars. I was lucky that was all I ended up with. And that one was a work accident. I used to work on a Christmas tree farm and a tree got stuck in a machine and spit out splinters. Again, I was lucky."

"Wow. Are you accident prone?"

He shook his head. "Not usually. Freak things more than anything else."

"Any other scars?"

He raised an eyebrow. "I have one on my thigh."

"Oh, um, cool."

"Elise, we don't have to do anything," he said quietly, leaning away from me.

"What do you mean?"

He sighed. "You're not ready, and that's okay. We can just watch the rest of the movie."

I shook my head. "I want you, Colin. But I don't know how to seduce a man. I don't know how to tell you all I want is for you to yank off all my clothes and have your way with me. I want to feel you inside me and know I'm not completely broken because I can have sex with a man I like. I—"

Colin stood with me on his lap. I squealed and wrapped my legs around him.

"I'm too heavy. Put me down."

"You're perfect. And if you want me to yank all your clothes off, I kind of need you to come with me."

"You…I…"

"Yes or no, Elise?" he asked, pausing in the middle of my living room.

"Yes. God, please, yes."

He carried me the rest of the way to my bed and set me

down on the edge. He stared at me for a long moment. He tucked my hair behind my ear and said, "You want me to stop at any point, and I will. I promise you."

I nodded. "I trust you, Colin. Just, um, don't touch my neck. Don't put your hands around my neck or anything like that."

He nodded. "Got it. Anything else?"

"No. I don't think so."

He smiled and leaned over me. "Are you ready for me to yank your clothes off?"

I grinned back. "Hell, yes."

He grabbed the edges of my yoga pants and hooked his fingers into my panties and tugged both off in one move. He pressed me back so I laid on the bed and just stared at me.

I wanted to cover myself with my hands, but the look in his eyes said he wasn't bothered by the way I looked.

"You're even more stunning than that day in the pond. I wanted you so much that day, Elise. It's gotten even harder to resist you as I've gotten to know you."

"I feel the same way," I admitted. "I don't know if I'd be able to say no to you about anything."

"You can always say no, Elise. Always."

I nodded. "Thank you."

He leaned over me and rested his weight gently on my body. His chest pressed against mine, his scratchy chest hair rubbing against my sensitive nipples. His cock nestled between my thighs. His lips covered mine, parting to take a taste of my lips. I wrapped my arms around him and pulled him closer, needing to feel more of him on top of me. I opened my mouth and sucked his tongue inside, tasting him.

He supported his weight on his elbows while he kissed me. He took his time, tasting and teasing me until I wiggled beneath him impatiently.

He pulled back and ran his tongue down my neck. He

kissed his way to my nipples and tortured me more with his tongue and teeth. When he abandoned my breasts and kept moving down, I realized what he was doing.

"You don't have to."

"Do you not enjoy it?"

"I…um, I don't know. I've never…"

"Are you willing to try? You can say no."

"I, um, I don't want you to feel like you have to."

"I want to, but if you don't want me to, that's okay."

"We can try. If you're sure."

He nodded and stood. He towered over me before he covered me again and kissed me hard. He didn't slow down or pause before he plunged his tongue between my lips and pressed my thighs wide with his hips. His hands cupped my breasts. It was a full body assault, one I never wanted to stop.

I moaned and tried to wrap my legs around his hips. As soon as I did, he pulled back and grinned at me.

"I had to make sure you were okay with it."

I grinned as he sank to his knees next to my bed. He stared at me and licked his lips. His hands pressed my thighs wide, but my body resisted. Everything about Colin was new and different and terrifying.

"Elise," he said softly. He kissed one thigh, then the other. "You smell so good. I can't wait to get a taste of you. To make you feel good. To know I'm the only man who's done this."

As he talked, my thighs relaxed and eased to let him in. He traced my seam with one finger, and I almost flew off the bed.

He kissed my thighs again, getting closer and closer to my core. I realized as he was about to kiss me that I never shaved down there. Like ever.

I almost stopped him, but his tongue slid over my clit and all thoughts ceased.

Colin started off slow, his tongue slicking over my sensitive flesh. He licked all over, teasing me when he dipped his tongue inside me.

"Holy shit," I breathed.

Colin groaned in agreement, then slid his tongue to my clit and drew a circle around it. I bucked against his face, wondering why I didn't demand this of every man I'd ever met.

He slid a finger around my entrance and ramped up my desire to about seven thousand. Between his tongue and his finger, I couldn't focus. The two together were driving me quickly out of my mind, and I was enjoying the trip.

He thumped my clit with his tongue, and I gasped. I was close. If I was alone, I'd be furiously sliding my fingers over my clit to finish, but Colin wasn't in a hurry to finish. He was dragging it out, and I wasn't entirely mad about it.

My pulse roared in my ears, and every cell in my body fought the urge to take over. I panted and sighed and groaned. Then I resorted to begging. "Please, Colin. Please."

He sucked hard on my clit and thrust his finger inside me, and the world exploded. Fireworks and shooting stars and everything good about the world all came together and burst inside me, sending me into another world where all that existed was peace and joy and pleasure. So damn much pleasure.

Colin kissed my thighs and stared up at me while I figured out which way was up. I smiled at him and crooked my finger for him to come closer. He kissed me, letting me taste myself on him. It was a weird sensation, but I wasn't going to let anything stop me from kissing him.

I wrapped my arms around his neck and my legs around his waist and realized he was still dressed from the waist down.

"Why didn't you take your pants off?" I asked when I pulled back.

"Because this is for you, Elise."

"I thought you were going to take off my clothes and have your way with me."

"I just did."

"But…"

He kissed me again, but I wasn't done. I wanted more.

"I was hoping you having your way with me involved sex."

"You told me last time not to have sex with you even if you begged. I figured there was no way that's changed in only a few days."

"It has."

"I didn't bring any condoms," he said with a sheepish smile like that was the end of it.

Silly, silly man.

"$\mathcal{I}$ have condoms," I told him, feeling both embarrassed and hopeful. "I've never brought anyone here, but just in case, I bought some. I mean, I know that's weird, but—"

"Elise, you're killing me. I feel like an asshole if I say yes and an idiot if I say no."

"Then say yes because I don't think you're an asshole. I think you'll be doing me a really big favor. I want you, Colin. Please."

I watched the war in his eyes and decided to play dirty. I lifted one of my breasts in my hand and slid my thumb over my nipple. I opened my mouth in a silent moan, then reached for him and teased his nipple. He tensed and groaned.

"You're not being fair."

"I never promised to be fair."

"I can't resist you, Elise."

I slid a hand between us. "Then don't."

I eased my hand into his jeans and wrapped it around his cock. He jerked against my palm and moaned. "Elise."

"Don't say no, Colin. Please."

"Are you sure about this?" he asked.

I nodded. "Yes, please. I promise. I want you, Colin."

He eased away from me and unzipped his jeans. He dropped them to the floor and I lost all train of thought. He was stunning without clothes on. His cock was thick and long and standing up. A nest of dark hair circled the base. I wanted to taste him. I wanted to feel the weight of him in my hand. I wanted him inside me.

I rolled over and opened the drawer where I'd stashed condoms. I opened the box and pulled one out. Instead of handing it to him, I ripped the foil wrapper and turned back to him.

He stood there, watching me the whole time. He nodded when I made a move to put the condom on him. I held the tip and rolled it down his erection. He jerked against my hand and groaned when I squeezed him.

"Fuck, Elise."

I kissed his stomach and went up on my knees so I could kiss the rest of the way up to his lips. He eagerly kissed me back, his arms tightening around me and holding me close while his tongue probed my mouth and his cock throbbed between us.

Colin turned us and flopped onto the bed, pulling me on top of him. "Aah!" I screamed, not expecting the move. Colin righted us with my knees on either side of his thighs and my body on top of his.

"You're in charge, Elise," he said softly, pulling my hair back from my face. His fingers tangled in my hair and pulled a little.

"I'm not used to that. I've never been on top."

"Try it," he urged me. "Sit up and guide me in when you're ready."

I hesitated, but I wanted to feel him inside me. I eased up and let him help me position our bodies right. His cock brushed against my entrance, and I grew bolder. I slid down a little, taking him in, then lifted and lowered the rest of the way until he was fully seated inside me.

"Jesus, you feel good," Colin groaned. "Fuck, Elise."

"So damn good," I agreed with a moan.

My body took a few seconds to adjust to his size. Once I did, I lifted up and lowered back down onto him slowly. We both groaned with each stroke of him in and out of me. I didn't want to rush it, but I also needed to get a feel for what I was doing.

He felt good. Too good. Sex had never been so good for me. He caressed my skin and whispered sexy words to me. He kissed my palms and ran his hands all over my body. And he let me be in charge.

"So beautiful," he said. "Feel so good. You fit me. Can't get enough of you."

"Me, too," I murmured in reply.

My thighs ached, but I didn't want to stop. I loved the feeling of calling the shots. There was something to be said for a man who took charge, but being the woman in charge wasn't all bad either.

He thrust up to meet my next stroke and I moaned loudly. My body tightened, every inch of me focused on getting to the finish line. I was close, so close.

Colin's hand eased between us as our eyes locked. He stroked my clit with his thumb, and my body jerked. He started off gentle, but the faster I moved, the faster he rubbed my clit. He pressed harder and everything tightened inside me. The feel of his hard cock inside me, the press of his thumb on my clit, and the pinch of my nipple pushed me higher and higher until everything exploded inside me.

"Oh, God, yes. Colin. Yes!"

"Oh, Elise. Fuck. So fucking beautiful," he moaned. His hands locked on my hips as he helped me continue up and down on him. His fingers bit into my flesh, but I knew he wasn't trying to hurt me.

I struggled for strength and used the last bit I had to bounce up and down on him until he came. "Elise," he groaned, sucking my nipple hard into his mouth while he pulsed deep inside me.

I collapsed onto him, both of us sinking into my bed. I made a move to roll off him, but he held me still. "I'm not ready for you to leave yet. If that's okay."

I nodded and settled against him. My muscles trembled but they felt good. Everything felt good.

After a minute, Colin chuckled. "We forgot about the pie."

"That's a treat for later, I guess," I said.

He shook his head. "You're the only treat I need."

I snorted. "That was corny."

"Yeah, but it was true. We'll get pie soon. Right now I just want to lie here with you for another minute."

I nodded. "Sounds good to me."

WHEN WE FINALLY HAD ENOUGH energy to get out of bed, Colin went to the bathroom and I headed for the kitchen. I grabbed his shirt on my way and pulled it over my head. It pulled tight across my breasts and belly, but it covered my butt.

I grabbed a knife and took the pie out of the fridge. It smelled good, sweet with a touch of maple that made my mouth water. I cut two large pieces and put them on plates. When I turned around, Colin was watching me.

He'd pulled his jeans on and they hung low on his hips. He zipped them but left the button undone. The vee on his abdomen was visible and made my mouth water even more than the pie did.

"Hey," he said, his eyes slowly sliding down my body and back up.

"Hey. I figured we could have the pie."

He nodded and walked closer. When he reached me, he took both plates from my hands and set them on the counter behind me. His body pressed against mine, letting me feel his erection. "You in my shirt is better than any fantasy."

"It's a little tight."

"It's hot as fuck, Elise." He leaned down and suckled gently on my ear then pressed his nose to my shoulder. "I'm never going to wash this shirt again. It smells like you. Like us."

I wrapped my arms around his neck and smiled when he lifted his head and kissed me.

"I think you've turned me into an animal. I'm not going to be able to think about anything except you now that I've tasted you. Nothing else is going to taste nearly as good."

I moaned and pressed my curves to his body. He slid his hands under my shirt and groaned.

"And you're not wearing anything underneath? I'm not going to survive."

"But you brought pie. We need pie."

He chuckled. "You're right. We do need pie. Because nothing goes better with amazing sex than pie."

I laughed with him and grinned when he picked up the plates and carried them to the couch. He sat down on one end and waited for me to join him before handing over my slice. And yes, I noticed he gave me the one that was slightly bigger.

"Another movie?" he asked.

I nodded. "Sounds good. I think I need a breather."

He grinned. "I know what you mean."

We sat back and ate our pie. It was good. Really good. It was like a cross between banana cream pie and pecan pie. I was pretty sure the maple glaze was from his farm, and the crunch inside was definitely nuts and chocolate crunch and something else. The crust was good, and the cream on top was to die for.

"This is amazing," I told him.

He nodded. "Right? An old friend of my grandmother's makes them. We sell them in the store, but they're always gone within a few minutes of her bringing them by. I asked her to make one for us."

I raised my eyebrows. "Really?"

He nodded. "The only payment she would accept was a recap of the night. I think I'll have to amend the details."

I laughed at the look of horror on his face.

"I did not expect to have anything like this to share when I made the deal."

I leaned over and kissed him. "Thank you. For not expecting it and for giving in when I begged you."

"Like I keep telling you, you're in charge, Elise. I can't say no to you."

I smiled, feeling more than a little pleased with his answer.

We finished our slices of pie and cuddled on the couch. It wasn't long before hands started wandering. When he slid his hand under my shirt and teased the inside of my thigh, I admitted I wasn't at all interested in the movie.

"How many more condoms do you have?" Colin asked as I spread my thighs for him to slide a finger inside me.

"Oh, fuck. Lots more. Lots and lots more."

"Good," he whispered.

He teased my sensitive skin while he gently probed inside me. I wasn't scared this time, or shy, and spread my thighs wide for him to explore. He held my gaze the entire time he touched me, kissing me and telling me how beautiful I was as he sent me up and over the edge.

"I want to taste you," I told him when he made a move to get off the couch.

"Elise," he groaned.

"Just for a minute," I said. "Get a condom, too."

He shucked off his jeans and jogged across the room naked. He grabbed a condom and raced back to me. He pulled me to my feet and kissed the hell out of me.

"Where do you want me?" he asked when he finally released me.

"On the couch," I said, pointing.

He sat down and leaned back, stroking his cock a few times and wiping the tip.

I kneeled in front of him. Andy was a big fan of blow jobs, but I hated it with him. I hadn't tried with another man since, but with Colin, I wanted to.

"It's been a while," I told him.

He cupped my jaw and met my gaze. "You don't have to."

I nodded. "I know, but I want to. You might have to tell me what you like."

"Your lips on my cock are going to be like heaven, Elise. Trust me, I'll be holding back from the moment you touch me."

I smiled and leaned forward. He shifted to bring his cock up to my lips. I opened my mouth and licked the tip of him. He groaned long and low, and he tensed.

"Oh, fucking hell, Elise."

His hands touched my head for the briefest of moments, then immediately disappeared. Both landed on my upper arms and squeezed.

I took him deeper into my mouth and pulled back when he hit my throat. I sucked a little on the tip, and he groaned again.

"Fuuuuck."

I smiled around his cock, loving that I could please him. It had been a long time since I was able to enjoy pleasing a man. It wasn't about making sure he was happy, it was about making sure he felt good. It was about enjoying the fact that he felt good. And the tingling between my thighs and the wetness coating my flesh said I was definitely enjoying making him feel good.

His hands slid up and down my arms, squeezing and relaxing as he held himself still. I could feel his need to move, but I wasn't sure I could take it. Even in the middle of his pleasure, he was thinking of me.

"Elise," he groaned.

I looked up at him and found him watching me.

"You are amazing. So fucking hot. Your pretty pink lips wrapped around me. I need to stop you soon. I'm not going to be able to stop. Oh, God."

I sucked harder on him and took him in just a little deeper. He groaned and pushed me away.

"I'm sorry, Elise. Fuck. I'm so sorry," he whispered. "Are you okay?"

I nodded. "I'm great. Thank you."

"I'm sorry I was rough with you."

I shook my head and smiled. "You didn't touch my neck. I'm good. I promise. Better than good, actually. That was amazing."

"Yeah?"

I nodded. "Oh, yeah."

"Come here, Elise," he said, reaching for me. "Let me feel what that did to you."

I moved closer and let him run a hand up my thigh. When he slid a finger deep inside me, we both groaned.

"All that from sucking me?"

I nodded and moaned when he dragged his finger back out and pulsed in again with two.

"Come for me, Elise."

I rode his hand right there on my knees in front of the couch. He toyed and teased me until my thighs ached and my body throbbed.

"Don't hold back, Elise. Come for me. Let me hear you again."

"Oh, yes," I moaned. "Colin. Yes!" I let go, giving him everything. He held me the whole time, until I collapsed on the floor in front of him.

He smiled down at me. "You're so beautiful when you come. It looks like I might need to get you to bed, though."

"Only if you come with me," I said.

He nodded.

"Bring the condom."

He did as I requested and followed me to bed. I laid down and spread my thighs. "Are you sure?"

I nodded. "I don't have the strength to be on top again, but I still want you."

He rolled the condom on and positioned himself between my legs. He teased me, sliding himself up and down my wet flesh. I jumped with every brush of him against my clit until my thighs were clenching around him.

He slid inside in one smooth stroke. He leaned over me once he was seated inside. "Thank you."

I smiled. "Thank you."

We locked eyes while he slid in and out of me. Each thrust was another pulse in my heart telling me he was different. He wasn't like Andy. He wasn't like anyone I'd ever known. He was special, and that meant I could let go.

I didn't come, but when he did, I felt it inside me. His arms gave out and he collapsed on top of me, both of us panting for breath. He rolled us to the side, staying connected while we held on to each other.

Colin got up a few minutes later to get rid of the condom, then came back and crawled into bed with me. "I will leave soon, but I wanted to lay with you for just a minute. Is that okay?"

I nodded. I wasn't ready for him to go either. The morning would come soon enough, but for the moment, all that mattered was Colin and me.

"Just for a minute," I whispered as my eyes closed. "You feel good. We might need more pie, too." Then I was out.

20

COLIN

I stretched and smiled in my sleep. Elise was still there. My leg brushed hers. My hand slid up and cupped her breast.

I thought it was a dream, the best kind of dream, but when I blinked my eyes open, she was there in the bed.

I smiled deeper until I looked around and realized I wasn't home. I was still at her place.

She was pretty adamant that she doesn't do sleepovers, but there were a few other things she said she didn't do before last night so I hoped it was okay that I passed out in bed with her after round three, or was it four?

I nuzzled against her neck and immediately realized that was the wrong move. She went from pliable with sleep to fully awake and tense.

"It's just me, Elise. I fell asleep."

She jumped out of bed and faced me. Her body distracted me, her curves on full display for me to see, until she yanked the sheet off and wrapped it around herself.

"I thought you were leaving," she said. Her tone was accusatory and her face said she was angry.

I eased out of bed on the other side and moved slowly toward her. "I planned to, but I fell asleep. I just woke up a minute ago."

"You need to go. Now. You can't be here."

"Why not?"

"Because you can't!"

There was a part of me that wanted to press her for a better reason than that, but I also knew trying to get someone to talk when they weren't ready to say what needed to be said was useless.

I gathered my clothes and got dressed while she watched my every move. When I had everything on, I turned to her. "Can I kiss you?"

She hesitated for a second, then shook her head.

Her entire body was trembling. She was afraid of me. Or maybe she was just afraid, but she was not willing to let me come any closer.

I nodded once and said, "I'll talk to you later, Elise. I had fun last night. I'm sorry I stayed."

She nodded back but didn't reply.

I let myself out of her trailer and heard the lock click back into place as soon as I closed the door.

"Why are you still here? Did you hurt her?" Mrs. Carter said. She was standing at the edge of her trailer, glaring at me. "My husband was a cop, and I still have friends. I can find out anything I want to about you, Mr. Jones."

I walked over to her. "Can I ask you a favor, Mrs. Carter?"

She was clearly taken aback by the request. She nodded.

"Will you check on Elise? She asked me not to stay, but I fell asleep. She was really upset just now."

"What did you do to her?"

"I didn't do anything that wasn't mutual, Mrs. Carter. I swear on my life that's the truth. And if that wasn't, I think you know, as the wife of a cop, I wouldn't be asking you to make sure she's okay. I'd be running as fast as possible and saying I did nothing wrong."

"You said you did nothing wrong," Mrs. Carter argued. She narrowed her eyes and glared at me. It didn't matter that she was in a bathrobe and slippers, she was the one in charge.

"I said everything was mutual. There is a difference. It wasn't wrong, but if Elise has regrets now that it's morning, please tell her I'm sorry."

Mrs. Carter stared up at me for a long moment. "You care about her, don't you?"

I looked closely at her and nodded. "I do. Very much. I'd never do anything to intentionally hurt her. I know she didn't want me to stay, and I would have left, but I fell asleep with her in my arms. I didn't mean to stay."

Mrs. Carter's face changed. She smiled at me. "She's had a lot of pain in her life. She needs a man who will love her the way she deserves to be loved."

I nodded. "I agree. And I want to be that man."

Mrs. Carter grinned. "Good. I'll check on our girl. I'll bring my tea over with something good for breakfast. Now, you run on to your farm. We need some girl talk."

I smiled, not the least bit surprised Mrs. Carter knew more about me than she'd let on. I thanked her and got in my truck then drove home, thankful the rest of Elise's neighbors didn't stop me.

When I got home, I parked at my house and ran inside for a quick shower. I knew Nicky was at the sugarhouse, but I needed a minute to wake up before I faced him. I brewed a pot of coffee while I showered and poured it into a large mug before I headed over to check on how the day started.

"Well, look who finally decided to come to work," Nicky teased. He was in his standard uniform of well worn jeans and a Jones Farm sweatshirt. The sugarhouse got warm most days, but Nicky always wore a sweatshirt. "I'd say I'm happy you took the morning off, but I drove by your house and saw your truck wasn't there early. Where did you go this morning?"

"I was at Elise's," I admitted, unable to come up with a lie before the truth spilled out. It wasn't that I didn't want to tell Nicky, it was more that I didn't want to admit how our date ended.

Nicky whistled. "Well, damn, kid. Good for you. She's a beautiful girl. You could have taken today off and spent it with her. I wouldn't have minded."

I shook my head. "Nah, I needed to get back here."

"No, you didn't," Nicky argued. "You should have stayed in bed with your girl. Girls like that stuff. You could have taken her to breakfast or, better yet, made her breakfast in bed. You need to learn to be more romantic, kid."

"She threw me out," I admitted.

Nicky's grin fell. "Why?"

I shrugged. "I don't know. I woke up in her bed, and when she realized I was there, she was upset. She doesn't like to do sleepovers, but I fell asleep. I didn't mean to stay."

"What's wrong with her that she doesn't like sleepovers? Those are the best nights, when you wear each other out so much that neither of you can move. I remember this one night—"

"God, please, don't tell me about sex with my grandmother," I groaned.

Nicky stopped talking and rubbed his hand over his head. "Sorry, kid. I kind of forgot who I was talking to for a minute."

I nodded. "It's fine. Let's just work."

"Did you hurt that girl?" Nicky asked, his voice dark and deadly.

I stared at him and shook my head. "No. I'm not that kind of man. I would never hurt anyone, but especially her. I lo—" I cut myself off.

"You love her?"

I hesitated and nodded. "I haven't told her yet, but yes. She's…she doesn't have the best track record with relationships. She's cautious. I'm hoping her getting upset was because of that and not because she regretted our night. I wouldn't be able to live with myself if I knew I did something that hurt her or scared her."

Nicky nodded. "I'm sure everything will be okay."

I nodded, but I didn't have his confidence. I hoped everything was okay with Elise, and I hoped Mrs. Carter checked on her like she said she would. I just wanted Elise to be okay.

Nicky and I worked side-by-side for the rest of the morning. It flew by for me, which was a good thing. I managed to push Elise out of my mind while I worked and get a lot done. But as soon as we took a break and I was in my office alone, she came rushing back.

The way she smelled, the way she tasted, the way she laughed, the way she came. Everything about her made me fall even more in love with her. I thought the night was good. Almost perfect. I meant to leave, but I fell asleep.

I pulled out my phone and checked for any messages. I didn't have any from her, so I pulled up the app, the way we'd communicated mostly. Our last exchange was there, but there wasn't anything new.

SWEETSTUFF

I'm sorry about this morning. I meant to leave.

I stared at my phone, hoping she would reply soon. Thankfully, she did.

CAPTAIN

Okay.

SWEETSTUFF

I didn't mean to fall asleep. I promise, it will never happen again.

CAPTAIN

That's good.

SWEETSTUFF

Are you okay?

CAPTAIN

I'm still trying to decide that.

SWEETSTUFF

I'm sorry. For what it's worth, I had a great time last night. That sounds cheesy, but it's true. I enjoy spending time with you.

CAPTAIN

Me, too. Thank you. Sorry, but I have to get to work.

SWEETSTUFF

Can I call you later?

CAPTAIN

I don't know. I think I need a little time.

SWEETSTUFF

Okay. I understand. I'll be here when you're ready to talk.

Short answers and a brush off did not make me feel better. But she replied, which was good. I still wasn't sure where it left us. If she was going to freak out when I spent the night...I wasn't going to worry about it yet.

I checked on a few things in the office and was almost ready to do my daily walk around the farm when my phone rang. I smiled at my dad's face looking back at me. I took the picture on one of my visits home over a year ago. I surprised him with the visit, and it showed on his face. Even though we lived close then, we didn't see each other as much as either of us would have liked.

"Hey, Dad."

"Hey, Colin. How are ya?"

"I'm good. What's going on? Is everything okay?"

"What, I can't call my son?"

I shook my head. "It's not that. Usually you call at night."

"Well, I wanted to see if that invite to visit the farm is still open. I was thinking of coming the weekend after this one. If your old man won't be cramping your style."

"Of course, Dad. You're welcome any time you want to come."

"Good, except you don't sound so happy about that."

I shook my head. "No, Dad, it would be great to have you come up. I'd love to know what you think of the place."

"And what about your girl? Do you want to know what I think of her, too?"

I sighed and shook my head. Leave it to my dad to hear something else in my voice.

"Things not going well with her?" he asked.

"I don't know, to be honest. We…I spent the night with her last night. She asked me to leave before I fell asleep. I knew it, and I was okay with it because I got why she didn't want me to stay. I fell asleep and woke up this morning still in her bed."

My dad chuckled. "You always were a hard sleeper. I remember trying to wake you up for school one morning. You were so out I couldn't get you up. At all. I ended up needing to let you sleep because you just wouldn't wake up. I went in every thirty minutes to make sure you were still breathing, but you were just passed out hard."

"Maybe you can tell Elise that story if you ever meet her. Make her feel better about me not leaving her place."

"I'm sure she wasn't upset about you not leaving. It was likely something else that bothered her. I know the man you are, Colin. You'd never do anything to hurt a woman. Chances are she knows that, too. Even if she questions it at times."

"Her ex…"

"I figured. You need to be careful with her. It's hard for people to trust when they've been hurt like that. Give her time, and make sure she knows you're still there whenever she's ready to give you another chance."

I nodded. "I'm trying."

"Good. That's all you can do."

We talked for a few more minutes before my dad said he needed to get back to work. I had to do the same and thanked him for the advice. With any luck, everything with Elise would work out.

RAMSEY TOLD me he and the others had a standing Thursday night meetup at O'Kelley's. It was casual and whoever could make it would end up there at some point. I had a blanket invitation to join if I wanted to, and I needed the break from thinking about Elise.

It had been more than a day since she kicked me out of her home, and we hadn't spoken since we traded messages on the app. I thought about reaching out, but she said she needed time and space from me, so I didn't.

I parked a block away from O'Kelley's and took my time walking to the bar. It was a nice night, with a decent breeze coming off the water. People walked hand-in-hand on the riverfront, some stopping to sit and others continuing a lazy stroll. Summer was around the corner, and in two weeks, my fortieth birthday. I was definitely looking forward to one more than the other.

O'Kelley's was busy, which was just what I needed. Ramsey, Ian, and James were already at the bar with beers in front of them when I spotted them. They had an extra stool for me so I didn't have to fight the crowd.

"Thanks," I said to James. His jacket was reserving the stool.

He nodded. "People don't usually move my stuff. They're afraid I'll arrest them."

Hudson snorted. "No one is afraid of you."

James glared at him. "They are when I pull out the cuffs."

"Especially the women," Ramsey said with a chuckle.

Ian and Hudson joined him, and I couldn't resist.

James flipped all of us off. "Some friends you are."

"Oh, come on," Ramsey said, "that was too easy. You would have been disappointed if we didn't take advantage of that one."

James thought for a second then nodded. "True."

"It's just too bad no women have been close enough to him to use his cuffs lately," Hudson said.

James flipped him off. "And what would you know about my sex life?"

"Just that you don't have one." Hudson raised an eyebrow, daring James to argue.

"Fuck you."

"That's about as much action as you're getting. A threat to me." Hudson snickered and walked away.

Ian leaned forward and said, "I can share some stories so you can live vicariously. Blake and I have a great sex life. This morning, she—"

"Please don't," James said. "I don't want to think about you getting naked with anyone."

"Well, Melody—" Ramsey started.

"You either," James said firmly.

Ramsey and Ian laughed at him then Ramsey nodded at me. "Maybe Colin can tell you a story. Rumor has it he was sneaking out of Elise's yesterday morning."

"How the hell do you know that?" I blurted before I thought about what I was saying.

"Well, it was just a rumor before. Now we know it's true. Good for you, man. And good for her. As long as she wanted you there," Ian said.

"I'm not so sure."

All three of them turned and glared at me. If I was a weaker man, I might have pissed myself from the murderous looks on their faces.

"Not like that. Our date was good, but she doesn't do sleepovers. I passed out and she freaked out in the morning. I didn't do anything."

James leaned in close to me. "I can throw you in a cell so deep and dark that you'll wish you'd never been born. If you even think about—"

"I love her," I said. "I'd never hurt her. And I wouldn't have come here if I had. You already told me you would all kick my ass if I hurt her. I know you will, and if things don't work out with us, I hope you will with the next guy. But what happens between Elise and I is between us. You two might be okay telling stories about your women, but I'm not sharing shit with you about Elise. That's none of your fucking business."

James held my glare for a long moment then nodded. "Good. We don't have to kick your ass. We did need to make sure she was okay with you."

"What the hell are you talking about?"

"Our women talk," Ian said. "Elise was upset yesterday. If you showed up tonight, we were under orders to either kick your ass or find out what happened."

"And?" I asked.

"And now we can tell them you're not the asshole they feared you were. We all know Elise had a shitty ex. We don't know the details, but we watch out for her, for all of them. We needed to make sure you weren't like him."

"I'm nothing like him," I growled at them.

"You know?" James asked.

I nodded. "She told me everything."

James, Ian, and Ramsey exchanged a glance.

"Then she'll come around," James said. "If she let you in, there's a good reason. You just have to give her time and let her know you're there for her."

"My dad said the same thing," I admitted.

"Your dad is smart. Elise is like a scared witness. Tell her to call and every so often, remind her you're still interested in what she has to say. Eventually, she'll tell you what you want to hear," James said.

"Well, damn," Ian said. "I never would have expected you to be the one with relationship advice."

James rolled his eyes. "I know people. Just because all the women I date end up losing interest once the excitement of dating a cop wears off doesn't mean I don't know how to treat a woman."

"If you did, the excitement wouldn't be the only reason they were there," Hudson said as he delivered food.

"No one asked for your opinion," James snarled.

Hudson shrugged. "It's my bar. If you don't want my opinion, you can leave." Hudson crossed his arms and smirked at James.

James rolled his eyes again and shook his head. "It's a damn good thing you make the best quesadillas in town."

"Uh huh. And you're lucky you're a cop or you'd never get a date in the first place," Hudson said.

The two of them kept picking at each other while Ian, Ramsey, and I ate our food and laughed. They were like brothers fighting over the same girl. It was entertaining, and definitely took my mind off Elise for the night.

21

ELISE

I didn't know what to say to Colin, so I just didn't talk to him. It was cowardly, but it was the only thing I could do until I figured out how to talk to him.

When I woke up with him in my bed, I panicked. I hadn't shared a bed with a man since Andy, and my mind convinced me it was Andy in the bed with me. I'd had dreams about him being there before. About him coming after me. He was still in jail, and I didn't think he would ever try to contact me, but every once in a while, the fear took over and I freaked out.

Mrs. Carter was worried about me and brought breakfast. Before she left, she admitted Colin asked her to check in on me. It was sweet of him, and even through my irrational fear, I appreciated it.

Mrs. Carter made me feel better, and by the time she left, I knew I needed to apologize to Colin. I just didn't know how.

So, I put it off. When he reached out, I still put it off. I didn't know how to put it into words, so I delayed saying everything I needed to say.

By the weekend, I knew I was being a coward, but I was

back to the fear outweighing the desire to be with him. I told myself I was busy with work and the employee event we had that night. It was only partly true.

I worked Saturday with Ava and Cami. The three of us were starting to make a good team. They got along well, and all of us seemed to have a sixth sense for what the others needed. I was impressed with Cami's dedication and ease with customers, and she appreciated Ava and I helping her out and giving her tips.

When we finished our last tour of the day, we headed into the boat house to help Walter set up for the party. Since it was our first of the year, it was employees only. Usually the party involved some drinking, a lot of getting to know each other, and ice breaker games that no one really wanted to play.

"How's my dream team?" Walter asked when the three of us walked in.

"Good," Ava replied for us. "Doing really well."

"That's great to hear. Any progress on the job search, Ava?" Walter asked.

Ava shook her head. "I'm talking to different districts and sending out my resume, but so far I've only heard back from a few."

"My mom is asking around," I told her. "She said the offer still stands to teach with her if you want to, but I told her you were really hoping to get into middle school."

Ava nodded. "I am. I will have my certification for all of secondary, so I can teach seventh through high school, but I love middle school."

Cami shuddered. "I hated middle school. I don't think I could handle being there forever."

"Yeah, but as a teacher instead of a student, it's different. Think of everything you learned when you were in middle school. It's fun and exciting. In elementary school, everything is really basic. In high school, attitudes take over and kids stop trying. Middle school is when they're still kind of little but ready to learn more advanced stuff. It's fun," Ava said with a huge grin.

I shook my head. "And that's why you're a teacher and I'm not. I'm glad there are people like you who want to teach because I'd rather do just about anything else instead of teach."

"Anything?" Walter asked with a grin.

I nodded. "Just about. I, um, I actually wanted to talk to you about that. Do you have a minute?"

His smile faded, and he nodded. "Why don't you help me over here?"

I nodded and followed him, appreciative of his understanding that I wanted privacy.

He turned back to me and smiled. "So, how long?"

"How long what?"

"How long until you leave me? I know that segue. I've heard it before from others. We were talking about changing careers and you said you wanted to talk. So, how long? Are you leaving before the end of summer?"

I chuckled and shook my head. "No, I'm not. I'm actually not leaving at all, unless you want me to."

"You're not?" Walter asked.

I shook my head. "I wanted to ask your opinion on getting my captain's license. I'm thinking about maybe driving some instead of just giving tours."

"Well, I'll be damned. Are you really?" he asked.

I nodded. "If you don't think I'd be a good fit, that's okay. You can tell me. I just feel like I want to do something else. Something more. But I love being out there. I'm just trying to figure out if I want to be giving tours forever."

"Elise, you would be great. You can do anything, and if

this is what you want, I'd love to have you as one of our captains."

"Are you sure?"

Walter nodded. "Absolutely. Some of the guys are talking about slowing down some. It's not a tough job, but you know the hours aren't great. I've been looking for someone, but I haven't had anyone interested. If you are, I'll do everything I can to make sure you're set up. I'll pay for your course and give you time off. Training. Whatever you need."

"You don't have to do all that," I told him.

"Elise, you know this company is all I have. You guys are like my kids. Most of them are here for a year or two and then fly off. You've been with me for six years. You're like a daughter to me, to all of us. If this is what you want, I'm going to help you out."

"Thanks, Walter. That means a lot. I really wasn't sure if you would be okay with it."

"You got it, Elise. Let me know what you need and when you need it. And I'll talk to the captains and let them know to give you as much practice as they can. And tips."

"Thank you. So much, Walter. I do plan to stay on as a guide, too. We can talk about driving some next year, assuming I pass the test."

"I have no doubt you will. I'll help you study, too. Once upon a time I was a pretty good captain."

I grinned. "I have no doubt you were. Best captain ever, I'd guess."

He chuckled. "I don't know about that. These guys know tricks I never knew. Boats have changed a lot since I was driving one every day. I could do it, but I don't get out as much as I'd like."

"Maybe it's time for that to change, too," I suggested.

Walter nodded and rubbed his chin. "You know, you might be right. But first, it's time to party."

I laughed and went back to Ava and Cami while Walter greeted the other employees filtering in. He was in his element with all of us around. He could entertain a crowd without even trying.

"What was that about?" Ava asked when I rejoined them.

"I told Walter I've been thinking about getting my captain's license. I wanted to know what he thought of the idea."

"You are?" Ava asked. "You never told me that."

I shrugged. "I wasn't sure about it. I feel like I'm getting too old to keep making the same jokes about finding a man when I'll be thirty in less than a year. It won't be long before I look desperate instead of funny."

"It's still hilarious because they don't expect it. But I know what you mean. It's like there's an age where joking about being single is acceptable, and then you look a little crazy, but then when you're older again, it's okay. Of course, I also think people suck and it doesn't matter what they think of you half the time, so I'm probably not the best judge," Ava said.

"You don't care what people think of you?" I teased her.

She shook her head. "Nope. I had a realization after orientation when I went back to school. There was this guy that I had a crush on, but he was only interested in me because of my grades. He was using me to get a good grade in the class we had together. He flirted with me, but he had a girlfriend."

"I'm sorry, Ava," Cami said with a hand on Ava's arm.

"Thanks," Ava said. "But it taught me that people are going to see what they want to see and do what they want to do. It didn't matter that I helped this guy or that he was appreciative, he was still using me. And if a guy like him, who really is pretty much a nice guy, is going to do that, anyone will. So, screw them. Take care of yourself and do what feels good for you. If someone else doesn't like it, that's their problem."

"She's right," Cami agreed. "Of course, I was a theater major, so I clearly don't follow along with what people want me to do. My mom begged me to get a degree in something useful. My dad told me to start working and not bother racking up debt when I wasn't going to be able to pay it back on a theater salary. I ignored both of them, but now I understand why they said what they did. Still, I know it was the right choice for me."

"You guys are right, but I still want to try something new. I've been thinking about being a captain for a year or two. I think it's finally time to try it."

"Then good for you," Ava said. "Congratulations. I can't wait to be the guide on one of your cruises. That will be awesome."

"The dream team can live on," Cami said.

The three of us laughed and hugged.

As more people came into the room, we mingled and talked to the others. I kept my news to Ava, Cami, and Walter, but I was sure everyone else would know before the end of summer. For now, I just wanted to relax and get to know some of my coworkers.

I CONSIDERED INVITING Ava and Cami to girls' night out, but I hadn't done it yet. It was weird having two different groups of people I spent my time with. Even weirder would be mixing them together. I knew Ava would fit into the group, even though she was younger than all of us. Cami took a little more getting used to. She was nice, and I really liked her, but I'd only ever talked to her about work. When I was with my friends, we got really personal. I wasn't sure how Cami would feel about that.

None of that mattered when I walked into Book Boyfriends Unlimited Sunday night. I was with my best friends, which meant I didn't have to explain anything to anyone or do anything I didn't want to do. It was why I was in yoga shorts and a loose tee that was like wearing nothing at all. I was cozy, and I felt good.

Melody brought a pie that looked scary familiar. I didn't want to say anything, but she announced, "Colin said this maple cream pie is to die for. We bought two because he said they go as quickly as he gets them in. I thought it would be good for tonight."

My heart sank. I didn't want to think about Colin, or about how I left things with him. But I had no choice.

Melody cut the pie and groans worked their way around the room as everyone tried the sweet and savory pie. I could taste the sweetness before I even got a piece. The crunch made my mouth water. I knew it was going to be good, but it also brought back memories.

Memories of Colin smearing cream across my nipple and licking it clean.

Memories of wiping it on his erection and sucking it off.

Memories of everything we did after we devoured each other, inch by inch.

My cheeks burned with the dirty thoughts and my thighs ached. I missed him.

"Are you okay?" Melody asked me.

I looked up and smiled. "I'm good."

"Are you sure? Because you look like you're not feeling well."

I shook my head. "I'm just…Colin spent the night last week."

"What?" Laura asked.

"Seriously?" Karissa said.

I nodded.

"Why is that a big deal?" Trinity asked.

"I haven't spent the night with a man since Andy."

"I never spend the night," Trinity said. "Too much pressure the next morning."

"Andy tried to kill me when I was sleeping. I woke up with his hands around my throat," I admitted softly.

"Did Colin…?" Melody asked.

I shook my head. "He was just there. And it scared me. But before that, he brought this same pie over."

Trinity grinned. "And judging by the look on your face, it was a really good night. It was just the morning after that wasn't so great."

I nodded. "I hate that Andy is still having an impact on my life. I wanted Colin to stay. I didn't tell him that, but I didn't want him to go. When I fell asleep, I felt safe. It was only when I woke up and he was there, nuzzling against my neck, that I realized how terrifying it was to have someone else there when I was sleeping and unaware of everything."

"Was it him being there or was it him touching your neck?" Melody asked.

"I—" I was sure I knew the answer to that until Melody asked me. Only then did I realize that it wasn't the fact that he stayed that bothered me. It was him touching my neck at all that I couldn't handle.

"I give you a lot of credit, Elise," Trinity said. "I really do. You talk to us about this stuff all the time. I don't think I'd be as brave as you are. I don't know if I could share so much with people. You're willing to try, and you're willing to talk. You're amazing."

I smiled at her. "Thank you. That means a lot."

"She's right," Laura said. "You've changed in the last few months, but especially since you met Colin. He's made you more open. And I have no idea what it's like to go through what you went through with Andy, but I remember how scared you were when I got you that one day. I tell people they have cancer every day, but I'd never seen anyone as terrified as you were. To have turned your life around and let someone else in, and to be sitting here talking to us about it, tells me you're not willing to walk away from Colin."

I shook my head. "I'm not. I like him. A lot. And I'm not ready for that to be over."

"Then don't let it be over. Talk to him," Blake said. "Tell him what you're thinking. Don't hide from him because you're scared. Let him in because he's not Andy. He's better than that. And I think he's good for you. You two work together."

"You do," Melody agreed.

The others nodded along.

"Thanks everyone. We do. Hopefully Colin understands."

"Call him," Finley said.

I shook my head. "Not right now. But I am going to send a message."

I opened the app and asked Colin if he was free to get together sometime soon.

SWEETSTUFF

Any time.

CAPTAIN

I know you have work and a life. I'm off tomorrow and Wednesday.

SWEETSTUFF

I will make time for you, Elise. You tell me what works, and I'll be there. Wherever you want me to be.

CAPTAIN

Tomorrow. Lunch?

SWEETSTUFF
See you then. And Elise?

CAPTAIN
Yeah?

SWEETSTUFF
Thank you for reaching out.

CAPTAIN
Thank you for answering.

SWEETSTUFF
I'll always be here.

I smiled because I believed him. He was that kind of man.

22

COLIN

I tried not to be anxious for my lunch with Elise, but I was worried. She was either going to explain and things would go back to normal, whatever that was, or she was going to tell me she couldn't do this and we would be done.

I was pretty sure it was going to be the second one.

I got there a little early and didn't see her. I found a table toward the back of the small restaurant and told the server I was meeting someone. She brought two waters over and said she'd come back once she saw another person here.

I watched the door, wanting to flag Elise down as soon as she walked in. I sipped my water and glanced at the menu, but until I knew what she was going to say, my stomach was in knots.

I'd never been like this over a woman before. When friends told me about that feeling, I thought they were crazy, but now, I regretted picking on them. It was pure torture.

Elise walked in a minute or two before we were supposed to meet. She smiled at the hostess and looked around while they spoke. When she saw me, she pointed and waved to the hostess. I wondered if they knew each other, then remembered everyone knew everyone in MacKellar Cove.

"Hey," Elise said, sliding into the booth opposite me. "Thanks for meeting me here."

I nodded. "Of course. It's one of the many places in town I've never been."

Elise smiled and looked around. "I worked here when I was in high school. It's one of my favorite places to eat."

"High praise. I'll have to come back again."

"You should. There are too many good things on the menu to only come here once."

I nodded and pretended to look at the menu. There was a Mediterranean restaurant near where I lived before, so I knew I liked the food, but I couldn't focus on food with the tension between us. I wanted her to say whatever she came here to say so we could move on, either together or separately, but she was acting like things weren't completely awkward between us.

We ordered our lunch and sipped our drinks, and with each second, things grew more and more tense.

"This is uncomfortable," Elise finally said.

I nodded.

"I'm sorry."

"For what?"

She smiled, a tight, tense smile. "I like you, Colin. A lot. I really do. And I know I owe you an explanation for the other morning."

I shook my head and leaned back. "You don't. I always said you didn't have to tell me anything you didn't want to. I shouldn't have stayed. I didn't mean to. And it obviously won't happen again."

"Why do you say that?"

I raised an eyebrow and met her gaze. "You're here to end

things. I can see it in your eyes. I appreciate you not telling me over text, but having lunch isn't necessary."

She was shaking her head, but she didn't refute my statement. She just kept shaking her head. Then she laughed. "I seem to have trouble expressing myself lately. This is the second time in just a few days I've tried to say something and started it completely wrong. I'm not here to end things."

"You're not?"

She shook her head again. "I'm not. I wanted to apologize for freaking out on you and tell you it had nothing to do with you."

I shrugged. "I figured, but regardless of that, I scared you."

She nodded. "You did, because you brushed against my neck. When Andy…"

She paused and rubbed her throat. It was a nervous habit of hers, and one I never connected until that moment. She rubbed her neck because of him. When she was anxious. Because he put his hands there and tried to kill her.

She took a deep breath and looked up at me again. "When Andy choked me, I was asleep. I'd locked myself in our bedroom because he hit me. He picked the lock while I was sleeping, and I woke up with his hands around my neck. When I woke up with you touching my neck, even though it wasn't your hands, it put me right back in that moment. It was a flashback, and I thought you were him."

I sighed heavily. "Elise, I'm so sorry. I didn't even think about kissing you there."

She shook her head. Her eyes filled with tears that she swiped away quickly. "It's not your fault. I didn't know I would have that kind of reaction."

The server showed up with our lunch, forcing us to stop our conversation. Elise forced a smile and almost looked like everything was okay. Apparently not close enough because the server shot me a dirty look for making my date cry.

"I'm glad she already brought the food because if she hadn't, she definitely would have spit in mine for making you so upset," I said.

Elise chuckled. "Sorry. I didn't mean to make you look bad."

I shook my head. "Your opinion is the one that matters to me the most right now. Are you okay?"

She nodded. "I'm better now. I thought I was over everything with him, at least I thought I knew what would set me off, but I haven't spent the night—"

"I know, and I'm sorry," I said quickly. "I didn't mean to stay."

She smiled and put her hand on mine. I turned my palm over and held her hand, my fingers brushing her wrist. "I didn't want you to leave, but I didn't want to freak out on you either. None of this had anything to do with you, and I'm sorry I've taken so long to talk to you. I figured you probably had enough crazy from me and needed some space."

I shook my head. "Not even a little. I'll take all the crazy you have."

She smiled and laughed. "Are you sure? Because I'd be willing to bet I have more."

I nodded. "I can take it, as long as you're willing to talk to me. Help me avoid scaring you as much as possible."

"I will."

"Good. I do have one favor to ask you."

She tilted her head to the side.

"Would you be willing to meet my dad this weekend?"

She grinned. "I'd love to."

I COULDN'T REMEMBER LAUGHING SO MUCH in my entire life. I chuckled to myself at the grill, listening to Nicky, Dad, and

Elise get to know each other. It was like they were all in competition to see who could tell the most outrageous story.

"What did you say?" Dad asked Elise.

She was telling them about one of her tours where a client got drunk and asked if he could pee while they went over the US / Canada border.

"I told him it was illegal," Elise said, as serious as could be.

"Is it?" Nicky asked.

Elise shook her head. "Technically, no, but it is illegal for him to whip out his junk in public. I figured it didn't matter which law I was using to explain why the drunk guy who could barely stand up straight should not climb up on the edge of a boat and pee into the River."

Dad and Nicky laughed with Elise. I glanced over my shoulder at the three of them and shook my head. It was good to see smiles that big.

"How are those steaks coming?" my dad asked.

"Almost done," I told him.

He got up and walked over, leaving Elise and Nicky to talk. Dad bumped my shoulder and grinned. "I really like her," he said softly.

I nodded. "Me, too."

"Have you told her yet?"

"Told her what?" I asked, even though I knew what he was talking about.

"That you love her?"

I shook my head. "She's skittish. I told you she doesn't have a good history with relationships."

Dad shrugged. "No one does. That's why we keep trying until we find the right one. It's kind of like looking for my keys. I don't keep looking after I found them in case I find keys for a better truck. I stop looking because I like the one I've got."

I looked back at Elise. She laughed at something Nicky

said. She looked relaxed there on the deck. Nothing was bothering her. All the tension I'd seen in her so many times was gone, and she was just a regular woman having a good day. It was nice to see.

"You two should head out to the swimming hole after lunch. Nicky was going to show me around a little."

"I thought we were going to spend time together," I said. I turned the grill off and put the steaks on one plate and the vegetables on another.

Dad nodded. "We are, but just because I'm here doesn't mean you shouldn't spend time with Elise also. Besides, I'm going to need some time to myself. I'm happy I came up here, but it's still tough."

"I'm sorry, Dad. You don't have to stay through the weekend if you don't want to."

He chuckled. "I want to. Being back here…it almost makes me want to move back, but you have your life here. You don't need me cramping it."

"You wouldn't. The house is huge, and we can add on if we need to."

He shook his head. "That house is made for a family. Not for a family and your old man."

"I don't have a family yet, and I'd love if it you came up here."

Dad nodded. "I'll think about it. Maybe I can get a place in town."

I shook my head. "Dad, stay."

He grinned. "You're going to need to talk that over with your Elise, not me."

I looked at her again. She was watching us and smiling softly. She winked at me.

"She's a keeper, son. I don't want to jeopardize that."

"You won't, Dad. I think she likes me more now that she knows you," I said, carrying the food to the table.

Elise set it earlier with bright and cheery plates she found in the cabinet. She said a home should have things that make people smile, and that food should be presented in a way that makes people excited for it. I never paid much attention to the plates I ate off of, but the bright yellows and purples and blues against the dark wood table looked good. Everything with Elise's touch was so much better.

"You're just lucky he's not twenty years younger. He might have given you a run for your money," Elise said with a cheeky grin.

"Is that so?" I asked.

She laughed.

"No steak for you."

"Ah, hey! That's not fair," she said.

"Here you go, Elise. You can have mine," Dad said, trading plates with her.

"At least I know someone around here likes me," she said. She stuck her tongue out at me.

I leaned down and stole a kiss from her. I whispered, "I think all of us like you a lot."

She put her hand on my chest and smiled when I pulled back. "The feeling is mutual."

We talked while we ate and laughed so much my cheeks hurt. Elise and Dad cleaned up when we were done, and Nicky echoed my dad's words.

"I like her a lot."

"Me, too."

He laughed. "Yeah, I know. Your dad wants to give you two some time together and asked me to wander with him. We'll stay away from the swimming hole, though. He said you two were headed up there."

I grinned. "Probably a good idea."

Elise tried to argue with Dad and Nicky about going on the farm without us, but Dad told her he wanted to some to himself, too, and she gave in. When they wandered off, she turned and said to me, "Well, I have the rest of the day off. Do you want to do something until dinner?"

I nodded and moved closer to her. She let me pull her into my arms and hold her. I hadn't held her since the night before she chased me out of her home. Even though we'd cleared the air and were good, our work schedules made it a busy week for both of us and we hadn't spent much time together aside from lunch. She traded a day off earlier in the week so she could be there to meet my dad.

"I'm sorry," she whispered.

"For what?" I asked.

"For making things weird between us."

I kissed her quickly and pulled back. "How about we go swimming and forget all about it?"

"Really?"

I nodded.

She smirked. "But I didn't bring a bathing suit."

I shrugged. "It's a good thing you don't need one."

We walked through the woods, half casually like we were in no hurry and half rushed like we couldn't wait to get there. I wasn't sure how Elise felt, but I was nervous, just like the first time we went there.

When the pond came into view, Elise's breath hitched. Sunlight streamed through the trees, highlighting the water like it was a pond sent straight from heaven. It felt even more isolated than the first time we were there with the trees fuller now. The water ran a little faster over the rocks, making the waterfall louder than it had been. Everything about it was different, but the magic of being there was definitely the same.

We stopped at the edge and stared down into the depths

of the water. I knew it was still cold, but the sunlight would help. The air temperature was almost twenty degrees higher than the first time, so drying off would be easier since, again, I didn't think to bring towels.

"Well, I guess you don't have to turn around this time," she said with a squeeze of my hand.

"I can if you'd feel more comfortable."

She shook her head and released my hand. Her shirt came off first, followed by her sandals. Her arms were a golden color from being on tour boats, but her chest was pale from the lack of sun she'd had outside her uniform. She tugged off her capris, then looked up at me.

She stood in front of me in her bra and panties. They were dark green and matched. The curve of her belly and the softness of her body called to me, but I didn't move. I couldn't move. She was perfect.

"Are you not going in?"

I cleared my throat and shook my head. "No, I am. I was just…"

"Staring at my boobs?"

I breathed a laugh and nodded. "They are pretty fantastic."

"Want a closer look?" she asked. She reached behind her back and unclasped her bra.

I sucked in a sharp breath when she let it fall to the ground at her feet. Then she hooked her fingers in the sides of her panties and dropped them, too.

She was always beautiful. The first time I saw her, she was beautiful. But standing in the woods completely naked, just for me, she was the most stunning woman I'd ever seen in my life.

"Elise," I groaned.

She smiled. "I'm going swimming. If you want that closer look, you should join me."

She smirked and turned and jumped into the water. Before she surfaced, I was halfway naked and aching to follow her.

The water was cold, but it didn't do anything to chill my body with Elise right there. She swam away from me, but she didn't get far before I caught up to her.

"Be careful. The last time we were here, you almost let us drown," she said with a grin.

I groaned. "I'm never going to live that down, am I?"

She shook her head. "Probably not."

She swam forward and kissed me on the lips. Our bodies brushed, but neither of us made a move to deepen the kiss. We were content to share slow kisses and feel like we had all day together. Maybe forever.

I couldn't remember the last time I felt so at peace. Happy was an easy emotion, but peaceful never was. I always wanted to be on the move. Doing something.

Busywork, my dad called it. He said I couldn't sit still for five minutes.

But watching her glide through the water, her curvy body lazily floating before she turned and dove under. The droplets of water streaming down her cheeks. Her dark hair slicked back.

The joy in her amber eyes. Pure, real, unhindered joy. That was what did it for me. That was what made me want to pull her closer and wrap my arms around her. That was what gave me peace.

"What?" she asked, her lips curled up on the side.

I shook my head. "Nothing."

She raised an eyebrow. "It doesn't look like nothing. What are you thinking?"

"I'm thinking you bring me peace."

"Peace?" she asked, that eyebrow going back up.

I nodded. "Peace."

She chuckled. "I don't think anyone has ever told me I bring them peace. Usually I'm more of a headache than anything else."

I shook my head. "Not for me. Definitely peace."

She ducked her chin and stared into the depths of the water. When she looked back up at me, my breath hitched. Maybe peace was the wrong word. Maybe she didn't bring me peace at all. Maybe she just brought me clarity. A soul deep knowledge of exactly what I'd been looking for my whole life.

Her.

23

ELISE

The look in Colin's eyes shook off all the chill the cool pond had soaked into me. He'd barely touched me, even though I was completely naked. I knew he wanted me. His long, thick cock told me that much. But he was keeping his distance.

I swam over to him again and treaded water in front of where he was. His eyes were locked on mine, not daring to drift beneath the surface of the water where my naked body glowed in the afternoon sun. My arms and legs were tan, but the rest of me was pale and pasty, a perfect farmer's tan.

"This was a good idea," I told him. "Coming out here again."

He nodded.

"It's very peaceful here."

Another nod.

"Are you going to say anything or just nod?"

He shrugged, and we both laughed.

"I really like your dad."

He groaned. "I don't think my dad is a good topic of conversation right now."

I chuckled. "Probably true. I don't really know what to say to you."

"Why not?"

I shrugged. "I keep messing things up."

He shook his head and moved closer to me. "You didn't mess anything up. I did. I never meant to scare you or hurt you."

"You didn't," I assured him.

He smiled, but it didn't reach his eyes.

"So, um, have you ever had sex here?"

His grin changed, and that one did reach his eyes. "No."

"Why not?"

"I didn't grow up here. I was young when we moved, and we didn't visit much, not at all in a while. You're the only woman I've ever been here with."

"At all?"

He nodded.

I looked around at the trees surrounding the pond, giving it a private and intimate feel. The waterfall was romantic. The water was sensual. But none of it mattered without the man I was there with.

"This place is like every woman's fantasy," I said softly.

He came up behind me, his legs brushing mine. "I don't care about anyone else. I only want to know your fantasies."

"I have one," I admitted. "I've never told anyone, but I love being outdoors and I've always wanted to have sex outside. A place like this where I don't feel exposed. Private, intimate."

"In the water or out?"

"Both? Either one, I guess. No, in. I'm not a small woman, and I've always wanted to be able to wrap my legs around a man's waist and have him hold me up during sex. I think in the water because then we could do that."

"I could hold you, Elise."

I turned and slid my hands down his arms. "You are pretty strong."

He grinned, his eyes crinkling at the edges.

"Hi," I whispered when I realized just how close he was.

"Hi," he whispered back.

We swam toward the edge of the pond together, only stopping when my back hit the side. A stone ledge was just above my hip, and the perfect height. I eased myself onto it.

Colin set his hands on either side of my hips and leaned closer. He held my gaze with his dark one until his lips touched mine. My eyes slid closed, and my body relaxed. Colin. Everything would be okay because Colin was there.

He kissed me softly at first, then he licked his way into my mouth. His tongue slid slowly along mine, letting me taste him. His erection rested on my thigh, while his legs floated behind him.

He tilted his head to the side and deepened the kiss. I clung to him, desperate for more as he pressed his chest to mine. The water made our bodies slippery. I floated my hand over his muscles, touching all of them and learning his body. In my bed, we touched, but everything was hurried because it was new. In the afternoon sun, in the wide open, I look my time learning every inch of him. Every dip of his muscles, every plane of his body, every spot that made him groan.

When I leaned back and spread my thighs, he pulled back from me. He groaned and pressed the side of his head to mine.

"I don't have condoms with me," he admitted. "I didn't come here to seduce you. Hell, I forgot towels again. I'm clearly not very good at planning things when you're around to make me forget everything."

I took his face in my hands and pulled him back to look at me. I studied him carefully and made a decision. "I haven't had sex without a condom in more than eight years. I've required it of everyone I've been with since him. I'm on birth control and get tested regularly. I know I haven't given you a lot of reasons to trust me—"

"I trust you with my life, Elise. But this is a big thing. More for you than me."

I pulled back just enough for him to know I didn't understand.

"I haven't been with anyone before you in a long time. Years. I'm clean, but if he—"

"He's not taking anything else from me. He's almost taken you more than once, and he stole years from me. I've been living in fear. I'm done, Colin. But that doesn't mean we have to have sex without a condom. I know it's a really big deal, and if you aren't sure…"

"I'm sure about everything with you, Elise. Everything. I don't doubt you. But I don't want to hurt you again."

I smiled. "You won't. I'm…I want this. I want you."

He covered my mouth and kissed me hard. He didn't hold back, just forced his tongue into my eager mouth and kissed me. The assault was exactly what I needed to stop thinking and let my body take over. Thoughts of Andy were obliterated with each pulse of Colin's tongue inside my mouth.

Then he slid a hand up my thigh, and I didn't think about anything at all.

"Oh, Elise," he groaned when his finger slid inside me. "You're so wet."

"I've been staring at you for a long time. Teasing me with your perfect body."

He shook his head. "You're the tease, Elise. When you laid back and your breasts popped out of the water I almost died. And don't even get me started on how I felt when you stripped down to nothing on those rocks over there. I nearly came in my shorts right then and there."

"Is that why you didn't touch me when we first got in?"

He chuckled and nodded. "I knew if I did, I'd embarrass myself."

"No need to be embarrassed now," I said, followed quickly by a moan.

"Come for me first, Elise. I wish I could taste you right now. Let me hear you and feel you."

His fingers sank in deeper, and my entire body trembled. Whatever part of me he was touching sent fire sparking through all of me. I'd tried with many vibrators to have the same effects, but nothing compared to Colin's hand.

He pressed his thumb to my clit, and I jerked off the rock I rested on. "Oh, God," I moaned loudly, forgetting we were outside. "Please, tell me your dad and Nicky aren't anywhere close to here."

Colin shook his head. "They're staying far away."

"Thank Gooooood," I moaned. "Oh, fuck, Colin. So good. Yes."

He leaned down and captured one of my nipples. It was barely above the water, giving him a face-full every time I moved, but he didn't stop.

I supported myself on my hands and pumped my hips in time with Colin's strokes. He thrust harder into me until everything around me went dark and bright lights burst behind my eyes.

His fingers withdrew instantly, and I moaned at the loss, hovering in the middle of my orgasm. On the edge, about to fall, but barely hanging on.

Then he thrust hard into me in one long stroke, and I broke all around him. He held the rock ledge with one hand and wrapped my legs around his hips with the other. He brought me right to the edge, where I could fall off with the wrong move, and pounded into me.

My body was sensitive from my first orgasm and quickly spun up into another. I hung on to Colin's shoulders, along for the ride of my life as he carried us both toward the finish line.

"Oh, Elise," he grunted. "So fucking perfect. Beautiful. Elise. Yes, Elise."

He movements were erratic, but it didn't matter to me. I was as gone as he was, close but barely out of reach of where I needed to be. I tightened my legs around him, and he shifted just slightly, and we both moaned loudly.

"Yes," we said together.

His thrusts deepened, and my breath vanished. I couldn't breathe. All I could do was feel. Colin. Colin. Colin.

His head rested on my shoulder. Sweat dripped from his forehead. But he didn't stop. He kept going, harder, faster, and deeper until I started to shake.

"Oh, God. Oh, yes," I moaned. "Colin. Oh, fuck."

"Touch yourself, Elise," he growled. "I...I'm trying. Put your hand between us and help yourself."

I did as he said, but I'd barely touched my clit when my entire body clenched tight around him and I came. I dragged my fingers down his back, needing something to grab on to. My other hand was trapped between us, my fingertips grazing my clit with every jerk of our bodies together.

Then he swelled inside me and spilled himself in me.

I wrapped my legs and arms around him and held him to me when he collapsed. We laid right there, on that flat rock, our bodies entwined and connected for a long time.

Colin pulled back first, sliding out of me with a tug at the end. My body didn't want him to go either. He brushed my wild, wet hair back from my face and smiled at me.

"That was unbelievable."

I nodded. "Yes, it was."

"Did I hurt you?"

I shook my head. "Not even a little. You felt amazing."

"Elise," he said softly.

I looked up at him and smiled.

"I love you, Elise."

My smile faded instantly. "We barely know each other." I pushed him off me and climbed out of the pond.

"We know a lot about each other, Elise. And that has nothing to do with loving you."

"Don't say that. No. You can't. You don't."

I picked up my clothes and shoved my feet into my sandals and started running. He called after me, but I didn't stop.

I tugged my shirt over my head even though it hurt to run without a bra on. I skipped into my capris, wishing I'd worn shorts after I tripped and almost face-planted. I shoved my panties in my pocket and held onto my boobs, my bra flapping behind me, and I ran.

When I reached my car, I jumped in and tore out, thankful I never carried a purse or left anything in someone's home. My keys were in my pocket, and my purse was in the car.

I tried to pull my hair back on the drive home so Mrs. Lockhart didn't ask too many questions when I pulled into the neighborhood. Thankfully, she just waved and kept sweeping her porch.

I pulled into my parking space instead of backing in like normal just in case Colin followed me. I locked my car and raced into my trailer.

I peeked out the windows and panted for air. I was standing there for five minutes before I convinced myself he wasn't coming after me and went to sit down.

My capris were uncomfortable without panties, so I dug them out and put them on. I debated taking a shower, but someone knocked on my door.

I pulled up the video doorbell on my phone and sighed

with relief when I saw Chelsea on my doorstep instead of Colin.

"Hey," I said in what I hoped was a happy and normal voice. "What are you doing here?"

She opened the door and stepped in. "I wanted to visit my cousin. Is that okay? Did you just get out of the shower?"

I touched my wet hair and shook my head. "Ah, no. And yes, of course it's okay. It's always okay."

She gave me a look but didn't say anything.

"Do you want a drink or something?"

"Sounds good. You look like you could use a glass of wine." She raised her eyebrow.

I smiled. "Still able to see through me, huh?"

She nodded. "Like I could tell there was more going on with Colin Jones than you were just talking. It sounds like things are going well between you two."

"Well, yeah, um, they were. I guess. Maybe."

"Is this another one of those Andy things where you fall for a guy and forget about everyone else in your life or is there something wrong?"

I had my back to her when she asked the question. It was ironic to me that she phrased it that way. Like with Andy things were okay, but with Colin they weren't.

I poured two glasses of wine and handed her one.

"Both and neither, at the same time."

She raised an eyebrow. "Uh, how does that work?"

"Let's sit, and I'll explain," I said.

I led Chelsea to the couch and told her everything. From how abusive Andy was to how things ended. I told her about my life after Andy and trying to regain some sense of control. And then I told her about Colin and learning to trust a man again with him.

"I am so sorry you went through all that," Chelsea said, wiping tears from her eyes. "And that I wasn't there for you through any of it. I thought you were just one of those girls who chose the boyfriend and cut ties with everyone else. I had no idea."

"I didn't want you to know. I was ashamed of all of it."

"You know you didn't do anything wrong, right?"

I nodded. "I do, but it's hard to feel it sometimes. I feel like I should have left the first time. Or any of the other times before the end."

"It sounds like he was a master manipulator. He knew exactly how far to push you to get what he wanted."

I nodded. "He definitely did. And I let him. I kept trusting him. That's been the hardest thing with Colin. Trusting him."

"I don't think it's trusting him. I think it's trusting yourself. You have to know you're making the smart choice. It isn't really about him. Who the guy is doesn't matter. What matters is if you make the right choice about trusting a guy who is good or not trusting a guy who isn't."

"Colin is a good man. Everything that's happened between us tells me he's a good man."

"Well, then I'm happy for you. You fell for a good one this time," Chelsea said.

"Fell for him? No. No, no, no."

Chelsea chuckled. "Of course you did. Why are you saying you didn't?"

"Because I don't. I don't love him. I barely know him."

Chelsea shook her head. "That doesn't mean you don't love him. It only means you get to discover more about him."

"But—"

"Listen, Elise, it's terrifying. Letting someone in is the scariest thing in the world. It's enough to make you insane, but how many times have our moms talked to us about love?"

I snickered. "Thousands."

"And how many times did they say they needed a certain amount of time to know they were in love?"

I smiled. "None."

"Exactly. I've had my heart broken, cuz. I've been hurt and I've cried and I've sworn off love, but every time, I come back for more because love like our parents have is worth it. I have to believe that."

"But how do we know if it's real? How do you know it's the good one and not the bad one?"

Chelsea grinned. "You don't. That's the scary part. But when it's right, you should say it."

I took a deep breath. "He said it earlier."

Chelsea raised an eyebrow. "The gorgeous man you've been dating told you he loved you earlier today, and instead of screaming it back between his sheets, you're having a pity party here with me? What is wrong with you?"

"Lots," I said.

Chelsea snorted. "True. Is that why your hair was wet? You were with him?"

I nodded. "We went skinny dipping at a pond on the farm. He told me he loved me right after the best sex of my life."

"Elise, if you won't tell the man you love him, I'm going to tell him I do and steal him from you because he is a keeper."

I chuckled.

"Why did you run? Seriously."

I smiled. "Because I don't know how to love someone."

Chelsea reached over and took my hand. She squeezed it and said, "Yes, you do. You've been loving our family your whole life. And your friends. And hopefully yourself, Elise. Real love isn't what happened with Andy."

I shook my head. "I thought it was. When I was with him, I thought I loved him."

"Maybe you did, but he wasn't worthy of your love. Colin is. Love him. Let him in. You both deserve it." Chelsea drained her wine and carried her glass to the kitchen.

"I should go see him."

Chelsea nodded. "You should. But you might want to shower first. And I could do your hair for you."

There was a knock on the door that had both of us looking at each other.

"It's not my house. Whoever it is is clearly not here for me," Chelsea said.

I pulled up my phone and saw Colin standing outside. Tears welled in my eyes. "It's Colin," I said, turning the phone to show Chelsea.

"Aw, and he brought flowers. Please tell me you don't want him so I can have him."

I shook my head.

"Damn. Does he have a brother?"

"Just a cousin, but he's married."

"Happily?" Chelsea asked.

"Chelsea!"

She rolled her eyes. "I'm just kidding. Mostly."

"Chelsea!"

"Yeah, yeah, I'm leaving. But I'm walking out the front door so I can meet this man. Our moms will never forgive me for meeting him before them. You better invite him to the next dinner," she hissed.

I nodded and laughed.

Chelsea opened the door to Colin's hand raised to knock again.

"Well, Colin Jones. It is so nice to finally meet you."

He looked between us and pasted on a grin. "You as well, Chelsea. You look just like your picture from when you two were younger."

"Oh, you are a charmer. Are you sure—?"

"Chelsea!"

"Fine, fine, I'm going. See you both soon!" Chelsea said with a wave, leaving Colin and I alone.

24

COLIN

"Can I come in?" I asked, standing on her doorstep. I'd hoped to be more prepared or eloquent or something, but as soon as I saw her, all I wanted was to wrap her up and never let her go again.

She nodded and moved back. She chewed on her lip, her gaze flicking from me to the flowers and back.

"Um, I brought these for you. I saw them on my walk back and wanted you to have them."

"Thank you," she said. She reached out for the flowers and pressed them to her nose. "They smell like the farm."

I smiled and tried to breathe while she carried the flowers to the kitchen and put them in a pitcher.

When she came back, I opened my mouth, but Elise beat me to it.

"I'm sorry," she said.

I pressed my lips into a line. She was constantly apologizing.

"I shouldn't have told you how you felt. I had no right."

I took a breath and nodded. Not what I was hoping she would say. "Um, okay."

"Aside from my family and my friends, I've never known what love was like. I watch movies where people fall in love in like five minutes, but it always seems so ridiculous. You have to know someone, really know them, to know if you love them."

I opened my mouth to say something again, but she paced away from me and kept talking.

"There's always some big secret people are keeping or some skeleton in the closet or something, and you fall for someone and then find out and say it wasn't really love. You thought it was love. But if you thought it was love, why wasn't it? You know? I mean, either it was or it wasn't, right?"

I opened my mouth, but she talked over me.

"But maybe there are different degrees of love. Like burns. First degree is like when you think you know a person, but there's a lot buried deep. More layers of them to uncover before you really know. Second degree is when you get closer, you know more. It's harder to heal when it ends, and you might have scars, but they're not noticeable to everyone else. But third degree...that's the one that almost kills you. The one that, if it ends, makes you feel like you will, too. It's the one that goes deep, all the way inside of you. It's the one you don't ever recover from. Your scars are permanent and they're ugly. But if it doesn't end, if it lasts, that person becomes a part of you."

I wasn't sure whether to be horrified or agree with her, but she wasn't looking for an answer anyway.

"With any burn, it can happen quickly. You touch the stove or a candle. An explosion or house fire. Something that would be a minor burn can get worse if you keep holding on, but time isn't always a factor with burns. Sometimes there's a person who ignites you with one look or one touch. Maybe it's a kind word, and you know, without a doubt, that you're the one who will ruin me forever. That if I let you get too close, I'll die if I have to let you go."

She looked up at me with tears streaming down her face.

"You're my third degree, Colin. I'm terrified to get too close to you because I know if you walk away, I will be left with scars too deep to heal."

"I'm not walking away," I told her.

The tears kept coming. "And that scares me, too. Because what if I'm only a first degree love for you? What if you think I could be a third degree, but you peel back another layer and don't like what you find?"

I pulled her into my arms and held on to her. My chest ached with the pain she was feeling. The fear. "I've been telling you for weeks you're the one in charge, Elise. I'm following your lead. You call the shots. It's not because you're a first degree love for me. You're it. You're the house fire with an explosion that knocked me off my feet and burned me to the core. There is no coming back from this for me. And I came here because I'm not going to let you run away again. I'm not going to let you push me away again. I don't care about your scars. I see them, and I think they make you even more beautiful. I want to spend the rest of my life showing you how much I love you."

She sobbed and nodded. "Are you sure? Because I have some pretty scary layers."

I grinned. "Trust me, I want to see all of them, and I can take it."

"But what about—"

"All of it, Elise. I know you thought you were in love before. I guess you were, like you said. Maybe Andy was a third degree love for you. One that should have been first degree, but you held on too long and he destroyed you. I don't know, but what I do know is love was never like this for me before. I never put everything else aside for a woman before I met you. I wasn't single my entire life, but I never had a third degree love. I never had you, Elise."

"But you—"

"No buts. Not anymore. No sorry and no but and no arguing. I love you, Elise. I love you so much it kills me to stand here and look at you and not know if you feel the same way. It kills me to wonder if you think I'm your third degree love, but you find out one day I'm just another first degree one you held onto too long. I'm here, Elise. I'm going to keep coming back. For you."

She threw herself into my arms and wrapped her legs around me. I caught her and held her. "I love you, Colin," she breathed.

I groaned and kissed her and carried her to her room to live out another one of her fantasies.

"I CAN'T BELIEVE you didn't tell me your birthday was so close," Elise said with a scowl. "You should have told me."

I shook my head. "It isn't usually a big deal."

"But you're turning forty. Can I call you my Old Man?"

"Only if I can call you my Jail Bait."

She wrinkled her nose. "That's creepy."

I nodded. "Yep, it is."

She sighed. "Fine. I'll just call you…"

"How about you call me Colin."

She rolled her eyes. "Fine."

I chuckled and pulled her closer. Everything had changed in the last few days for us. My dad decided to stick around through the week to celebrate my birthday on the actual day, and Elise and I opened up to each other even more. I'd never been closer to another person.

"Where are we staying tonight?" she asked.

That was another big change. She liked spending the night together. We spent the first night at her place, and when we woke up, she climbed on top of me and told me how much she loved me while she rode me.

The next night we stayed at my place, but with my dad on the other side of the hall, it was a little less adventurous.

Elise insisted I spend time with my dad, though, so when she worked early, we stayed at the farm, and when she worked later in the day, we stayed up all night at her place, taking advantage of having the place to ourselves.

"Do you work tomorrow?" I asked. I nipped at her ear and slicked my tongue along the shell.

She shook her head.

"Then we definitely need to stay at your place. Because I plan to start my birthday buried inside you."

She moaned softly and tilted her chin up for a kiss. "I like that plan a lot."

"We could start now," I suggested.

"Hey, guys," one of her friends said, setting a pitcher of beer down in the center of the table. Loudly.

"Hey, Finley. This is Colin. Colin, do you remember Finley? You met a while ago when we were here for dinner."

I nodded, finally placing her. "Good to see you again."

"You, too," she said with a smirk.

Another woman joined us a second later.

"This is Karissa. She's Finley's roommate and the app designer," Elise said.

"Ah, nice to meet you. And thank you."

Karissa grinned. "Happy couples are great for my business. Although you two kind of had a head start. I'll still count it."

I laughed.

Ian walked over with his arm around a curvy brunette who he introduced as Blake. Then Ian and Melody joined us with apologies for being late since Amber was with a babysitter.

"We never hired a babysitter until a few months ago. Amber and Willow were buddies, but I just can't ask her anymore," Melody said.

Ramsey filled me in on the shitshow that led to Melody and her sister not speaking. I didn't blame Melody or Ramsey a bit for not trusting her with their kid, or anything else, after she tried to break them up. And almost succeeded.

Trinity and a blonde woman, who introduced herself as Laura, joined us. After another minute, Hudson pulled up a chair and made a space for himself next to Laura.

"Where's James?" Ian asked.

"He's on his way. Something came up," Ramsey said.

"We can't toast to the birthday boy before everyone is here," Trinity said.

I shook my head. "You don't need to toast to me at all."

"But we do. Birthdays are special around here. And we celebrate them," Blake said. "Trinity's is in a few weeks. She shared one with Karissa's mom."

I looked at Trinity and nodded. "You're next, huh?"

Trinity smiled. "I am, but my birthday marks one year since I moved here, so I'm kind of excited about it."

"You moved here on your birthday?"

She nodded. "Karissa's mom and I met the year before and realized we shared a birthday. I told her I thought the area was beautiful, and she convinced me to move. It took me a year, but I did it. I'm so happy I did."

Elise told me about Karissa's mom. She sounded like an amazing woman, and someone I would have liked. Of course, it was hard to imagine anyone not liking her. "I wish I'd known her," I told Karissa. "Elise has lots of great stories."

Karissa nodded. "My mom was special. One of a kind."

"So was mine. I imagine they would have been good friends if the situations were different."

Karissa nodded. Losing your mother, no matter what age, was something a person never recovered from. Imagining their life if they had lived was a comfort, sometimes the only one you had.

"There he is," Hudson said, lifting his glass. "We can finally toast."

Ian pulled Blake onto his lap and offered James Blake's chair. James sat and poured himself a beer, then lifted his glass. "To not being an asshole."

I chuckled. "Interesting toast."

James shrugged. "It's been a day. I'm happy with anyone who isn't an asshole right now."

"To not being an asshole," Hudson reiterated, glass raised.

Everyone else laughed and raised their glasses. I clinked glasses with the people closest to me and sipped the beer.

Elise was a part of every conversation happening around us. She chimed in with Blake and Finley arguing about a book, then said something to Melody about her sister, and to Hudson and James about the bar. I didn't know how she kept up with all the conversations at once, but she did it.

I sat back and took it all in. When I moved to MacKellar Cove, I figured I'd spend all my time on the farm making it what it was when I was a kid. Instead, I followed in my dad's footsteps and fell in love.

When the night was over, Elise hugged her friends and thanked them all for joining us. I thanked them, too, since they were mostly Elise's friends instead of mine. Ian, Ramsey, James, and Hudson said I had to buy the first round the following week since I never told them it was my birthday. I wasn't sure if they were serious, but I said okay.

Hanging out with my lawyer was turning out to be a good thing.

Elise sat close to me in my truck on the drive to her place. We waved to Mrs. Lockhart, who'd gotten used to seeing my truck and accepted me as one of them. Even Mrs. Carter asked if she could bake pies to stock at the farm, free of charge because she liked me. I insisted we pay her, but she kept arguing. Elise told me it meant she liked me, so I gave in and decided I'd find something to do with the money. Maybe a donation to the police department in honor of her late husband.

I let us in with the key Elise gave me the day before. She said she wanted me to know she trusted me. I gave her a key to the farmhouse also, but I told her it was rarely ever locked.

We sat on the couch and turned on a movie, as had become our evening ritual. She snuggled up next to me and told me she loved me before resting her head on my shoulder.

"My dad is thinking of moving back up here," I told her when the movie ended.

"That's awesome. He should."

I nodded. "I told him the same thing, but he's not entirely sure."

"I can't imagine how hard it is for him to go back to his third degree burn and live in it."

I nodded. "If I ever lost you, I'd feel the same way he did. I'd leave. I couldn't stand living there without you. I see you everywhere."

"I'm not going anywhere," she said softly.

"I know." We were quiet for a few minutes, then I said, "My dad wanted to know what you thought about him moving up here."

She shrugged. "I already said it would be great. But it's not my decision."

"Well, he was thinking of living in my grandmother's house with me."

She sat up and held my gaze. "Okay. It's your house."

"Yes, but my dad is figuring one day it'll be your house, too."

"Oh," she breathed. "I really hadn't thought about it."

"I'm not saying right now or anything. I know I want to spend the rest of my life with you, but I am enjoying where we're at right now. I just wanted to let you know why he keeps asking me to talk to you about him moving up here."

"Well, that's sweet of him, but we have to do the things that make us happy. If living at the farm makes your dad happy, then he should be there. It doesn't matter if I'm there with you or not, if that's where he wants to be, that's where he should be."

I hesitated for half a second then kissed her. I couldn't hold myself back. She thought she didn't know how to love people, but with everything she said and did, she proved herself wrong. She was the most loving person I'd ever met.

"What was that for?" she asked with a laugh when I pulled back.

"For loving my father, too."

"Well, he did say if he was twenty years younger," she teased.

I stood and pulled her off the couch. I scooped her up and squeezed her ass while she wrapped her legs around my hips and yelped.

"Don't drop me."

"I didn't drop you last time," I reminded her. "And I have no plans to put you down any time soon. It's almost midnight, and that means I'm ready to start my birthday celebration."

Her eyes drooped low and sexy, and her body melted against mine. I loved the way she let me in. There was nothing more perfect in the world than the woman who set mine on fire. And no one I'd rather spend my birthday with than her.

EPILOGUE

TRINITY

There was a part of me that didn't really want to celebrate my birthday. I thought about going to visit my mom and grandmother, but they insisted I stay and have fun with my friends instead of visiting a couple of old ladies.

Age was definitely just a number with those two.

My birthday wasn't what I expected when I moved to MacKellar Cove. Ms. Georgia was the kind of person who wrapped you up and made you believe anything was possible. Knowing she died was something that scared me every day. She was immortal in my mind, and the rest of us just tried to be half as good as her.

When I lost my dad, life changed. Of course it did, but life wasn't something everyone was entitled to after that. Life was precious, and not everyone got the same amount of time. Losing my dad taught me that lesson at thirteen, and losing Ms. Georgia taught me the same lesson all over again.

When I left home for college, I told myself I was independent and that I didn't need anyone. My mom relied on my grandmother when my dad died, and then on me with her ex. She was a strong woman, but she couldn't do it alone. I didn't want to be like that. I wanted to be like the woman Ms. Georgia said she saw in me. A strong, confident, independent woman who could do anything she wanted.

That was why I moved to MacKellar Cove. It was beautiful, and I fell in love with the place on my first trip. Living there was like a fantasy, but the fantasy wasn't quite as fanciful as I expected. Bad things still happened in MacKellar Cove. People still got cancer and died. People still got hurt. People still treated each other like shit sometimes.

But I was trying to live in the moment. I was trying to enjoy every day because there was no reason not to. Life was going to happen, whether we were involved or not. So, I pulled up my big girl panties and got involved.

Which meant going to my birthday party and having fun no matter what.

Finley and Karissa said they'd meet me in the lobby of our building at eight, so I headed down a few minutes before. No one was there when I stepped off the bottom step, so I pulled out my phone to see if I'd missed a text from either of them.

I checked my email since there wasn't a text and waited for them to show up. I smiled and put my phone away when I heard their voices and laughter coming down the stairwell.

"There's the birthday girl!" Finley said. "Let me see what new stuff you made today."

I told everyone at girls' night that I was going to make something new to wear for my birthday. I wasn't sure if it was going to work out, but it was better than I'd expected.

A clear resin pendant with a four-leaf clover hung around my neck. I matched it with a resin bracelet that had trimmed sprigs of baby's breath. My earrings were simple green studs, but they were the same green, matching without being too perfect.

"That's awesome," Finley gushed. "Is that a real four-leaf clover?"

I nodded. "It is. I found a few last week but they died almost as soon as I got them home. I pressed them and laminated them, but I couldn't use them for jewelry. Since I knew they didn't last long, I went out looking yesterday for more and found just this one. I had everything ready to make the pendant. I love how it turned out."

"It's beautiful," Karissa agreed. "Truly unique."

I grinned. Karissa was trying to convince me to let her design an app for my business. I hadn't given in yet, but she was pushing the fact that it would make me just a little more unique than the other jewelry designers out there. Yes, the big names had apps, but small designers like me didn't.

Karissa and Finley also had ideas on branding and business design that they were pushing. They knew about things I'd never considered before, especially since most of my business before I moved to MacKellar Cove was B2B. Selling directly to a customer instead of to a business who then sold to the customer was new, but exciting.

"You should totally use that in your marketing," Finley said. "Truly unique. It could be one of your three points."

"I said the same thing," Karissa agreed.

I just shook my head and followed them out the door.

"Who's coming tonight?" Karissa asked.

"I know Ian and Blake will be there," Finley said. "Melody and Ramsey, Elise and Colin. Laura was a yes, right?"

Karissa nodded. "Yep. And I think Elise invited her cousin and a friend from work. Did she tell you that?"

I nodded. "She asked me. I told her it was supposed to be a party."

Finley grinned. "Hell, yeah, it is. Last year was sad, but this year, we can do a little more celebrating. Ms. Georgia will always be a part of us, but we can celebrate Trinity's birthday this year."

"Absolutely," Karissa said.

The walk to O'Kelley's was short, and the crowd was big. It was a Friday night, so the place was usually packed, but it felt busier than usual.

"Ugh," Karissa groaned. "Too many people."

"Something must be going on. Hang on, Trin!" Finley said, reaching for my hand.

The three of us wound our way through the crowd near the door to the tables. Elise and Colin were already at a table, but they were clearly having trouble keeping all the seats by themselves.

"Ian and Ramsey went to get drinks. It's nuts in here," Elise said.

"What is going on?" Finley asked.

"Some kind of sporting event or something," Colin said. "I didn't even know there was anything big this close."

"Must be over the border," Karissa said. "There's nothing for hours around here."

"Rugby," Ian said when he made it to the table with two pitchers of beer. Ramsey was right behind him with two more. "They're a bunch of rugby players, and they're nuts."

"They definitely don't mind pushing. I hope Hudson has James on stand-by," Ramsey added.

Officer James Rucker. Boy did he rub me the wrong way. We met my first day in town, and he thought I was a tourist trying to steal things from locals. I parked my car outside my new apartment building and ended up locking myself out. My car keys were in the apartment and my apartment keys were in the car. With no one to call for help, I tried to break into my own car. When he saw me, he stopped me and threatened to arrest me when I couldn't prove that I lived there.

Such an asshole.

If I'd met him under any other circumstance, I might be able to admit that he was the sexiest thing in town, but with that know-it-all attitude and the don't-fuck-with-me looks he gave me, I would swear under oath that he didn't do a damn thing for me if I had to.

Because it didn't matter how good looking he was, he was a first class ass. And I did not have time for men like him in my life. I was all about fun and freedom and living life to the fullest.

Officer James Rucker was a pin in the balloon of fun. And I was over men like him.

THANK **you** so much for reading Elise and Colin's story! When I visited the area (fictional) MacKellar Cove is in, there was a maple farm I wanted to go see. They were closed while we were there, but I loved the romance of a farm and privacy while in the great outdoors. It seemed like an amazing place to fall in love.

Trinity and James's story is next. Trinity is looking to expand her business and enjoy her life, but she keeps crossing paths with Officer Rucker. James rubs her in all the wrong ways, but when she needs his help, she starts to wonder if she was wrong about him the whole time. His Curvy Frustration is available now!

CAN'T GET ENOUGH of Elise and Colin? Subscribers get a free, exclusive bonus epilogue of Elise helping Colin on the farm! Sign up now!

. . .

NEED MORE? Sawyer packs up and moves to Hawaii, but things don't go as planned when he meets his new boss. She's curvy and sexy and catches him checking her out before he even starts work. Not the best start. Read Order vs. Chaos today!

ABOUT THE AUTHOR

USA TODAY Bestselling Author Mary E Thompson spent most of her childhood wishing she had a few less curves. She hid in the pages of books because her favorite characters never cared what size her clothes were. Now, neither does Mary, and she writes stories that celebrate women like her. Real women who have curves, chase dreams, and find love, because we should all be happy, no matter our dress size.

Mary spends her non-writing time with her husband and two kids, watching too much TV, cheering for her home-town football team (Go Bills!), and hiding chocolate from her family.

Visit https://MaryEThompson.com/ to sign up for Mary's newsletter, **Romancing the Curves**. Subscribers get free ebooks and other fun stuff, like exclusive, members only content and giveaways, plus are the first to know about new releases and sales!

www.ingramcontent.com/pod-product-compliance
Lightning Source LLC
Chambersburg PA
CBHW030349200726
48286CB00013B/590